**Her heart slammed against her chest,
pounding erratically.**

Kiss me! she thought, crazily, wildly. As if a kiss would fix everything. She tossed her head and pursed her lips, mentally daring him to do it.

He looked hard into her eyes, as if assessing the depth of her soul. Their lungs moved in tandem, drawing in great gasps of ragged air. There was such raw hunger in his eyes she couldn't help but gasp. The look was naked, completely without guile, a mirror image of her heart.

He cupped her face with his left hand, tilted her chin up to look at him. This time she did gasp. The harsh sound echoed in the tiny room.

Was he going to kiss her?

Also by Lori Wilde

Second Chance
HERO

LORI WILDE

FOREVER

NEW YORK   BOSTON

Copyright © 2008 by Laurie Vanzura
Excerpt from *Rocky Mountain Heat*, previously published as *All of Me* © copyright 2009 by Laurie Vanzura

Hachette Book Group supports the right to free expression and the value of copyright. The purpose of copyright is to encourage writers and artists to produce the creative works that enrich our culture.

The scanning, uploading, and distribution of this book without permission is a theft of the author's intellectual property. If you would like permission to use material from the book (other than for review purposes), please contact permissions@hbgusa.com. Thank you for your support of the author's rights.

Forever
Hachette Book Group
1290 Avenue of the Americas, New York, NY 10104
read-forever.com
twitter.com/readforeverpub

Originally published as *Once Smitten, Twice Shy* by Forever in January 2008
Reissued: August 2019

Forever is an imprint of Grand Central Publishing. The Forever name and logo are trademarks of Hachette Book Group, Inc.

The publisher is not responsible for websites (or their content) that are not owned by the publisher.

The Hachette Speakers Bureau provides a wide range of authors for speaking events. To find out more, go to www.hachettespeakersbureau.com or call (866) 376-6591.

ISBNs: 978-1-5387-0020-4 (mass market reissue), 978-0-446-55340-7 (ebook)

Printed in the United States of America

OPM

10 9 8 7 6 5 4 3 2 1

This book is dedicated to my parents,
Fred and Maxine Blalock, who lost two children
but never lost their faith or love in each other.

Acknowledgments

No one writes a book alone. It feels like it sometimes, all those hours spent in front of a computer wrestling with the words, but if it weren't for the following people propping me up, I wouldn't be able to make the magic happen.

To my husband, Bill, who takes care of all the domestic details so I don't have to worry about any of that and who loves me unfailingly. I'm the luckiest person on earth.

To my editor, Michele Bidelspach, who gently nudges me in the right direction.

To my agent, Jenny Bent, who keeps my spirits up when the publishing business closes in.

To the people of my hometown, who from Jay, Melinda, and June at the post office who smilingly accept my numerous packages to Leah Western at Freedom House to Linda Bagwell at Weatherford College, I'm blessed to know you all. Thank you for all your support over the years.

Second Chance
HERO

Chapter 1

From behind his high-end designer sunglasses, Secret Service agent Shane Tremont scanned the crowd gathered for the groundbreaking of the Nathan Benedict wing at the University of Texas campus.

His elbows were loose, his breathing regular, his stance commanding and self-confident. The perimeter had been secured. The crowd controlled. His Sig Sauer P229 357-caliber pistol nestled comfortably in his shoulder holster, freshly cleaned and loaded, along with a full capacity of ammunition clips stowed in the holster pockets and a bulletproof vest molded against his chest.

Although Nathan Benedict, the President of the United States, was being honored at his alma mater, he wasn't attending the ceremony. In Nathan's place was his twenty-two-year-old daughter, Elysee, who'd been entrusted with clipping the ceremonial ribbon in her father's absence.

Everyone loved sweet-natured Elysee, and it was Shane's job to guard her life with his own. His nerves might be relaxed, but his muscles were tense as coiled springs, cocked and ready for action.

The sky was clear and blue and balmy—the perfect mid-October afternoon in Texas. He was acutely aware of the political protesters. They carried signs scrawled with anti-Benedict sentiment. The Austin police held them at bay behind the picket line several hundred yards from the groundbreaking site.

Potential assassins, all of them. From the smiling young mother with a towheaded toddler in her lap to the elderly man leaning on a cane, to the trio of cocoa-skinned, dark-haired men gathered at the periphery of the crowd.

Shane narrowed his eyes and took a second look at the three men. They fit a profile that was politically correct to ignore, but he was Secret Service. Political correctness didn't figure into it. A whiff of Al-Qaeda and his adrenaline kicked into hyperdrive. He touched his earpiece and quietly mouthed a coded message that sent another Secret Service agent closer to the trio. Better safe than sorry.

"Everything okay?" Elysee laid a hand on his elbow.

"Yes, miss."

"Miss? Getting formal on me, Agent Tremont?" Her eyes twinkled.

"We're in public. I'm on high alert." He resisted the urge to smile.

"The crowd looks pretty tame to me."

"Protesters lined up on the sidewalk."

"Ubiquitous," she said. "I'm surprised. Usually there's more."

"It's because it's you here and not your father. Few are eager to protest a true lady."

"Why, Agent Tremont." A soft smile touched her lips. "What a gentlemanly thing to say."

He gave her a conspiratorial wink and her smile widened.

"Your tie's crooked," she said and reached up to give his plain black necktie a gentle tug, then passed the flat of her hand over his shoulder. "There now. Spit-polish perfect."

"What does that mean?" he teased.

"I don't know. Just something my mother always said to my dad when she hustled him out the door each morning."

Shane and Elysee and her entourage were standing on a small platform suspended over the site of the ground-breaking. A fat yellow backhoe, along with several other heavy construction vehicles, sat with their engines powered up and running, ready to get to work as soon as Elysee sliced through the thick scarlet ribbon.

Some committee had decided a ballet of earthmoving equipment would be more cinematic than Elysee shoveling dirt. Although in the end, cinematography had turned out to be a nonissue. A devastating category four hurricane had just crashed ashore along the South Carolina coastline, pulling news crews eastward. Other than a few print journalists, the groundbreaking ceremony was devoid of the usual media brouhaha.

Shane swung his gaze back to the President's daughter. He had been assigned to her detail for the past thirteen months and in that time they'd become close friends. The relationship between a bodyguard and his protectee bore many similarities to that between a psychiatrist and his patient. Elysee told him things she couldn't tell anyone else. He listened, sympathized, and kept his mouth shut.

The intimacy had created a special connection. Shane liked her, even though she was seven years younger than he. This unexpected emotional bond wasn't something his training had fully prepared him for.

Elysee was petite and soft-spoken, with earnest opinions and tender sensibilities. She loved fully, completely, and without reservation, although men were always breaking her heart.

Shane couldn't understand why she hadn't become hardened or cynical about love. Her capacity to pick up her crumpled spirit and move on with the same degree of hope, trust, and optimism impressed him.

He thought of his ex-wife and his own heart—which was finally, finally starting to mend—swelled, testing the tentative seams of its emotional stitches. Two years divorced and thoughts of Tish still made him shaky. He'd loved her so damned much and she'd disappointed him so deeply. No pain had ever cut like Tish's secrecy and betrayal.

Many times over the past twenty-four months he'd tried to convince himself that he hated her. His anger was a red-hot flame he held close to his chest and stoked whenever his mind wandered to tender memories. But he couldn't hate her. Not really. Not when it counted.

Thing was, no matter how hard he tried to suppress his weakness, in the dark of midnight, he found himself longing for Tish and all that they'd lost.

He still ached for the feel of her curvy body nestled against his. Still longed to smell the spicy scent of her lush auburn hair. Still yearned to taste the rich flavor of her femininity lingering on his tongue. Even here, in the brightness of the noonday sun, surrounded by a crowd, he felt it.

Dry. Empty. Desperately alone.

The tip of his left thumb strayed to the back of his

ring finger, feeling for the weight of the band that was no longer there. He swallowed past the unexpected lump in his throat.

Head in the game, Tremont.

Shane clenched his jaw to keep from thinking about Tish. Channeling all his attention onto safeguarding Elysee. This was his life now. Without a wife. Without a real home. The job was the only thing that defined him. He was a bodyguard, a protector, a sentinel. He was descended from war heroes. It was in his blood. In his very DNA.

The University of Texas chancellor stepped to the microphone and made a speech about Nathan Benedict and the dedication of the new Poli-Sci wing in his honor. Then he introduced Elysee.

A cheer went up. She *was* a crowd pleaser.

Elysee smiled and cameras clicked. An award-winning high school marching band that had been recruited for the event struck up "God Bless America." Shane's eyes never stopped assessing; his brain never ceased analyzing.

An assistant handed Elysee a pair of scissors so outrageously large that she had to grab onto them with both hands. Laughing, she raised the Gulliver-sized shears. Whenever she smiled, Elysee was transformed. Her bland blue eyes sparkled and her thin mouth widened and she tossed her hair in a carefree gesture. For one brief moment she looked as beautiful as any runway model.

Elysee snipped.

The thick red ribbon fell away.

The backhoe dipped for dirt at the same moment the bulldozer's blade went to ground and the road grader's engine revved.

The crowd, including the protesters behind the picket line, cheered again and applauded politely. Nearby, the backhoe operator was apparently having trouble with the equipment. It moved jerkily as its bucket rose. Elysee was perched precariously close to the platform's edge.

The backhoe arm swung wide.

In that instant Shane saw pure panic on the backhoe operator's face and realized the man had lost control of the machinery. The bucket zoomed straight for Elysee.

Shane reacted.

He felt no fear, only a solid determination to protect the President's daughter at all costs.

But it felt as if he were moving in slow motion, his legs locked in molasses, his arms slogging through ballistics gel. He lunged, flinging his body at Elysee.

He hit her with his shoulder. She cried out, fell to her knees.

Spinning, Shane turned to face the earthmoving equipment, hand simultaneously diving for his duty weapon at the same second the backhoe bucket sluiced through the air, slinging loamy soil.

His arm went up, gun raised.

The bucket caught his right hand, yanking him up off the platform. He heard the awful crunch, but the pain didn't immediately register. He was jerked from his feet. He tried to pull the trigger, not even knowing what he was shooting at, just reacting instinctively to danger. He'd kill for Elysee, if that's what it took.

But his fingers refused to comply. What the hell was wrong with his fingers? Shane frowned, puzzled.

The driver looked horrified as his gaze met Shane's. He was dangling from the bucket right before the operator's eyes as the man frantically grabbed levers and fumbled with controls.

Distantly, Shane heard Elysee screaming his name. Was she hurt? In pain? Had someone gotten to her? Was she being kidnapped? Was the runaway backhoe all a ruse to deflect attention from hostage takers? The questions pelted his mind, hard as stones.

People were running and screaming, rushing in all directions, ducking and dodging, tripping and falling. He feared a stampede.

Shane swiveled his head, trying to locate Elysee in the confusion. Why couldn't he feel the pistol in his hand? Dammit, why couldn't he feel his hand?

"Elysee!" Her name tore from his throat in a guttural growl.

The backhoe arm slung Shane up high, and then slammed him down hard onto the cab of the earthmoving vehicle.

Metal contacted with bone.

Pain exploded inside his skull, a starburst of bright searing light.

Then his vision went dark as he tumbled toward the hardpacked ground and slumped into the inky-black tunnel of unconsciousness.

Chapter 2

Affluence attracts affluence.

Tish Gallagher repeated her mother's favorite mantra to herself as she wriggled into a fifteen-hundred-dollar gray tweed Chanel suit. Her potential client was a banker and quite conservative.

After a quick peek into her closet, she added a lavender silk blouse to the ensemble. The color complimented her deep auburn hair. She removed four earrings from the multiple piercings in her ears, leaving only a single pair of simple gold studs. She clipped a strand of pearls around her neck and then donned four-inch, open-toed, lavender-and-gray Christian Louboutin stilettos. Because, hey, an artistic girl's just gotta wear *something* whimsical.

Although it was mid-October, the weather in Houston was still in the upper eighties and dastardly humid. But Tish knew La Maison Vert, the upscale French restaurant where she was meeting Addison James and her daughter, Felicity, kept their dining room chilled like fine champagne. Hence the long-sleeved tweed jacket. This job was very important. She couldn't afford to shiver throughout the interview.

As she studied herself in the full-length mirror mounted on the inside door of her closet, Tish spied the price tag dangling from her sleeve. "Uh-oh, that won't do."

Since her divorce, she'd lived in a one-bedroom garage apartment behind a lavish manor house in the old-money section of River Oaks. The apartment had once served as maid quarters and its 1950s décor, with black-and-white tiled floors and foam green appliances, held a certain kind of retro charm. Not to mention that the six-hundred-dollar-a-month rent was a salve to her strained budget.

The elegant neighborhood was quiet. The only drawback to the apartment was that her bedroom had to double as her office. Consequently, everything was always in disarray. Cameras hung from hooks on the wall, a bank of editing monitors vied for space on the bedroom furniture, and papers and files were stacked on the floor.

A search for the scotch tape amid the disorganized, overflowing room finally turned up the dispenser, lurking beneath a tote bag on her computer desk, but not before she almost knocked the bookend off.

Her fingers traced over the weighted statuette of a little girl with a pail of water in her hand. The bookend had been carved from the burl of two banyan trees that had twined and grown together.

Her ex-husband, Shane, had bought the Jill half of the Jack and Jill bookends for her at a rummage sale while they were on their honeymoon. She'd fallen in love with the bookend the moment she'd seen it, although Shane had tried to discourage her from getting it because it was just one lone bookend. But she'd wanted it so much, he'd used Jill's singleness as a bargaining chip to get the price down.

Seeing how happy the bookend made her, he'd promised he would search the Internet and haunt garage sales until he found the missing Jack and reunited him with his Jill.

An empty feeling settled in her stomach. That was another promise Shane hadn't kept.

Tish shook her head, shook away Shane. Water under the bridge.

She peeled off a strip of adhesive tape and carefully taped the price tag up inside the sleeve of her suit jacket so she could return it to Nordstrom's for a refund on her credit card once her meeting was over.

Then, she took another spin in front of the mirror. Yes. She exuded money, polish, and sophistication. Never mind that deep inside she still felt poor, tarnished, and from the wrong side of town. "Please, please, let me get this job."

Her car payment was two months overdue and she'd been eating Ramen noodles at every meal for the past two weeks. She was hoping to procure a down payment from Addison so she could zip it to the bank before the check she'd written for the stilettos ended up costing her thirty bucks in overdraft protection.

For five years now she'd been struggling to get her fledgling business off the ground. She was a damned good videographer and she knew it, but she couldn't seem to catch a break. She wasn't one to give up on her dreams, but at some point didn't prudence step in? When did common sense shout that your dreams were going to destroy you and you'd better let go of them before you lost everything that was important to you?

Like Shane.

Tish winced and bit down on her bottom lip. The love of her life. The man she'd foolishly allowed to get away. But she wasn't going to think about him. Not today, dammit.

Sometimes, in spite of her best attempts to look on the bright side of life, it felt as if everything was slipping, spreading, festooning headlong into a disaster she could neither name nor predict. Her throat tightened and she shook her head against the dark, creeping thoughts.

No, no. She wasn't the sort to dwell on unhappy things. Onward and upward. That was her motto. She was just about to shut her closet door when she caught sight of the wedding veil in her peripheral vision.

The three-hundred-year-old veil was carefully folded and sealed in a special bag. Her best friend in the whole world, Delaney Cartwright, had given Tish the veil for good luck after her own wedding the previous December.

Tish remembered the day they'd found the veil in a tiny consignment shop. Delaney had immediately fallen under the spell of it, but Tish had been skeptical. Then the mysterious shopkeeper, Claire Kelley, had told them a fantastical tale about the veil that Tish did not believe.

Still, it had been a compelling fable and she recalled it with clarity. For some reason, the story had stuck with her.

Once upon a time, according to the legend, *in long-ago Ireland, there lived a beautiful young witch named Morag who possessed a great talent for tatting lace. People came from far and wide to buy the lovely wedding veils she created, but there were other women in the community who were envious of Morag's beauty and talent.*

These women made up a lie and told the magistrate that Morag was casting spells on the men of the village. The magistrate arrested Morag, but fell madly in love with her. Convinced that she must have cast a spell upon him as well, he moved to have her tried for practicing witchcraft.

If found guilty, she would be burned at the stake.

But in the end, the magistrate could not resist the power of true love. On the eve before Morag was to stand trial, he kidnapped her from the jail in the dead of night and spirited her away to America, giving up everything for her love.

To prove that she had not cast a spell over him, Morag promised never to use magic again. As her final act of witchcraft, she made one last wedding veil, investing it with the power to grant the deepest wish of the wearer's soul.

She wore the veil on her own wedding day, wishing for true and lasting love. Morag and the magistrate were blessed with many children and much happiness. They lived to a ripe old age and died in each other's arms.

Claire Kelley had gone on to claim that whoever wished upon the veil would get their heart's deepest desire.

Delaney had believed. She'd wished upon the veil and ended up finding her true love in Houston Police Department undercover cop Nick Vinetti.

Tish was truly happy for Delaney, but magical wedding veil or not, she wasn't sinking all her hopes into happily ever after. She'd thought she'd found true love with Shane, and look what had happened. The old familiar misery rose up in her, the misery she'd struggled for two long years to exorcise.

She took the veil from the bag and fingered it, wrestled with the idea of making a wish. It seemed silly.

But what would it hurt? Even if you don't believe?

Good point. Tish slipped the veil from the hanger. The lace felt strangely warm to the touch.

Tentatively, she settled it on her head and examined herself in the mirror. The design was constructed of tiny roses grouped to form a larger pattern of butterflies. The veil was so white it was almost phosphorescent.

Her scalp tingled. Her pulse quickened. There was something undeniably magnetic about the veil, even to a die-hard cynic.

"I wish," Tish said out loud. "I wish, I wish, I wish . . ."

Her voice tapered off. Oddly, the veil seemed to shimmer until it looked like butterfly wings were fluttering all around her.

Eerie.

She swallowed hard. Goose bumps danced across her forearms. "I wish to get out of debt. I wish I didn't have to struggle over money. Oh hell, I'm just going to come out and say it. I wish for my career to skyrocket into the stratosphere and I'll become rich beyond my wildest dreams."

Instant heat swamped her body. The tingling at her scalp intensified. Her lungs felt at once both breathless and overly oxygenated.

She almost ripped off the veil, but something held her back. She stared into the mirror. Stared and stared and stared.

The looking glass blurred.

She'd skipped breakfast that morning. Was that why she was feeling weak and a little dizzy?

Tish blinked, shook her head. Her reflection swept in and out, her mirror image fading before her eyes as if she were in a slow, dreamy faint.

A face appeared. Indistinct at first. Fuzzy.

A man's face.

Not just any face, but a familiar one. A face she loved. Joy, full and unexpected, filled her heart.

"Shane," she whispered breathlessly. "Shane."

And then she could see all of him. He was dressed the way she'd seen him last, in his Secret Service black suit, white shirt, and black tie. Her man in black. Even through his clothes she could see the steel of his muscles and she knew that beneath the tailored material his body was ripped, perfectly defined.

His jaw was clenched, his brow furrowed. Some who did not know him might think him angry. But she knew that look. She saw it in the edges of his mouth, the corner of his eyes. He was in pain.

"Tish, I need you. I'm lost and I can't find my way back. Help me, Tish, help me."

Mesmerized, she reached out a hand to touch him, but her fingers met the hard surface of the looking glass.

Tish gasped as if she'd been splashed with cold water.

The vision vanished.

She stumbled backward, her temples pounding, eyes wide with awe and terror. She was back in her bedroom, back in the closet, gaping at the mirror, struggling to breathe.

The cursed veil lay on the floor at her feet.

Her stomach pitched. Her knees swayed. Impossible.

She stared into the mirror, but nothing was there except her own frightened reflection. Tish couldn't explain what had just happened, but her body hummed and ached with raw energy, rattling her to the very core of her soul.

"Holy shit," she exclaimed. "Shit, shit, shit. Today of all days, I certainly didn't need this."

Consciousness filtered in by degrees.

First, Shane detected sounds. Distant, muted. He tried to make sense of them, but when he concentrated too hard the fog in his head thickened.

Squeaky wheels on a rolling cart. Voices dark and soft. A rough scratchy kind of noise, like Velcro pulled apart. He heard a steady blipping. A heartbeat. Was it his?

Where was he? What had happened? Was he dead? Was this hell? He tried to think, but his memory was a curtain, heavy and black. It hurt too much to think. His brain burned. He willed himself back down from where he'd climbed. Willed the pain away and slept once more.

Time passed.

During his second swim up from unconsciousness, his nerve endings swarmed with feeling, buzzed with pain. *Fuck-o-fuck*, his head hurt like there was a steel beam jammed through it.

And his hand. What in the hell had happened to his hand?

Then a wisp of memory was there. Tenuous as a broken spiderweb. Free-floating and sticky. Something bad had happened. He didn't know how long he'd been out, but his body identified the minutes, hours. Days? Surely not weeks. Please, God, not weeks.

His skin ached. His joints were stiff. He tried to move, but his mind did not seem connected to his limbs.

Move your hand, he commanded, but he didn't want to

move it because he knew it was going to hurt like seven levels of hell. He gritted his teeth. He concentrated, but he could not feel his fingers respond to his brain's demands.

Open your eyes.

Nothing.

The air smelled foreign—like hard plastic mattresses and sterile sheets, like powdered eggs and stale blood. The thick earthy scents made him want to gag. What were these smells? Where was this place? Why couldn't he move?

He found no answers to these disturbing questions. Abject despair propelled Shane to dive back into the pool of darkness, seeking solace in the oblivion of drugged sleep.

All the way to the restaurant Tish's mind kept drifting back to the vision she'd had in her closet and the awful feeling that something bad had happened to Shane.

"You're imagining things. Shane is perfectly fine," she told herself, but her gut didn't believe it.

Tish nibbled a thumbnail, then forced herself to stop. Chipped nail polish would not earn her any brownie points with Addison James.

At an intersection, she missed the green light and had to sit through the red. Shriners made their way through traffic, soliciting donations from passing motorists. Tish dug in her purse for change. She only had a ten-dollar bill. She rolled down her window and waved the ten. The man in a tasseled fez thanked her for her donation just as the light changed and she zoomed off.

She pulled into the parking lot of La Maison Vert, gathered up the things she needed for her presentation, and rushed inside. The hostess escorted her to a back table where Addison and her daughter were sitting.

"You're three and a half minutes late," Addison said coolly, glancing at her Rolex. "Not an auspicious beginning."

"My deepest apologies for keeping you waiting." Tish slid into her seat feeling as if she was already behind the eight ball.

After they'd eaten and the dishes had been cleared away, Tish set up her DVD player in the middle of the table and ran the wedding montage she'd put together to showcase her work.

Addison was nodding and Felicity was smiling, and Tish thought she might be close to winning them over.

Don't do anything to screw this up.

If she were selected as the James-Yarobrough videographer—following on the heels of documenting Delaney's wedding to her dreamy hunk of a husband—Tish would be in with the elite of Houston's crème de la crème. And all her money problems would disappear.

"So when's the big day?" she asked Felicity.

"Next June."

"Good thing you're starting early. I book up quickly," Tish fibbed and hoped God wouldn't hold the little white lie against her. Sometimes in this business you had to stretch the truth to get what you needed, and Tish badly needed this wedding.

"We're starting right on schedule." Addison James pulled a checklist from her purse. "Nine months before the wedding, book the videographer," she read.

Tish kept smiling. Clearly, Addison was one of those by-the-book people. Just like Shane. Tish didn't do well with sticklers.

Beggars can't be choosers; you need this job.

"If we hire you," Addison asked in a snotty tone, "will you be three and a half minutes late for the wedding?"

"No, no, of course not. I'll be there hours before the wedding," Tish promised.

"Mom," Felicity said. "I really like what Tish has shown us. She's got a way of drawing out people that makes for great video. She's the sixth videographer we've spoken to and I like her presentation the best."

"What have I taught you?" Addison chided.

"Never act in haste," Felicity replied dutifully.

"That's right. We've got four more videographer interviews scheduled."

Their waiter approached the table. "Dessert, ladies?"

"None for me," Addison said. "I have a size-six mother-of-the-bride dress to fit into."

"I'm fine," Felicity said.

"Could you just bring us the check?" Tish asked.

"Most certainly." The waiter scooted off after the check.

"What are your rates?" Addison steepled her fingertips and slanted Tish a calculating glance.

She quoted a price that was slightly higher than her stiffest competition's. She based her fees on another one of her mother's mantras, *If you want people to think you're the best, charge like you're worth it.*

The waiter brought the check and Tish gulped at the total. Praying she wasn't over her credit limit, she pulled out her Visa card and handed it over to him. He disappeared to run her card.

"That's more than your competitors charge," Addison commented.

"Do you want the best? Or the most affordable? I can

understand if budget restrictions knock me out of the running." Tish reached across the table to turn off the DVD player and hoped her strategy would cause Addison to rise to the occasion rather than get up and walk away.

"I'm not going to pretend I don't appreciate a bargain, but when it comes to my daughter's wedding, we want only the best."

"And that's what you'll get if you hire me." Tish stashed the DVD player in her briefcase. Yes, okay, it was an egotistical thing to say, but she could back it up. She was damned good at her job. Why let false modesty sell her short?

"Mother, I really want Tish to video our wedding," Felicity wheedled.

Addison shot her daughter a quelling glance and said to Tish, "You put together a very compelling video. It's the best we've seen. But there are other considerations. I also want to make sure you're of upstanding moral character. Last year, my friend June hired a videographer who turned out to have a criminal record. He got access to their security code when he came over to interview June's daughter and during the wedding, his accomplices burglarized their home."

"I can assure you, Mrs. James, I don't have a criminal record. But feel free to run a background check on me if that would ease your mind."

"Ms. Gallagher"—the waiter came back to the table looking distressed—"I'm afraid your credit card has been declined."

Tish tried to make her face a blank slate as she inwardly cringed. She couldn't let Mrs. James see her sweat. Smiling back the huge lump of trepidation in her throat, she said, "There must have been a mistake. Can you run it through again, please?"

The waiter shifted his weight. "I've been told by the credit card company to cut it up."

He pulled a pair of scissors from his pocket. Right in front of Addison James, the conservative banker with concerns about Tish's moral character, he chopped the card neatly in half.

Humiliation sank its fangs into her. Her heart lurched. The waiter was killing her lifeline. Tish kept the smile plastered to her face and pulled another card from her wallet. "Here, try the MasterCard."

"Yes, ma'am." He left her murdered Visa behind and trotted off with the MasterCard.

"There's got to be some sort of mix-up," Tish said. "I'll call my credit card company as soon as I get home and find out what's going on here. I hope it's not identity theft."

Addison shot her a judgmental look. Tish felt the deal slipping away.

The waiter returned a moment later, shaking his head, her MasterCard in one hand, scissors in the other.

Not again! Fear struck her then, hard and vicious. How on earth could she be over the limit on both credit cards? It wasn't possible. Maybe someone *had* stolen her identity.

Snip, snip went the scissors. The desecrated Master-Card fell into pieces beside the Visa.

She felt fractured, disjointed, as if she, the real Tish, was separate from the woman who did dumb things like this. It was a feeling that dwelled in the fringes of her consciousness, a ghost of something she'd never been able to pinpoint. A feeling that she could never be whole, no matter how hard she struggled to integrate herself. It was a desolate sensation and made her want to run out and buy something expensive.

"What next?" the waiter asked. "Where do we go from here?"

"I'll pay for the lunch," Addison James said icily. She took out her wallet and counted out the correct amount of cash to cover the bill.

A deep silence fell over the table after the waiter departed. Tish worked up the courage to look Addison in the eyes. "I'm deeply sorry for that. I'll reimburse you."

Fury drew Addison's brows down tight in a disapproving frown and her lips thinned out. "What kind of business professional does something like this? Invites clients to lunch and tries to pay for it with not one, but two maxed-out credit cards?"

The air leaked from Tish's lungs. She couldn't breathe, could hardly speak. "I . . . I . . ."

Addison pushed back her chair and got to her feet. "Come on, Felicity. We have somewhere else to be."

"Please, wait." Tish put a hand to the woman's wrist.

Addison glowered at Tish's arm. The price tag had fallen out of her sleeve and was dangling there for everyone to see.

"You were planning on returning that suit after you wore it, weren't you?" Addison accused.

The deal was lost. No point lying at this juncture.

"Yes."

"You are so pathetic," Addison hissed. "Talented perhaps, but pathetic. Until you can pull your life together, stop shooting for the stars."

Reeling, Tish watched her meal ticket, daughter in tow, sweep out of the restaurant. Feeling as if her arms

had been amputated, Tish fumbled for the pieces of her
massacred credit cards and stuffed them in the pocket
of the suit that she had to return to Nordstrom's for a
refund.

Loser.

She raised her head and saw people were watching.
Peeved with herself, she glared at an owl-eyed woman at
the next table staring at her as if she had the avian flu.

Embarrassed but proud, Tish raised her head, pushed
back her chair, and got to her feet. At the same time a
waiter, zigzagging around tables with a big tray of
butter-slick crawfish balanced over his head on the palm
of his hand, zipped past.

The leg of Tish's chair clipped his ankle.

The waiter stumbled. His tray slipped. The crawfish
attacked—pelting Tish's suit with red, buttery bits of sea-
food hail.

Horrified, she gasped.

"Oh, gosh, ma'am," the waiter apologized as he
brushed crawfish from her clothing. He lifted his head
and met her gaze. His eyes narrowed, his lips curled.
"Oh, it's you," he said out loud, and then under his breath
he muttered, "deadbeat."

Tish's cheeks burned and her heart pounded. She
wanted to throw back her head and bawl. This wasn't the
waiter's fault. She was in a mess of her own making.

Again.

Accusing eyes scalded, judging her.

Flicking a crawfish off her lapel, she gathered up her
briefcase, slung her purse over her shoulder, and strode
from the restaurant. Shame tasted like heated aluminum
foil in her mouth—hot, sharp, and metallic.

She dug her car keys from her purse and pressed the

alarm button to locate her Ford Focus in the overflowing parking lot. No reassuring *chirp-chirp* indicated her car door had been unlocked. She hurried to the area where she remembered parking, hitting the alarm button a second time.

Nothing.

Tish was certain she'd been in this section of the lot. But an SUV sat where she thought she'd parked. Maybe, in her humiliation over what had just happened to her inside the restaurant, she was mistaken.

She retraced her steps. Yes, she was almost one hundred percent sure this was where she'd parked.

Clearly not. Your car isn't here.

She stalked up and down the aisles, the humid Houston heat causing sweat to pool under her collar. Her stilettos were made for showing off, not for walking, and her toes throbbed beneath the leather straps. She felt a blister forming. The heels kept sticking in the heat-softened asphalt and Tish stumbled twice. Where was her car?

Dread, sudden as lightning in a cloudless sky, struck her. Someone had stolen her car!

She dug into her pocket for her cell phone and turned it on. Just as she pressed the 9 of 9-1-1 an image rose in her mind. She recalled the stack of unpaid bills on her kitchen table.

There'd been a letter or two from the finance company threatening to take back her car if payment wasn't made soon. She thought of the phone calls left on her answering machine that she hadn't returned.

And she realized the awful truth. Her car hadn't been stolen.

It had been repossessed.

Chapter 3

Elysee Benedict was in love with love. She adored the heady rush of early romance—the kisses, the long, lingering glances, the surprise gifts, and the undivided attention. Her mother, Catherine Prosper Benedict, God rest her soul, had instilled in Elysee the staunch belief of happily ever after.

When she was young, her mother would occasionally take her out of school early on the pretext of a dental appointment. Instead, they would slip off to the matinee and watch romantic movies, eating popcorn from the same box and giggling like best girlfriends over handsome movie star heroes. Elysee loved those surprise outings in the darkened theater with her mother.

When she was ten, Catherine passed on her dog-eared copies of romance novels with muscular, longhaired men on the covers. Reading the stories had made her heart beat faster and she yearned for a romance of her very own.

When she was eleven, her mother was diagnosed with terminal bone cancer. "I'm not going to be around to see you fall in love and get married," Catherine had told her. "So you must listen to me now."

"Yes, Mama."

"True love is out there for you, Elysee, if you just believe it."

"I believe," she vowed, believing as only a young child could.

Her mother squeezed her hand. "Don't give up until you find him."

"But how will I know when I meet the right one?"

"You'll feel it." Her mother laid her hand over Elysee's heart. "Deep down inside here."

"What will he be like?"

"He'll be kind and strong and he'll fight for you and he'll protect you, even if it means he must give up his own life to save you, and he'll be your very best friend."

Six months later her mother was dead and Elysee's longing to find her true love was stronger than ever. The problem was, she saw love everywhere, in any masculine face that smiled. She went through crush after crush, each time feeling it deep within her heart, each time thinking, *It's him. He's the one.*

"She's too much like her mother," she'd once heard her father tell her nanny, Rana Singh, not long after Catherine had died. "Head in the clouds, mind filled with silly romantic notions about life. I don't know what to do with her."

Much to her father's consternation, at twenty-two she'd already been engaged three times. Elysee had been on the front page of too many tabloids, their ugly headlines burned into her brain.

First Daughter's First Romance Fizzles.
Elysee Benedict: Fickle Princess or Lonely Teen?

Beau Number Three Breaks Heart of Prez's Only Child.

Yes, okay, she'd made a lot of mistakes, picked the wrong kind of men, gone for flash over substance.

Shane Tremont, however, was different. For one thing, he was older. For another thing, her father liked and respected him. And there was the fact he'd saved her life, just as her mother had said her true love would do. Quiet, strong, steady Shane.

She'd stayed at his bedside from the beginning. Her father had tried to talk her out of it, but she insisted on being there when he woke up. He'd been her bodyguard for over a year and while she'd always thought of him as a good-looking man, she'd never considered him in a romantic way until he'd sacrificed himself for her.

Before that, well, he'd scared her just a little with his tough masculinity. In the past she'd favored polished, soft-featured, erudite men, and Shane certainly wasn't that. But seeing him in that hospital bed, with those tubes coming out of him and his head wrapped in bandages, he'd looked so lost and vulnerable she'd wanted to scoop him into her arms and cuddle him. He wasn't so big and tough and scary after all.

Elysee realized what she felt for Shane was different from what she had felt for her other three fiancés. This was a quiet love, a soft love, a mature love. This was the kind of love her father told her she needed, and she'd begun to realize that this was what true love must be—a deep, abiding friendship grown stronger through sacrifice and devotion.

So what if there was no electricity? No sparks. That was the point. Chemistry had led her down the wrong path before, caused her to make foolish choices. Sometimes, she missed her mother so much, it was a physical ache. She wished Catherine was here to confirm her belief that Shane was indeed The One. True friendship was the ingredient that had been missing from her other love relationships.

Elysee sat at Shane's bedside day in and day out. Willing him well, willing him to love her back the way she was coming to love him. And if she squeezed her eyes closed and concentrated really hard, she could feel it deep inside her heart.

Yes. Shane Tremont was indeed her true love. Now all she had to do was convince him of it.

"Häagen-Dazs is not the answer," Tish's best friend Delaney scolded her as she pried the empty cup of what had once contained coffee-flavored ice cream from her hand.

"Creamery-ista," Tish said to the woman behind the counter at the Häagen-Dazs kiosk in the Galleria mall, "I'll have another round. This time serve up a double scoop of Dulce de Leche."

Delaney shook her head at the woman and narrowed her eyes. "Don't make me stage an intervention, Tish Gallagher. Put down the sample spoon and step away from the Häagen-Dazs."

Tish gripped the spoon tighter, anxiety clotting her throat. She knew her friend had her best interests at heart. She also knew gorging herself wasn't an antidote. She'd screwed up big time and now here she was, trying to drown her sorrows in high-fat premium ice cream.

Two weeks had passed since the incident with Addison James. Two miserable weeks dodging bill collectors and begging rides to work from friends and neighbors. Her cable service had been shut off for nonpayment and she'd had to cancel both her Netflix subscription and her broadband service.

She'd been without television or online access since her car had been repossessed. She'd nixed her morning trip to Starbucks and stopped picking up newsstand copies of *People* and *Entertainment Weekly* to read during her treadmill workouts. Hell, she couldn't even go to the gym because she was behind on her membership dues.

Tish felt isolated, cut off. She had no idea what was going on in the world. For the last two weeks she'd spent her leisure time listening to mournful CDs and leafing through old photo albums, trying to figure out where things had gone so wrong. Addison James was correct: She *was* pathetic.

Stop whining, commanded the voice in the back of her head. *You're not a whiner. Pull yourself up by the bootstraps.*

But the straps were gone off the proverbial boots and she had nothing left to pull herself up by. She was divorced from a man she was still in love with, her car had been repossessed, she carried over eleven thousand dollars in credit card debt, and she hadn't been on a date in six months. Young and single in the city was not what television cracked it up to be.

"Give me the spoon." Delaney waited, palm outstretched.

Biting down on the inside of her cheek to keep from crying, Tish put the tiny pink plastic spoon in her friend's hand.

"Thank you." Delaney tossed the spoon in the trash. She took Tish by the elbow, propelled her past Victoria's Secret and The Gap to a wooden park bench underneath a trellis of fake yellow roses positioned beside a cement mermaid fountain. "Sit."

Tish sat.

"Why don't you let me loan you some money?" Delaney pulled a checkbook from her Prada purse. "To tide you over."

"Friends shouldn't borrow money from friends."

"What kind of friend would I be if I let you flounder?"

"A smart one."

"Tish, stubborn pride won't help you."

"I'm the idiot who dug myself into this hole. It's not your problem."

"But you ran up the credit cards getting your business going and surviving after your divorce. Those are extenuating circumstances. I know you're going to come out on top in the end."

"Most people would tell me to get a real job, to stop pipe dreaming."

It's what she'd been telling herself, too. But she hated so badly to give up on her dream that she'd ignored the mound of debts piling up and simply prayed it would all go away.

"I'm not most people and you know that I understand. Getting your own business up on its legs isn't easy." Delaney did understand. She had her own house-staging business, but she also had a trust fund.

"Maybe some people aren't meant to have their heart's desire," she mumbled, thinking of Shane.

Delaney patted her hand. "You're just in a down cycle. You're a fabulous videographer, Tish. If you can just hang in there, your career is going to take off big time. I know it."

"I appreciate you, Delaney." Tish shook her head. "But I can't let you bail me out of this." The same stubborn pride that had kept her from asking Shane not to walk out the door clutched her tight as a closed fist.

"Why not?"

"I've got to do this on my own," Tish said, knowing she was tripping over her pride, but not knowing how to get out of her own way. "But thank you."

"So what do you plan to do?" Delaney asked softly. She tilted her head and Tish felt the heat of her gaze.

"I'm going to get a real job. Two if it comes to that."

"And how are you going to get to those jobs with no car, and no money or the credit rating to buy one?"

There was the major kink in her plans.

"Well," Delaney said, putting her checkbook away. "If you won't take my money, at least let me loan you a car."

"How are you going to get around?"

"My parents have a spare car I can borrow."

"No, it'll be too big an inconvenience."

"I don't expect you to have to borrow it for long, because I'm going to put a bee in the ear of every dowager with a marriage-minded daughter in River Oaks and tell them what a wonderful videographer you are."

"You didn't much like it when your mother helped your business."

"That's because my mother was trying to meddle in my life. I'm your friend. I don't want to control you or tell you what to do. I just want to help. It hurts my heart to see you in distress."

Her friend's kindness was too much. Tish felt tears pushing at the back of her eyes, threatening to flow down her cheeks. Aw, damn. She wasn't a crier. She was tough. She prided herself on it.

Delaney reached over and hugged her. "Everything is going to be all right. I promise."

When Delaney said it, Tish could almost believe it. But there was a small ugly voice inside her that kept whispering, *Who do you think you are? Daring to dream big dreams? You don't stand a chance. You're just like your mother. Every time you get something good you ruin it.*

Like your credit rating.

Like Shane.

Two years later and the pain still washed over her, fresh as the day he'd walked out—the day she'd let him go forever. It was the biggest mistake of her life. She knew it now and she'd known it as she was letting him slip away. Something in her weird psyche kept thinking that if he loved her, he would understand her. That she shouldn't have to say anything. He should just *know* what she was feeling. But he hadn't known and he'd left because she could not tell him how much he meant to her. And she could not forgive him for not being there when she needed him the most.

Delaney jangled her car keys. "The Acura's yours for as long as you need it."

Swallow your stupid pride for once. Take her up on this.

She'd been unable to fix her marriage, but maybe she could fix her career. Humbled, Tish held out her palm, and closed her fingers around the keys. What else could she do? "Thank you."

"There's more, isn't there? Something else is bothering you."

Tish felt strange talking about the wedding veil, about

the odd vision she'd seen and her irrational fear that Shane was in some kind of trouble. Two weeks had passed and she still couldn't forget what she'd viewed in the mirror. She'd been too afraid of what she would see to put the veil back on again.

"It's safe. You can tell me anything."

"Do you really think your wedding veil has magical powers?" Tish whispered. "Do you really believe in all that wish fulfillment nonsense?"

"You had a vision." It was a statement, not a question.

"How did you know?"

"It's what happened to me in Claire Kelley's consignment shop, the first time I touched the veil."

"How come you never said anything?"

Delaney shrugged. "How do you admit something like that?"

"Point taken." Tish stared across the mall unseeingly, thinking about her disturbing vision.

"You saw the face of your true love, didn't you?"

"No."

"No?" Delaney arched an eyebrow.

"I saw Shane. And I got the awful feeling he was in trouble. Tell me I'm just being silly. It's stupid to think the veil has some kind of magical power, right?"

Delaney shifted on the bench. She looked uncomfortable. "I'm not sure how to answer that. In my vision I saw Nick and then when I met him in person I knew instantly he was the man I was supposed to spend the rest of my life with, even though I was engaged to Evan at the time."

"No fantasy man for me. Just Shane."

"Do you think your mind could have created the vision as a smoke screen for your problems? That you're projecting your fears onto Shane so you don't have to face what's going on in your own life?"

"Maybe."

"It's time to let go of Shane." Delaney's eyes were kind. "You've been holding on to the possibility that he would come back. It's been two years. He's not coming back, Tish."

"I know," she whispered. "We were too different. The maverick wild child and the stalwart soldier. But the deal is, whenever we were good together, we were really, *really* good. Shane connected me to a part of myself I didn't even know existed. He grounded me. Made me feel secure in a way I never felt before or since. When I was around him I felt like more. You know?"

Delaney smiled with understanding. "I do know."

"I screwed it all up, Delaney." Tish's breath hitched.

"There are two sides to every story, Tish, and it seems to me that Shane doesn't know how to forgive. And if he couldn't forgive you for being human, how could he have truly loved you unconditionally? We all make mistakes. Shane's mistake was letting his anger rule his heart."

Tish wanted to cry, but she'd learned a long time ago tears were a weakness she couldn't afford. Delaney was right.

It was time to let go.

The next time Shane surfaced things seemed brighter, lighter. Was that sun on his face? Had someone opened a window?

A soft touch squeezed the fingers of his left hand. A woman's hand. His heart leaped with hope.

"Tish," he whispered, barely able to push his wife's name across his dry, cracked lips.

"It's Elysee." Her voice was quiet, reassuring.

Disappointment locked him in a stone fist. It wasn't Tish. "Elysee?"

"I'm here. Open your eyes. Open your eyes and look at me."

He wanted to look at her, but it wasn't as easy as she made it sound. His eyelids lay heavy as gold medallions. Stubborn. Hanging on to the darkness.

Slowly, he managed to force them open and he saw Elysee Benedict sitting at his bedside, her fingers clasped around his. There was a forlorn expression in her gentle blue eyes that he'd never seen before.

He noticed something else. His right hand was bandaged like a mummy, his whole arm cradled in a sling that slipped over his neck, and it hurt. Throbbing, blinding pain blunted from his fingertips, up through his wrist. He gritted his teeth and forced himself to ignore the pain. He was Secret Service. He knew how to accomplish it.

Elysee sucked in a breath through the cute little gap in her front teeth. "I'm afraid that I have bad news."

"Wh . . . ?" His mouth was so damned dry, his tongue was glued to the roof of his mouth. "What happened?"

"You don't remember?"

He tried to shake his head, but movement hurt too much. "No."

"The groundbreaking at the University of Texas?"

His memory was foggy. He frowned, trying to call up the scene.

"You saved my life." The smile on her face was wistful, but warm. The sight of it caught him low in the gut.

He felt as if he'd stumbled in from a frigid blizzard and she was a hot, crackling fire welcoming him home.

"I did?"

"You did. And I've been here with you ever since."

"How long?" Shane tried to moisten his lips with an arid tongue.

"Thirteen days."

"Thirteen days?" It seemed impossible. How could he have checked out for so long?

"Almost fourteen, actually."

The news flattened him. He felt at once both restless and leaden. "You've been here with me for two weeks? But you have duties, appointments, and responsibilities."

"All canceled. Nothing is as important to me as your recovery."

"It's not necessary."

"Shane, you're not only my bodyguard, but my friend. I'm staying."

She looked so fiercely loyal that he had to smile even if it hurt.

"You gave us quite a scare in the beginning," she went on. "When the backhoe bucket hit you, it caused your brain to bleed. You had surgery."

Her voice went softer and he could tell by the tears swimming in her eyes that he'd been close to death. The realization didn't frighten him, but her emotional reaction did.

"Surgery?"

"They shaved your head. All that beautiful dark hair." She sighed.

He reached up a hand to touch his scalp. It was prickly with hair stubble. He'd been burred before. In the Air Force. In boot camp. He didn't care about the hair. His fingers crept to his right temple, the spot that ached, and he found the raw seam of stitches four fingers long.

"I hate to be the one to have to tell you this, but that's not everything." She smoothed the bedcovers with her fingers, and she couldn't meet his gaze.

He laughed. He didn't mean to laugh at her. It just came out. "No?"

"Your hand."

His chest tightened. She didn't have to say it. He guessed. "Yeah?"

"It was crushed by the backhoe. They managed to save your hand, but it's very doubtful you'll ever regain full use. You're probably going to have to give up protective detail for a desk job."

He couldn't absorb that information. Not now. Not yet. To hear the news that he could no longer be a Secret Service agent on protective detail was more than he could handle at the moment. So he refused to acknowledge it. If he didn't acknowledge it, then how could it be true?

"How are you?" He tightened the fingers of his good hand around hers. "Are you doing all right?"

"Unscathed except for skinned knees when you knocked me down and a little worn out from this bedside vigil. Otherwise A-okay." She canted her head, smiled wryly.

His memory finally flashed and he saw himself pushing Elysee to the platform as the backhoe bucket descended. "And the backhoe operator?"

"He's fine, too."

"No," Shane said. "I mean why was the bastard trying to kill you?"

Elysee gave a gentle laugh. "He wasn't trying to kill me. He'd been up all night because his wife had been giving birth to their first child, but he didn't tell his boss he was sleep-deprived because he wanted to be at the groundbreaking to meet me. He just made a mistake. Pushed the wrong levers, then panicked and kept pushing them."

"You could have been killed."

"But I wasn't, because of you."

The tenderness in her eyes separated his heart from his chest. He felt it free-falling straight to his feet.

"You saved my life," Elysee whispered, her cheeks pinking. "You saved me, Shane. At great personal cost to your own safety."

He'd done his job. Elysee was safe. That's all that mattered.

"I called your parents," she said. "I thought they should know."

"Are they here? In Austin?" His parents were supposed to be on an around-the-world cruise celebrating his father's retirement. They'd been looking forward to this trip their entire lives. He hated to think that they'd been forced to cut their travels short because of him.

"No, I downplayed your injuries. I hope that's okay." Elysee looked anxious. "I remembered you told me how important this trip was to them and I knew you'd hate being responsible for ruining it. I felt a little guilty myself. If you hadn't been rescuing me, you wouldn't have gotten hurt."

"You did good," he said. "Thank you."

In that moment, in that serious exchange of glances, he felt as if he'd known her his entire life. Her calm energy was as comforting as a kitten's purr. He already knew her so well. She was predictable, safe. He liked that about her. With Tish things had always been exciting and electric, but keeping up with her boundless energy had taken constant effort. Elysee was effortless.

"Thank you." Her eyes glistened.

His ego inflated. To think she was looking at him, a scarred war dog, with such adoration and respect. Heady stuff. Was their friendship growing into something more?

It was a scary thought. This wasn't smart, these budding feelings he was having for her—he hadn't been involved with anyone since Tish. Right now, he was feeling pretty damned vulnerable.

Shane thought of Tish again. Wild and rebellious and passionate. Never a dull moment. Life with her had often mimicked an episode of *I Love Lucy*. Madcap, adventuresome, filled with irrepressible spirit. She'd been like a lit firecracker in his hand. Sizzling hot and ready to detonate.

And explode she had.

Their marriage had been the collateral damage.

Shane had learned the hard way that blistering passion was bound to blow up in your face. He'd followed his heart and not his head and it had nearly ruined him.

Elysee was Tish's polar opposite. Not a risk taker at all. It had made guarding her easy and being friends with her even easier. Being married to a woman like her would be serene. And right now, nothing seemed more appealing than serenity.

Shane closed his eyes, unable to keep them open any longer. Waking up, jogging his memory, learning that his skull had been cracked and his hand had been shattered had taken a toll.

He felt the gentle brush of Elysee's lips against his cheek. "That's right, darling," she whispered. "Sleep."

Darling?

The word befuddled him, but he was already sliding away, unable to make sense of why the President's daughter was kissing him and speaking in terms of endearment.

Chapter 4

Tish usually got over the blues by going shopping, but this time, shopping had caused her blues. How was she going to get over that?

At ten o'clock in the morning, she sat in Delaney's Acura outside the Galleria. She wanted to go in and buy a new outfit to cheer herself up, but she was broke. Completely tapped out. Ninety-seven dollars and fifty cents was all she had left in her savings account; there were no groceries in the house and no new wedding gigs in sight.

October was a slow month for weddings. She'd planned to make ends meet by taking the gray tweed suit back and living on her credit card until she had another wedding to photograph. But the suit had been ruined, her credit cards ruthlessly massacred, and her car repossessed.

Unless she could manage to sell a few of her used clothes on e-bay, she was royally screwed. And seriously regretting having closed out her Macy's account after paying it off with the money she'd earned from videotaping Delaney's wedding.

Go in. Go shopping. With ninety-seven fifty you could buy an accessory, or an autumn blouse, or a new pair of jeans.

E-bay. She'd do it tonight. In the meantime, the mall beckoned.

Tish opened the car door and swung her legs to the asphalt.

She poised there, half in, half out of the car, taking stock of her life and the mess she'd made of it.

Stop thinking. Just go shopping. Remember what Mom always taught you. Affluence attracts affluence. You wouldn't have met Delaney if you hadn't been following Mom's hard-and-fast rule.

Tish had met her best friend during college when she'd pledged Phi Beta Kappa at Rice University and had blown her entire IRS refund on a new wardrobe to look the part, with money originally earmarked for tuition.

She and Delaney had ended up rooming together, and if it hadn't been for Delaney feeding her and sharing her textbooks, Tish wouldn't have made it through. Even with Delaney's help, a night job, and the scholarships she'd received, Tish had barely finished college.

Promising herself that she was only going to window-shop, Tish climbed out of the car and headed inside the mall. Nordstrom's was having a sale. She felt the immediate squeeze of excitement. This wasn't just any sale, it was a fire sale—everything except new arrivals was listed at the lowest prices of the year.

Adrenaline streamed her down the aisles. Fossil watches normally priced at seventy-five dollars and up were marked thirty percent off.

Her heart beat faster.

Lingerie was slashed forty percent. Since she had no

one to wear sexy lingerie for, Tish skipped over to the next department.

Shoes. Omigosh, shoes!

Sixty percent off! Designer names. Stilettos and pumps and sandals and boots. Red and blue and black and tan.

Blood rushed through her ears. She felt breathless, faint. A sixty-percent-off sale on expensive designer shoes, and she was dead broke.

Not dead broke. You have ninety-seven fifty.

Tish paused. It wouldn't hurt just to try on a few pairs. Sixty percent off for great shoes. How often did one find a deal like that?

But you have no money and no credit cards.

She walked into the shoe department. Women were grabbing shoes, elbowing each other out of the way. The display racks were a mess. Shoes and shoeboxes were scattered everywhere. Harried salespeople ran to and fro, trying to find missing slippers for disgruntled Cinderellas. After circling the area a few times, Tish found an adorable pair of red Stuart Weitzman sandals.

And they were in her size.

Hands shaking, she took the sandals, sat down in an out-of-the-way area, and slipped them on her feet. They fit like a dream. She got up and walked around. Like walking on whipped cream. She was already halfway in love and she had the perfect red cocktail dress to go with them.

She went back to her seat and nervously lifted the box. They were regularly two hundred and fifteen dollars. She was lousy at math, but she thought she might just have enough.

Clutching the shoes to her chest, she waited in line for the cashier.

Put them back, Tish; this is insane.

She turned to get out of line, but then she thought of the shoes, how cute her feet looked in them. How they made her feel like a princess.

You've got six boxes of Ramen noodles in your pantry. You can hit a couple of happy-hour free buffets. Maybe you can call up an old boyfriend or two and see if you can finagle dinner. The shoes are worth it.

She thought of how it had felt when the waiter chopped up her credit cards, when Mrs. James walked out on her, when she'd discovered her car had been repossessed.

"Next," the cashier called out and Tish realized the woman was talking to her.

She hesitated.

Go ahead. You can always return them.

Tish stepped up and slid the shoes across the counter. She'd let fate decide. If the total came to more than ninety-seven fifty, well, it was out of her hands.

"Ninety-three seventy-two," the cashier said.

Feeling as if she'd just won the lottery, Tish grinned and ran her debit card through the card reader. But just as she punched in her debit code and the machine accepted it, the cahier said, "All sales are final. Absolutely no refunds."

Panic gripped her. She had shoes she did not need and less than four dollars in her checking account.

That's when she knew she'd hit rock bottom.

Hello, my name is Tish Gallagher and I'm a shopaholic.

Every night he was in the hospital, Shane dreamed of Tish. Whether it was the painkillers or his head injury or the combination of both he didn't know, but he just couldn't seem to peel his ex-wife off his subconscious mind.

He dreamed of the way she'd looked when he'd walked out the door, her mouth pressed into an unyielding line unable to say the words he needed to hear. Her jaw clenched, but her eyes begging him to forgive her, begging him to understand, begging him to stay.

But he'd just kept going. If she couldn't learn to ask for what she needed from him, he couldn't continue to try to read her mysterious mind. Now he realized how stubbornly stupid he'd been, how fragile Tish was, in spite of the toughness she projected. He'd wounded her. She'd wounded him. They'd stupidly wounded each other.

Then he'd wake up and look over at Elysee, his dear friend who would touch his good hand, murmur words of reassurance. She looked so serene. He came to expect her, looked forward to opening his eyes and seeing her face. A smile from Elysee sent his demons running for the shadows.

Three weeks he had been stuck in the hospital, enduring a series of tests, undergoing therapy, recovering from surgery. Elysee had steadfastly refused to leave his bedside for any length of time.

Her new bodyguard turned out to be his old partner Cal Ackerman. Cal lurked in the hallway, waiting patiently, watching for danger. Doing Shane's job while he was stuck in the bed.

Wounded. Infirm. Weak. He hated it.

The doctors had told him it would take several months of physical therapy for him to regain partial use of his right hand. They'd told him he would never have full range of motion. He couldn't make a fist, couldn't even hold a spoon. And although there would be no long-term damage from his head injury, he still had headaches. He felt as raw and vulnerable as he had during his first week at boot camp.

"You're being released tomorrow," Elysee said. "And you're going to need a place to recuperate."

"I'll be fine at home," he said, although he'd been dreading the thought of staring at the bare walls of his apartment, having no one to talk to, no place to go except physical therapy three times a week. He realized then how narrow his life had become since the Secret Service had promoted him to protective detail.

"I've spoken to Daddy," she said. "He's agreed the best place for you to recover is at our ranch in Katy."

"I appreciate the offer, Elysee, but this isn't your problem."

"You saved my life." She sounded hurt. "I thought we were friends.

His eyes met hers. She *was* hurt. "I'm sorry," he said gently. "I can't accept."

"I'll be at the ranch with you," she said. "You shouldn't be alone."

"You can't put your life on hold for me. You have duties in Washington. Your father needs you."

"Daddy understands that you need me more."

The dynamics in their relationship had shifted. He'd gone from protector to patient and he didn't like it. He wasn't the man he used to be and he didn't know how to find his way back.

"Elysee, I just don't think it's the best idea."

"Don't make me pull rank on you." She grinned. "I could have your Commander-in-Chief give you a direct order."

He thought again of his sparse, lonely apartment back in Georgetown, and then he looked into Elysee's eyes.

"Please," she said. "Do it for me."

In the back of his mind something was jangling, but his thoughts were still so jumbled he couldn't put a name to it. Too much damned Percodan. He had to lay off the stuff, blinding headaches or not. Because the tender way she looked at him both worried him and drew him to her.

He didn't know how it happened exactly, but Shane found himself saying what he feared wasn't in his best interest. He said the words for her, because she seemed to need to hear him say them. He said them for himself because he didn't want to be alone.

"Yes, okay, I'll recover at your father's ranch."

Five mornings later, Shane and Elysee ate breakfast in the dining room at her father's sprawling ranch house in Katy, with a handful of servants and her new bodyguards hanging around. Shane felt odd as a panda strolling up Broadway, sitting across from Nathan Benedict's daughter reading the *Washington Post* in his pajamas and bathrobe. Elysee leafed through her magazines, trying to catch up on the back issues she'd missed while nursing him through his recovery.

For one thing, the role reversal didn't fit. He should be guarding her, taking care of her, not making idle chitchat over cereal and cantaloupe. For another thing, he wasn't a pajama and bathrobe kind of guy. Nowadays, he preferred sleeping in the buff.

He used to be the sort who snoozed in his BVDs, but Tish had broken him of that habit. When they were married, he never knew when he would awaken to find her tugging at the waistband of his boxer briefs with a come-hither look in her eyes and making impatient get-naked noises at the back of her throat.

"Even though Hurricane Devon took top billing on the day of the UT groundbreaking," Elysee said, "we still managed to make page ten of *People* magazine. Look, here's a picture of you in the hospital."

She held up the magazine for him to see. Sure enough, there was a picture of him sitting up in the hospital bed, head bandaged, IV snaking from the back of his hand, looking like hammered dog crap. He had no idea when the photograph had been taken or who had snapped it.

Something else in the photograph caught his eye and caused Shane's chest to tighten. Elysee was sitting at his bedside, gazing at him with an expression of pure adoration. Cautiously, he shifted his gaze from the page to meet her frank stare from across the table.

She smiled, then ducked her head.

His lungs chuffed against his constricted chest. It wasn't his imagination. She was infatuated with him.

Shane gulped. Oh, shit. He didn't know how to feel about this discovery. The truth was it felt pretty damned nice being here with her, knowing how much she respected and admired him. Knowing he respected and admired her just as much. It was flattering.

It's hero worship is what it is. Don't let your ego swell out of control, Tremont.

"Omigosh," Elysee gasped and splayed a hand against her heart.

"What is it?"

"It's my old nanny, Rana." Elysee held up the magazine again, showing him a photograph of a woman in her early forties who looked to be of East Indian descent.

The woman's eyes blazed intensely. Her mouth was set in a serious expression. The headline read DEATHLIST TARGET.

"What's that all about?" he asked.

Elysee scanned the article. "Rana is a key player in a group called WorldFem that helps women in Third World and Middle Eastern countries escape honor killings at the hands of their families. Now she's being targeted herself for bringing shame on her country! Oh, this is terrible. What is wrong with people?"

It was a philosophical question Shane couldn't begin to answer. "This woman used to be your nanny?"

"Yes, when I was very small, for the couple of years my parents lived in London. Rana cared for me while my mother was getting her graduate degree at Oxford. She taught me how to speak Hindi. Then later, after Mother died, Dad hired her again while he was governor of Texas. She was with us a little over three years then, from the time I was eleven and a half until I turned fifteen."

"You speak Hindi?"

"Well, not fluently, but I can get by."

"I'm impressed. I didn't know that about you, Elysee. Who knew you were such a woman of mystery?"

"I know what you're trying to do." She smiled. "Thanks for that."

"Thanks for what?"

"Trying to get my mind off Rana's grim plight. I've got to speak to Dad, see if he'll throw some political muscle around and get the heat off Rana."

"You know next year is an election year."

"Meaning what?"

"Your father has to be careful what causes he champions if he wants to get re-elected."

"What's more important? Rana's life or winning an election?"

Shane raised his palms. "Hey, I'm on your side. I'm just pointing out your father's advisors might discourage him from wasting political energy on this issue."

"Well, he's got to do something. We just can't stand by and let whackos with crazy ideas kill Rana because she's trying to save women held down by an archaic system."

"You know it's more complicated than that."

"God." Her eyes flashed. It was the first time he'd seen her look so passionate. Her verve both surprised and delighted him. "I hate politics."

"You definitely should talk to your father. I was just pointing out it might not be a slam dunk."

Elysee closed the magazine. "I've got to get my mind off this. Nothing I can do until Dad drops by the ranch tomorrow. Why don't we take a walk in the garden this morning before your physical therapy session?"

"Sure."

"The chrysanthemums are in full bloom. I'd like you to see them. My mother planted the flowers before she died." Her voice saddened.

They finished their breakfast and Elysee waited patiently when he almost lost his balance getting up from the table and had to pause a moment. Since the surgery, if he moved too quickly he got dizzy. Damn this cursed weakness. He bit down on his bottom lip to keep from letting loose a string of foul words.

"Easier than yesterday," she said brightly.

If Tish were here, she would tell him it was okay to swear. She would probably even get the ball rolling with a few choice words of her own. Shane smiled, thinking about it.

"That's how I like to see you." Elysee tucked her arm through his. "With a nice big grin on your face."

When he looked at Elysee he saw all the ways she wasn't his ex-wife. Her hair was mousy brown; Tish's deep auburn. She was thin, petite; Tish busty and tall. She was quiet and thoughtful; Tish was energetic and spontaneous.

Something stirred inside him. Not desire, but something just as compelling for a man who was feeling vulnerable. Contentment. Around Elysee he felt content.

She maneuvered him out the back door. They picked their way across the patio, up and over the wooden deck, past the gazebo and down the walkway leading to the gardens. Once he was in motion, Shane's muscles relaxed and his joints loosened. His feet grew more self-assured over the cobblestones. No more dizziness.

The top of Elysee's head came to his chin and the smell of her gentle shampoo crowded his nose. Lavender. It had been his grandmother's favorite perfume. Tish preferred spicy fragrances. Like cinnamon and anise and ginger—exotic, sharp, and memorable.

Strangely, a lump formed in his throat. Damn injury brought his emotions too close to the surface. Shane swallowed back the bitter lump and clenched his jaw.

The late October weather had finally cooled from the intense dog-day summer heat. It had rained the night before and the damp morning breeze felt good against his skin. Fall flowers were in full flush. Pink and orange and rust-colored. Elysee leaned over to pick a petal. She straightened, the bloom held to her nose, and took a deep breath. "Smells like autumn."

The eastern sunlight dappled through the languid

limbs of willow trees and cast Elysee's face in an ethereal glow. Looking at her, Shane's chest tightened again.

She was so delicate, so fragile. Her soft blue eyes looked the way clouds felt. He found himself thinking crazily—*cumulus, stratus, cirrus*—and he had an irresistible urge to comb his fingers through the wisps of her flyaway hair. For the briefest of moments the sunlight tinged her hair auburn and she looked vaguely like Tish.

His eyes must have given away his impulse because she gave him a little smile and her gaze hung on his lips.

"Shane," she whispered and dropped the flower blossom. "Shane."

He leaned forward, surprised by how calm he felt, how utterly at peace. No raw passion. No disturbing chemistry. No volatile boom-boom of his heart like the first time he'd kissed Tish. Nothing except tranquil serenity. His lips brushed her mouth.

She kissed him back, tentatively curling one hand around his arm.

Safe, he thought. Safe and simple and comforting as mashed potatoes. Elysee would never max out his credit cards behind his back. She'd never challenge his authority, or question his motives.

The kiss was nice and sweet and reliable. Nothing to complain about. Everyone liked mashed potatoes.

But the minute the kiss was over and he caught the puppy-dog-in-love look in Elysee's eyes, Shane realized he'd just crossed a very important line that he hadn't meant to cross.

Chapter 5

The following day, the President arrived at the ranch for a weekend-long stay. Nathan Benedict was a tall, lean man, as aloof as his daughter was welcoming. He was fiercely intelligent and a moderate Republican who commanded respect from both parties. He was a man of few words, but when he spoke, everyone listened. Some compared him to Abraham Lincoln.

Shane's admiration for him was second only to his admiration for his own father and grandfather. Whenever he was in Nathan's presence, he felt as if a great honor had been bestowed upon him, but he was nervous as well, afraid that he wouldn't live up to the President's standards.

The dinner conversation was restrained. Nathan sat at one end of the table, Elysee down the length of the table at the other end, and Shane in the middle, feeling decidedly displaced. He should be outside the doorway with Cal, not dining on roasted chicken and tomato aspic with the leader of the free world.

He was especially self-conscious about his table man-

ners. The physical therapist had insisted he use his right
as much as possible, but not tonight. As awkward as eating with his non-dominant hand was, it was preferable
to anything his injured paw could accomplish. He ate
slowly, carefully, aware of each bite. A silence fell over
the table and he realized that Elysee was studying him.

And that Nathan was watching his daughter watch
Shane.

He shifted uncomfortably in his seat and put his fork
down.

Elysee coaxed a few stories from her father about his
trip to China, but ultimately she was the one who carried
the dinner conversation. Toward the end of the meal, she
brought up Rana Singh and what she'd read in *People*
magazine.

"Dad, you've got to do something to get Rana off that
death list."

"Sweetheart." Her father smiled at her kindly. "The
fact that she's been featured in *People* has effectively
guaranteed her safety. If she were murdered, everyone
would know who was responsible."

"So? It doesn't stop them from killing their daughters,
their wives, their granddaughters, their nieces over their
illogical sense of honor."

"Elysee, all of that takes place in other countries. Rana
lives here, in the U.S."

"But she goes overseas to help those women. Evil men
could kill her then and the U.S. couldn't touch them."

"Then Rana's just going to have to stay in the U.S."

"Well, what about those other women? If Rana's not
helping them, then who will? Can't you do something?
It's a horrifying practice."

"Agreed, but making moral and religious policy in other countries is beyond my scope."

"But you're the President of the United States! How can it be beyond your scope?"

"We had a similar conversation when you were thirteen and I was governor and you thought it was unfair that you had to pay adult prices at the movie theater, but you weren't allowed to vote, drink, or drive a car."

"It's not the same thing at all. You're comparing Rana's life to the price of a movie ticket?"

"You're taking it out of context, Elysee. What I'm saying is that I'm not the president of the world."

"Well, you should be."

"My opponents might disagree with you there."

"You might not want to help, Dad, but I've got to get involved with WorldFem."

"Be mindful of your position. You have a lot of influence. You must choose your causes with care."

"Exactly. What's the point of having influence if you can't effect change?"

"Just proceed with caution."

"I'm not a child, father. I understand my responsibilities."

Nathan frowned, but said nothing. Father and daughter exchanged a meaningful look. Shane couldn't help wondering if the President was thinking about Elysee's broken engagements and the men who'd taken advantage.

She pushed back from the table. "If you'll excuse me, I have a bit of a headache. I think I'll go to bed early."

"Good night."

Elysee paused at the door, and looked at him over her shoulder. "Shane?"

"Shane and I have a few things to discuss in private," her father said.

"You're not going to fire him off my detail just because he got hurt, are you?"

Was he? It was Shane's greatest fear.

"No, no, of course not. It's just the first time I've had a chance to speak with him in person since the incident."

"Oh. Okay." Looking appeased, Elysee left the room.

Nathan Benedict pushed back his chair, nodded at Shane. "A brandy in the study?"

"Sure." He didn't usually drink, but when the President of the United States suggested you take a brandy in the study, you took a brandy in the study. Shane followed Nathan past Cal Ackerman, standing sentry in the hallway.

He had the feeling his old buddy had been eavesdropping on their dinner conversation. It was a complication of the job, being privy to high-placed secrets but having to pretend that you didn't hear or see anything you weren't supposed to.

They exchanged glances, but Cal's face was unreadable. Shane wished he could change places with his former partner. He wanted his old role back. This strange new one didn't fit.

"Shut the door," Nathan said.

Shane entered the study behind him. He closed the door with his left hand, and kept his right hand tucked in his pocket.

"Let's see the hand."

"Excuse me, sir?"

"Your hand. I heard it was crushed. That you'll never be able to use a gun again."

"That's just one doctor's opinion." Shane shrugged.

"Let me see the hand," Nathan repeated.

He didn't want to comply. Was the man trying to humiliate him? Or use his injury as a reason to dismiss him, even though Benedict had promised Elysee he wouldn't?

The thought angered him. His eyes locked with the President's. "What for?"

"I want to see what you were willing to sacrifice for my daughter."

It was an odd statement. It effectively diffused Shane's anger, but not his embarrassment. Slowly, he pulled his hand from his pocket and thrust it under Nathan Benedict's nose. He steeled his jaw, hardened his feelings.

"Can you make a fist?"

Shane bent his fingertips as far they would go. His mangled paw wouldn't even make a good talon. His fingers felt stiff as concrete and almost as cold. They ached, but then again, they hadn't really stopped aching since he'd awakened from the coma. What good was a Secret Service agent who couldn't pull a trigger?

"They had to fuse the metacarpals in your hand." Nathan said it as a statement, as if he had already talked to Shane's doctors.

"Yes."

"You took a blow to the temple as well, survived a brain bleed without any lasting damage."

"That's what I've been told."

"You saved my daughter's life." Benedict headed for the wet bar in the corner of the room.

"I did what had to be done." Self-consciously, Shane eased his hand back into his pocket.

"You're a hero." Benedict poured the brandy and

turned back to him. He extended the brandy snifter toward Shane's left hand.

"I'm not." How could he be a hero when he couldn't even make a fist? "I was simply doing my job."

"It's more than that."

"Beg your pardon?" What was the man getting at?

"Your job is your identity. I know all about you, Tremont. I know your grandfather was killed at Normandy on D-day and your father is a decorated Vietnam POW. I know you saved a fellow recruit from friendly fire during boot camp maneuvers. Heroism is in your blood. I also know that you've had some sadness in your life and that your marriage broke up because of it."

As a Secret Service agent on protective duty in the White House, he knew he'd undergone the most extensive of background checks. He just hadn't realized how extensive. If the government knew the reasons his marriage had ended, then they knew everything there was to know about Shane Tremont.

"What's your point?" Shane asked bluntly.

At this juncture, he felt he had nothing else to lose. Elysee might believe her father wouldn't cut him loose from protective detail because of his injury. Shane, however, harbored no such illusions. He was useless as a bodyguard, at least until his hand was fully functional again.

If that ever happens.

He swallowed hard. No. He wasn't even going to entertain that thought. He would recover. Fully. Completely. He was determined.

Benedict took a sip of his brandy, but never took his eyes off Shane. "My daughter's in love with you."

Shane was bowled over. It wasn't what he'd expected to hear. "I'm aware of that, sir."

"Elysee told me that you kissed her."

He tensed. Where was this conversation headed? He'd done it. He'd kissed her and he wasn't a liar. "Yes, sir."

"Why?"

"It felt like the right thing to do at the time." Shane tried to gauge the President's reaction and was surprised when he nodded.

"Do you have tender feelings for her?"

"I'm very fond of Elysee. We're good friends."

"I'm aware of the psychological bond that develops between a bodyguard and the person he's protecting," Benedict said. "Especially when the bodyguard saves the protectee's life."

"What exactly are you trying to say, sir?" Shane took a swig of the stout brandy. It burned his throat as he swallowed back the biting mouthful.

"I respect you, Tremont. But more than that, I like you. You're honorable and straightforward. You don't pull any punches, but you can be trusted to keep your mouth shut."

"Thank you, sir."

"With someone like you, I wouldn't have to worry that Elysee would be taken care of," he said.

"No, sir," Shane said. "You have no worries on that score. I'd protect Elysee with my dying breath."

Yeah? And how are you going to do that with a useless hand?

"And you've proven it." Benedict kept nodding. "She couldn't do any better than to marry a man like you."

Marry?

Shane's gaze flew to Nathan Benedict's face. This

was the first time such a notion had crossed his mind, but he felt that any man would be damned lucky to marry Elysee.

"Until now, she's been picking these spineless peckerheads who are just interested in her because of who she is. But I don't have to tell you that. You've been her bodyguard for over a year. You know."

"Yes, sir."

"Then she gets her heart broken when her flash-in-the-pan boyfriends realize they'll have to sign a pre-nup agreement leaving them with nothing if they divorce her. Or they discover what it's really like living in the public eye and find out they're never going to be stars just because they've glommed on to her. But you, you're different. You really care."

"I do care about Elysee, sir." And he did. But just how deep did his feelings run? He was startled to realize how much he did care. It didn't compare to what he'd felt for Tish of course, but he never wanted to feel that kind of chaotic madness again.

Benedict polished off his brandy with a long gulp; for the first time Shane realized the man was as nervous as he was. "Have you ever considered getting remarried? I know this sounds strange, but I'm worried about my little girl. I was forty-eight when she was born and I'm not going to be around forever. I'd like to see her happily married to a good man who'll do right by her."

"Sir, I . . . ." Shane didn't know what to think, much less say.

Nathan Benedict held up a hand. "Elysee loves you and you're fond of her. You already know how easy she is to get along with. You kissed her. That means something."

Did it? Shane stroked his chin.

"Whatever you decide, you have my undying gratitude for saving her life. If you hadn't gotten between her and that backhoe . . ." Nathan let his voice trail off and Shane saw his eyes glisten with emotion. "You're going to be compensated for that. And I want you to stay here at the ranch until your doctors release you from their care."

"What about my job as Elysee's bodyguard?"

Benedict shifted his weight and didn't meet Shane's eyes. "I don't see how you can continue being her bodyguard, knowing she's in love with you. But if you regain full function of your hand, we'll find another protective detail for you."

"And if Elysee and I were to get married? What then? What kind of work would I do?"

"How would you feel about heading up the Secret Service? Marshal Vega is retiring next year. The position has a lot of power. You'd be effecting policy, in charge of all my personal security, my life," Nathan Benedict said with his unerring ability to read people. He'd figured out what motivated Shane most—the desire to protect and serve.

"Elysee is a wonderful girl."

"She is."

"Give it some thought, Shane. I'd be honored to call you son."

He looked at the President and a feeling he'd never wrestled with came over him. He felt flattered and intrigued, honored, and yet he didn't want to be given a job he hadn't earned just because he'd married the President's daughter. He also didn't want to marry Elysee simply because it was the easiest thing to do.

"I have to be honest, sir. I have no idea how I truly

feel. About Elysee. About the job. About myself." He indicated his injured hand.

"I understand." Benedict nodded. "You've got a lot to think about."

"Yes," he said. But deep within, Shane heard a soft voice whisper, *This is it. This is the way to let go of Tish forever.*

The next afternoon, Elysee took Shane horseback riding around the perimeter of the ranch. The kitchen staff packed them a picnic lunch and the day was all blue sky, cool breeze, and autumn wildflowers in full bloom.

They ate their lunch beside the lake, dining on chicken salad sandwiches, carrot sticks, and fresh fruit. Elysee talked animatedly about how she wanted to get involved with WorldFem. He could see the caring in her eyes, knew her heart ached over the injustices. They were so much alike in that respect. Both of them focused on making the world a better place, though each in their own way.

"What a team we could be," she said. "Going around the world, fighting for women's rights. I'd give speeches, visit women in need, head charity drives, raise funds, and you could be there to watch over me. Making it all possible. If only I could convince my father that I know what I'm doing and that with you at my side I wouldn't get taken advantage of."

"Elysee," he said softly, "I'm afraid I can't be your bodyguard."

Alarm spread across her. "How come?"

He laid his right hand on the picnic blanket between them. "I can't protect you, not with this."

"You're going to get full function back. You're dedicated to your physical therapy and you've got the right mental attitude," she encouraged.

"I'm trying my best, but I have to face the reality that no matter how hard I try, it might not ever happen. Besides, it's more than the hand."

"You're quitting? But why would you walk away from a job you love?"

"It's not that simple."

She leaned forward, bracing her chin in her palm. "Explain it to me."

He thought of his conversation with her father the night before. He thought about how lonely he'd been for the last two years. How much he'd loved being married until the worst had happened for him and Tish. How he'd like to have that kind of happiness back again. It was time to release the past and move on. And Elysee, the one he was closest to, was the perfect person to do it with.

"I can't continue being your bodyguard, under the circumstances."

"What circumstances?"

He didn't know what he was going to say. He hadn't planned it, hadn't even made up his mind for sure until the words were out of his mouth.

"Elysee Benedict, would you marry me?"

"What?" She blinked, looking completely caught off guard.

"Would you marry me?" he repeated.

Elysee squealed, knocking over the picnic basket on her way into his lap. She hugged his neck and rained kisses upon his face. "Yes, yes, yes!"

Shane blamed circumstances—his injury, their forced proximity, the beautiful autumn day. He blamed his job, his role as her hero. He blamed the way her eyes, blue as a robin's egg, promised to ease the loneliness he hadn't realized ran so deep. He blamed the earnestness on her face, her sweet scent, and her open honesty that made him want to tell her everything.

But most of all, he blamed himself. For missing being married so badly he wanted to do it again, and for failing Tish so spectacularly that he felt a burning need to make some kind of amends. He was crossing all kinds of boundaries, violating oaths, breaking taboos. Bottom line of the bodyguard's code—never, ever get emotionally involved with the person you're protecting.

What had he done?

"Elysee," he said, and then stopped. How did you go about taking back an impromptu marriage proposal? "Listen to me a minute, sweetheart, I . . ."

"I'm calling Daddy!" she cried and whipped her cell phone from her pocket. "I can't wait to tell him the good news. He really, really likes you. Oh, Shane, I'm so happy."

He looked down into her face, her eyes brimming with joyous tears, and his heart stilled with confusion and tenderness and a strange sort of peace. He liked taking care of people and Elysee let him take care of her. That was important for a man. To feel needed. It was something independent-minded Tish had never understood.

This was suddenly too real.

Tell her it was a mistake. Tell her you didn't mean to ask her to marry you just yet. Tell her you jumped the gun, spoke too soon. You don't even have a ring.

But he couldn't. She looked so happy and making her happy made him feel good. This was the right thing to do. No second-guessing. He'd made his decision and he was sticking with it.

"Daddy," Elysee bubbled into the phone, "guess what? Shane and I are getting married!"

And that's how Shane Tremont, middle-class boy from small-town America, found himself engaged to the President's daughter.

Chapter 6

Tish was sitting cross-legged on her couch, staring at the new Stuart Weitzman sandals propped on her coffee table and feeling like a binge eater who had just downed two boxes of double-stuffed Oreos, when the telephone rang.

She let it ring.

What if it's a job?

Forcing a smile so the caller couldn't tell she'd over-indulged on shoes two days ago and had the grand total of three dollars and seventy-eight cents in her checking account, she picked it up, answering with the name of her business. "Capture the Moment Videos."

"Tish Gallagher?"

"Yes. How may I help you?" Tish uncoiled her legs and sat up straight.

"Amber Wilson gave me your name. You videotaped her wedding and she can't stop raving about how great you are."

"Thank you." Her spirits soared on the praise.

"I'm getting married this Christmas Eve and while I

know it's rather short notice, I'm on the hunt for the best videographer in Houston."

"You've found her," Tish said with a smile.

"My name is Elysee Benedict—"

"Whoa, wait a minute. *The* Elysee Benedict?"

"That's my name." There was amusement in her voice.

"Elysee Benedict? As in the President's daughter?"

"Well, yes, but I'm going to have to ask you for complete confidentiality."

Tish couldn't believe it. The daughter of the President of the United States was calling?

Her bravado vanished and she was left breathless. This was the opportunity of a lifetime. If she snagged this job, she was set. All the fame and fortune she'd been dreaming of would fall right into her lap.

"Totally. Zipped lip. Tick a lock. Throw away the key."

Elysee laughed. "I'm interviewing videographers this afternoon at my father's ranch in Katy. Are you available to drop by, say, three o'clock–ish?"

"Absolutely." Tish would have found a way to go to the moon for Elysee Benedict. She couldn't believe it. The President's daughter.

"I'll tell security to expect you. Just check in at the front gate and they'll direct you around."

Several hours later, Tish arrived at the Benedict ranch, her heart filled with hope. She had changed outfits several times before deciding to go with a Bohemian style reflecting her personality—fresh, creative, fun. She wore a multi-colored circle skirt made of crinkle cloth with an expensive but simple turquoise V-neck tee. She put earrings in all four piercings in each ear, piled on the bracelets, and finished the ensemble with turquoise ballet-style slippers. She felt a hundred times more comfortable than in the Chanel suit she'd worn to meet Addison James.

After making it past the security checkpoints, Tish found herself standing on the front steps of a sprawling ranch house that put her in mind of Southfork, from the old television show *Dallas*. Her body tingled. She was here. At the Benedict ranch, about to have a meeting with the President's daughter.

A woman dressed in a simple black pantsuit and a stern expression met her at the door. "I'm Lola Zackary," she said, "Elysee's executive secretary."

"Good to meet you."

Lola ushered her into a sitting room furnished with polished antiques. "A female Secret Service agent will frisk you for weapons, ma'am."

The Secret Service agent came into the room and frisked her. The woman nodded at Tish's purse and the backpack containing her DVD player, video camera, and other equipment. "I'll need to look through your bags."

Tish surrendered her things and stood watching while the agent leafed through them.

"Take a seat, ma'am," Lola said when the agent had finished her job and left the room. "Miss Benedict will see you shortly."

Tish sat on a high-backed chair near the window and knotted her fingers in her lap. The minute the Secret Service woman had vanished from the room, doubts crowded in. They were the same doubts that had occasionally overwhelmed her in the middle of the night when she was married to Shane.

You're out of your element. Out of your league. For Pete's sake, you grew up on the south side of Houston. Who would want the likes of you?

But she'd come so very far from her early background and, excluding her problem with impulse shopping, she was a pretty decent person. She was loyal to her friends, volunteered at the local battered women's shelter a couple of hours a week. She was good at her job. But most of all, she genuinely cared about people.

"You're Tish?" Elysee Benedict came through the door with a warm, welcoming smile. She wore a simple pair of beige slacks and a black silk blouse that washed all the color from her skin. Her hair was pulled back with a headband. It wasn't a look that flattered her narrow face.

"You're too young to be getting married," Tish wanted to tell her, because she'd been Elysee's age when she'd gotten married. But instead she enthusiastically shook her hand and said, "Hi, I'm Tish."

"I love your outfit," Elysee said.

"Thank you."

"And such gorgeous hair." She gazed enviously at Tish's mass of corkscrew curls.

"It's an untamed terror, is what it is."

"Try working with this thin, fine mess." Elysee touched a poker-straight lock of mousy brown hair. "I'd kill for curls like yours."

"No one is ever satisfied with their hair. I bet Jennifer Aniston hates hers."

"Oh, I've met Jennifer," Elysee said.

"Really?" Tish widened her eyes. "She's my favorite actress."

"Mine, too."

"Is she going to be at the wedding?" Excitement made Tish's palms grow sweaty. She'd never thought that movie stars might be attending the ceremony.

"We're hoping to keep things fairly small. Two hundred guests. I don't have room for a celebrity list, plus it becomes such a security nightmare. Please, sit down." Elysee waved at the chair Tish had just vacated and took the adjacent seat.

Tish sat.

"So tell me a little about yourself." Elysee seemed so poised; but of course, growing up in the public eye, she'd received lots of coaching. Tish wished she'd had someone to coach her through the bumps in life.

Tish took a deep breath to calm her nerves. "I started my own wedding video business five years ago. I'm slowly starting to gain a reputation locally."

"No, no." Elysee shook her head. "Tell me about Tish the person. I already know you have gorgeous red hair and Jennifer Aniston is your favorite actress. I googled you so I know that you went to college at Rice. Are you married?"

"Divorced."

"That's a shame. I've gone through three broken engagements and while I'm not presuming to compare that to a divorce, I do know how painful breakups can be."

Tish wanted to tell her, *Honey, you don't know nothing until the love of your life ends your marriage on your first anniversary by walking out on you because you couldn't live up to his expectations.* Instead she said, "Three?"

"It's a lot, I know." Elysee shifted in her seat. "My father tells me I'm in love with love, and maybe I am. But my main problem has been that I have trouble sorting out the men who really like me for myself from those who want to be with me for who I am and what I can do for them."

Tish clicked her tongue in sympathy. "That's got to be rough."

"It is." Elysee smoothed imaginary wrinkles in the fabric of her slacks. "But that's the way it goes."

"How did you know this fiancé was a keeper?"

Elysee blushed. "For one thing, he saved my life."

"Literally?"

"Yes."

"That's a good start." Tish laughed. "At least you know he cares enough to put his life on the line for you."

Elysee leaned in and whispered, "He's my body-guard."

"You're marrying one of your Secret Service agents?"

"Uh-huh."

"Just like Susan Ford?"

"Uh-huh." This time she giggled, absurdly happy. Tish remembered being that giddy once.

"How romantic."

"It is." Elysee reached over and touched Tish's fore-arm. "But the best part is that what I feel for him isn't the kind of crazy, off-the-wall, gotta-have-him-or-I'll-die kind of love like I had with the other three fiancés. It's a steady and strong and mature love."

"Um, that's good." Tish struggled to keep her opinion from showing. She would never have married Shane if there hadn't been such seething chemistry between them. For one thing they were just too different. For another, without chemistry, well, what was the point? You might as well just marry your best friend. If every time she'd looked at him her knees hadn't gone weak and the breath hadn't squeezed from her lungs, if her womb hadn't ached and her mouth hadn't yearned for his kisses, she would never have taken the risk.

Even now, she would occasionally wake up in the middle of the night still burning for Shane's touch. Her body still craved him with a certain kind of wildness she'd never felt for another man before or since.

Then again, she was divorced. Maybe Elysee was on to something. Maybe steady, sweet, and mature was the way to go.

They talked for over an hour, discussing everything under the sun before they watched Tish's wedding montage DVD. They just seemed to click—she and the President's daughter. And it was easy, without any of the tension and need to prove herself that Tish had felt with Addison James.

"Oh my goodness." Elysee laughed. "I love how you humanize the guests by catching them in vulnerable moments. The sleeping baby. The canoodling grandparents. The teens sneaking kisses in the rectory. The friends of the groom opening up about their feelings for their buddy as they tie cans to the getaway car."

Elysee's words sent a warm pool of pride sliding into her belly. Even if Tish didn't get the assignment, she would come away from this interview feeling much better about her work. "Thank you for saying so."

"My father's warned me against making snap decisions," Elysee said. "Three broken engagements by age twenty-two and all that, but Tish, I like you. I like your work. And I want to hire you as my wedding videographer. What do you say? Can you do it? Are you available for Christmas Eve? It's already late October so I know that doesn't leave you much time for production, but I have my heart set on getting married on Christmas Eve. It would have been my parents' thirtieth anniversary if my mother had lived."

Every dream she'd ever had was coming true. Not only would Elysee's wedding go a long way toward getting Tish out of debt, but also, once word got out that she was the videographer to the President's daughter, the telephone would never stop ringing. "Oh, Elysee, that's so sweet and romantic."

"You don't have to answer right away. I'm sure you've got a lot to think about. This assignment isn't going to be easy with all the security details and confidentiality issues. Would you like a day or two to think it over?"

"I suppose I shouldn't make snap decisions either," Tish said, "but I can tell you're going to be such a dream to work with and I can't imagine a greater honor than videoing your Christmas Eve wedding. I can rise to the challenges. I'd be honored."

Elysee clapped her hands. "That's so great. I'm so excited!"

"Right, right." Tish nodded. "Leading up to the wedding, I'll need several sessions with you and your fiancé, interviewing you on your childhoods, going through old family photo albums and scrapbooks. Talking with your family and friends to get a real sense of who you are and what your union is all about. I want to capture the spirit of you both. I spend a lot of time on research, but it pays off in the quality of your video. This is a once in a lifetime affair and we want it be something you'll cherish and show your children and your grandchildren. I charge by the job, not by the hour, so you don't have to worry that the clock is ticking."

"Absolutely. That's exactly what I want. I'm so happy we're on the same page." Elysee grinned.

"Me, too."

"I want to introduce you to my fiancé. I don't think he'll have any objections, but since you will be working closely with him for the reception video, I want to make sure you guys click as well."

"Certainly." Tish nodded and prayed Elysee's fiancé loved her as much as Elysee seemed to.

"Could you stay for dinner?"

Dinner at the Benedict ranch or Ramen noodles in her apartment? Jeez, what a dilemma.

"I can stay."

"Excellent. Let me just get my secretary, Lola, to write you out a retainer check and we'll be good to go."

His physical therapy session had gone badly and Shane was in a foul mood. Determined to get the use of his hand back, he'd told the physical therapist, Pete Larkin, to challenge him. Larkin had been reluctant, insisting it was too soon, but Shane had been adamant.

And he'd failed miserably.

Not only had he been unable to complete the exercises, he'd ended up straining the muscles in his wrist and forearm as well, setting back his progress for days, and bringing on a fresh round of red-hot pain.

He'd suffered his defeat in stoic silence, but a dark cloud of anger gathered thickly over him. He hated being weak. And the therapy session had brought home an ugly truth.

He would never be the same again.

It was a disturbing realization that shook him to the very center of his masculinity. He had been a tough, strong man, with lightning-fast reflexes and deadly aim. But that was before the accident.

Who was he now?

What would he be if he couldn't be a bodyguard? His family history had indoctrinated him to be a hero. He'd never considered any other professional role. With these disparaging thoughts circling his brain he walked into the ranch house, telling himself he had to put on a cheery face for Elysee's sake. None of this was her fault.

"Honey, is that you?" Elysee's voice called to him from the sitting room.

He wanted to slide under the carpet and wait for his dark mood to pass before facing his bubbly bride-to-be, but he didn't have that option. She caught him in the hallway, took him by the left hand and, chattering like a three-year-old at her birthday party, dragged him toward the sitting room.

"I've found our videographer. She's the most dynamic, creative, interesting person and I know you're just going to love her."

"If you love her . . ." Shane intended on finishing the sentence with "I'll love her," but when he saw the woman sitting in front of the window, his heart just stopped.

No, it couldn't be.

Elysee hooked her elbow around his arm. "Honey, this is Tish Gallagher. Tish, meet my fiancé, Shane Tremont."

Tish stared into Shane's eyes. Time evaporated and the years fell away.

Her face instantly went ice cold as blood drained from her cheeks. Her heart rate dropped and she heard the slow, loud *boom, boom, boom* of blood beating against her eardrums. Dumbly, she stood there, mouth hanging open. Unable to speak. Unable to move. Unable to breathe.

Shane looked different now—older, leaner, with a hollow cast to his cheeks—but wiser, and if possible, even more handsome than she remembered. His hair was clipped close to his head in a precision military cut. When they had been married, she'd coaxed him into growing it out, but she had to admit the very short cut suited him.

And then she saw the scar at his temple.

Tish felt a sharp, sudden pain in her own temple at exactly the same spot as his wound. He was hurt. He'd had brain surgery. That was why his hair was so short.

She thought of what Elysee had said about her body-guard saving her life. The full impact hit her then. Elysee Benedict's fiancé was her ex-husband. For one microsecond, her heart just stopped. She'd told herself that she was over Shane, that she was no longer in love with him. But one look into his eyes and she knew it was all a vicious lie she'd been telling herself—a fairytale falsehood to keep the demons at bay.

Her initial impulse was to turn and flee as far from this house and her past as possible. But running was a luxury she could ill afford. If she wanted to achieve her life-long ambition and pay off her maxed-out credit cards, she had to stick this out.

Silence stretched into the room. It seemed to go on forever, until Tish was almost convinced she'd been ensnared in some sort of cosmic time warp. His gaze was on her face and no matter how hard she tried, she couldn't tear her eyes away. What to do?

Her right hand fluttered to her throat. This would be a very good time to faint. Unfortunately she wasn't the fainting type. Shane, her Shane, was engaged to marry the daughter of the President of the United States.

Snap out of it. You can't let Elysee know who you are or you'll lose the job and with it, all your cherished dreams. So what if she's engaged to Shane? He doesn't belong to you anymore.

Tish swallowed hard and pasted an artificial smile on her face. Honestly, someone should nominate her for a frickin' Oscar. She cleared her throat, put her hand out, and stepped the short distance between them.

"Hello," she said. "I'm very pleased to make your acquaintance, Mr. Tremont."

Shane didn't smile, didn't take her hand. It was only then she realized he had his right hand tucked into the pocket of his trousers.

Why wouldn't he shake her hand? Oh, God, was he going to make a big deal of this and ruin her chances at the opportunity of a lifetime, just because they were once married to each other?

"I don't shake hands," he said. "An accident."

"Oh," she said, feeling relieved that she didn't have to touch him, but at the same time sorry not to feel the heat of his hand against hers.

"So you're the best wedding videographer in the business?" he said.

"Yes," she replied and proudly raised her chin. "I am."

They used to have fights over her business. He claimed she spent too much money on camera equipment while they were trying to get a fledgling household started. He'd wanted her to take a part-time job to pay for her overhead. She'd accused him of not supporting her artistic vision.

Ha, so there. I made it without you. She'd gotten good enough at her craft to bag the President's daughter's wedding.

Hell, Tish, he's one-upped you again. Shane's bagged the President's daughter and you're going to have to film the whole ceremony.

Misery crawled through her, but she'd be damned

if she'd let him see how this development affected her. "Congratulations on your impending marriage," she said through clenched teeth.

"Thank you," he replied, sounding equally as tense.

"Did I tell you Shane saved my life?" Elysee interjected. She was gazing at Shane's face as if he'd created the sun.

"Yes, you did." Not surprising. He seemed to make a habit of rescuing damsels in distress and then asking them to marry him. "You sound like a real-life Sir Galahad, Shane."

Better watch out, honey. There's a real downside to these big burly guardian types.

"Oh, he is. Shane saved my life and now I've been nursing him back to health." Elysee stroked Shane's upper arm.

Yes, this story was sounding decidedly familiar. Tish thought of that first night she and Shane had spent together. How she'd tended the wounds he'd acquired in a bar fight while defending her honor. Far, far too familiar.

She suddenly felt sick to her stomach. "Um, Elysee," she said. "Is there a powder room I could use?"

"Oh, yes, sure, this way. Please make yourself at home."

Tish followed Elysee down the hallway, never looking back at Shane even though she could feel the heat of his gaze burning the back of her neck. She had to get by herself, calm down, and decide what she was going to do about this mess.

She stepped into the bathroom, shut the door, and took a deep breath. Stepping up to the washbasin, she dampened a washcloth and caught sight of her reflection in the mirror. Her throat was tight, her stomach even tighter as she assessed herself.

What had Shane seen when he'd looked at her? How had she changed over the course of the last two years? Was he sorry that he'd let her go? Or was he perfectly happy with sweet little Elysee?

Feeling short of breath and slightly disoriented, Tish closed her eyes. She pressed the damp cloth to her lips and then opened her eyes again.

Her mass of unruly corkscrew curls was longer now than when they'd been married, but they were still the same shade of burnished auburn. Thick ginger-colored lashes framed her kelly green eyes. Her peaches-and-cream complexion was still clear, but when she smiled she could see the faintest beginnings of crinkle lines around her mouth. Not old by any means at nearly twenty-six, but time was marching on.

People often told her she looked like a young Nicole Kidman, but she didn't think she was nearly that pretty. Her style was too funky and eclectic, from the four earrings in each ear to the henna tattoo scrolling around her upper right arm. Shane had liked her Bohemian flare, if not her Bohemian lifestyle. They'd been a severe case of opposites attracting.

And colliding.

Ha, that was the underassessment of the century.

A knock sounded on the door.

"Just a minute," she said.

"I'm coming in." The voice was dark, masculine.

Shane!

Her heart leapfrogged into her throat. She spun for the doorknob, determined to flip the lock and keep him out, but she was too slow.

Chapter 7

The bathroom door opened and Shane slipped inside. He reached behind him, clicking the lock in place.

Tish, who was already fumbling for the lock, ended up touching his hard, flat belly instead.

Electricity.

Hotter and quicker than ever. Lightning in a hail storm. It scared the hell out of her. She jerked her hand back at the contact. It gave her little satisfaction that Shane looked as unnerved as she. Being this close to him felt more dangerous than juggling fire.

"What are you doing in here?" she demanded. "You have to get out. What if I was using the toilet? You can't just barge in. We're divorced, remember?"

"We have to talk."

"Now? You want to talk now? Two years ago I wanted to talk, but you clammed up. Now you want to talk?"

"Yes, now."

"Where's little Miss Sunshine?" Tish tossed her head, trying to stall, trying to identify her emotions and figure out exactly how she felt without letting it show on her face.

"Elysee went to tell the cook to set an extra plate for you," he said.

"Aren't you worried what she's going to think when she catches us in here together?" Tish crossed her arms over her chest, both to stop her hands from trembling as well as putting up a barrier between them.

The room was claustrophobically small now with him in it. She'd forgotten just how masculine he was, with his big biceps and manly-smelling cologne.

"She's not going to catch us, because you're going to go tell her that while you're flattered by the offer, you just realized you have a scheduling conflict and can't serve as her wedding videographer," he said firmly.

"Don't you mean 'our' wedding videographer?"

He looked startled. "What?"

"You said 'her' wedding videographer. You're getting married, too. Shouldn't it be 'our' wedding videographer?"

"You're changing the subject."

"No, I'm not. I'm talking about *your* impending wedding."

"You're missing the point."

"But not the irony."

His eyes flared and her breath caught. She felt the old flutter in her chest. Divorced two years and with just one look he could still send her heart reeling.

But Shane had moved on with his life. He had someone else. A very nice someone else. Tish had absolutely no right to feel envious.

It sounded rational and well thought out. The problem was that her emotions weren't having any of it. She was jealous and angry and hurt. She wanted to throw back her head and howl for everything she'd let slip through her fingers. No, no, she wanted to run right out and buy the most expensive pair of shoes she could find.

What? You expected he would pine over you forever?

No, no. Yes.

Honestly, secretly, she'd always held on to the hope that some day, some way they'd find their way back to each other. When they'd both achieved their dream jobs and worked through their personal issues. How naïve was that?

If growing up with a mother who was always looking for love but never finding it had taught her anything, it was that happily ever after was nothing but a romantic myth. So why did she want so badly to believe in it?

Tish's eyes tracked over him. His shoulders were so broad they filled almost half of the wall behind him. Her gaze snagged on the scar running across his temple; unbidden fascination had her reaching up to touch it.

He grabbed her wrist before her fingers could graze his skin. "No," he said sharply, "no."

They stared into each other's eyes, both of them breathing hard. Her heart slammed against her chest, pounding erratically.

Kiss me! she thought, crazily, wildly. As if a kiss would fix everything. She tossed her head and pursed her lips, mentally daring him to do it.

He looked hard into her eyes, as if assessing the depth of her soul. Their lungs moved in tandem, drawing in great gasps of ragged air. There was such raw hunger in his eyes she couldn't help but gasp. The look was naked, completely without guile, a mirror image of her heart.

He cupped her face with his left hand, tilted her chin

up to look at him. This time she did gasp. The harsh sound echoed in the tiny room.

Was he going to kiss her?

She held her breath and waited. If she were to lay her palm against his chest would she feel the wild thunder crashing under her hand? She looked into his eyes and knew if she lived to be a hundred she'd never forget the starving look in his eyes at that moment.

He *hungered* for her.

Shane did not kiss her. In fact, he raised his head, let out his breath in quiet exhalation. Disappointment smashed down on her like a windowpane shattering.

But his eyes blazed black as lump coal. Heated, sizzling, eating her up.

I can still make this man . . . burn, she thought, and a powerful thrill rippled through her.

You could kiss him.

No. No way. Tish wasn't going to be the one to step across that line. If he wanted her, he was going to have to be the one to come after her.

"Why did you pretend not to know me?" he asked, sliding his hands down her shoulders to her upper arms. "Why didn't you tell Elysee who you were?"

"What? And blow my chances for videotaping this wedding?"

"You're not seriously thinking of going through with this. You can't take this job and not tell Elysee who you are," he said.

"Why not?" She wrenched her chin from his grasp. "I'm just trying to spare Elysee's feelings."

"And make your career." He clenched his teeth.

"What's wrong with that?"

"You haven't changed a bit," he said, bitterness tingeing his voice. A twist of panic went through her as his pupils constricted and his eyes darkened disapprovingly.

"What's that supposed to mean?"

"You're still hiding. Still keeping secrets."

She opened her mouth to deny it, but what was the point? He'd made up his mind about her. There was nothing she could say to change it. Instead she muttered, "I'm not the only one who keeps secrets."

Scowling, he drew himself up. "Is there something you want to say?"

Oh yeah. Things she should have said two years ago. But it was too late, water under the proverbial bridge and all that. They stood glaring at each other. The past was a brick wall between them that they couldn't climb over. They'd been at this impasse before. Unable to understand each other, unable to move forward.

"You're going to go back out there and tell Elysee who you are."

Defeat and despair crowded out any lingering hope. Not for the chance to videotape the President's daughter's wedding, but for the possibility that Shane still loved her in the same way she loved him.

"And if I don't?" Tish asked, challenging his authority.

Shane cocked his head and studied her face for a long moment. Same old Tish. She never accepted anything without question. It was one of the things he had always respected about her, but it had irritated him as well: her inability to put her faith in him.

Shane knew her distrust stemmed from the fact that Tish's father had taken off when she was a kid and that she'd rarely seen him after that. Men leave, she'd learned. Why should she trust him when he'd spectac-

ularly reinforced that lesson when he'd walked out on
their marriage?

He was sorry for it now. So damned sorry. His arms
ached to hold her. Lips burned to kiss her. There were no
words, which was just as well. It was too late.

How had this happened? The day after asking Elysee
to marry him, he found himself locked in the bathroom
with the one woman who could still send his senses reeling and his heart thumping.

"Well?" Tish's chin trembled defiantly. "Are you going
to tattle on me?"

"No," he answered quietly. "Because I know you'll do
the right thing and tell her yourself."

"Bastard," she said.

"That's beside the point." He quirked an eyebrow.

She flashed him a smile, brief, but it was there.

He grinned. "God, Tish, it's good to see you again."

"You mean it?"

"I missed you." Why had he said that? It was true, but
he was courting trouble.

"Really?"

"You find that so hard to believe?"

"Well, you are engaged to another woman."

"I'm just saying you look good."

"Thank you." Her earlobes pinked and she peered up
at him from underneath those long auburn eyelashes. His
heart knocked when he saw the vulnerability she struggled so hard to hide in those green depths. Her eyes narrowed, condensing the world to him.

Only him.

She raised a hand and nervously slipped her fingers
through her hair, trying to tame the springy curls that de-
fied taming. Her breasts rose and fell beneath the stretchy

material of her turquoise V-neck T-shirt. She looked damned good in turquoise, the way it contrasted with her red hair—like springtime in Arizona.

Her fingers dropped from her hair in one long graceful movement and fell to the pocket of her purple hippie skirt. Her fingernails, he noted, were painted an avantgarde color of silver, as always, flaunting convention.

He wondered, not for the first time, why she'd ever married him. Look up "conventional" in the dictionary, he thought, and you'd find a picture of Shane Tremont.

His eyes fixed on her lips. Rich, ripe, painted the color of sweet raspberries. He held his breath. Waiting for what, he did not know, but he was sure waiting for something.

Tish pulled a small round red-capped pot of cinnamon lip gloss from her pocket, unscrewed the lid and dipped the tip of her index finger into the petroleum jelly laced with cinnamon flavoring. She lifted her finger, slick and glistening, and slowly traced the glossy residue over her bottom lip with the cool certainty of a woman who knew just what it took to keep her lips supple and ready for a kissing. She recapped the lip gloss and slipped it back into her pocket, and the startling sienna-colored smell of cinnamon floated toward him.

The overhead lamp slanted a shaft of light across her face, bathing one half in light, the other in shadow. He looked down at her, glimpsing something melancholy there. Old feelings—both good and bad—rose between them like soap bubbles, rainbow-prism shiny and fragile as a whisper.

A balance was struck, only for a moment, but enough to pull the air from their lungs in a simultaneous exhale.

His heart slunk back against his spine in shame. What in God's name had he been thinking to ever let her go?

You were hurting.

But so was she, and he'd selfishly let his hurt mean more than hers. She'd betrayed him, yes, but in the end, hadn't he ultimately betrayed her more?

He fixed on those lips. Lips he craved to kiss. Lips that called to him late in the middle of the night, in the dark of his dreams. He leaned forward. Not thinking, just wanting.

She didn't draw away.

Shane never took his eyes off her face, and then suddenly realized their noses were almost touching. She used to give him what she called Eskimo kisses. Whimsically rubbing her nose back and forth against his, until he begged her to stop because it made him want to sneeze. How he wished for one of those Eskimo kisses right now.

It would be so easy for him to kiss her, Eskimo style or otherwise. The most natural thing in the world.

He felt the heat of her skin, so warm near his.

So damned easy.

But he could not. Would not. Should not.

She flicked out her tongue, tracing it over the lips that her fingertips had just touched, making the lip gloss application moot. The gesture wasn't calculated. She wasn't trying for seduction. She was just anxious. He recognized the nervous way she hugged her elbows against her body. Unsettled, just as he was, by the chemistry that time had not erased.

They stared at each other with a stunned mix of surprise and affection and stark sexual heat.

It was still there. The old spark. The embers that had never gone out. Two years and they were still burning.

Hope blossomed.

They were still undeniably connected. And that connection was incredibly complicated. Guilt clutched his gut in a slippery fist. He had no right to hope.

Then a knock sounded at the bathroom door, severing the tenuous chain.

Gently, Elysee knocked on the door a second time. She prayed her plan was going to work. It might be unorthodox, but it was the only way she could know for sure that Shane was indeed The One her mother had promised. She'd mistaken men for The One when they were not. This time, she was taking a different approach.

"Tish? Shane? Are you guys still in there?"

The door wrenched open to reveal Shane standing there, Tish hovering in the corner just behind him.

Elysee put a perky smile on her face. "Hi, guys."

Tish raised her hand in a halfhearted, guilty-looking wave. She *should* be feeling guilty. She hadn't come clean about her relationship with Shane, but Elysee understood why Tish had lied and didn't hold it against her. She believed in giving everyone the benefit of the doubt.

Even her fiancé's ex-wife.

Besides, she liked Tish. A lot more than she had thought she would. She could see why Shane had married her. Tish was passionate and beautiful and talented. What she didn't know was why they'd broken up.

That was the reason she'd asked Tish to video their wedding. She wanted to see if Shane could have a civil relationship with his ex. Elysee also had an added agenda. She wanted to discover how to avoid the problems Tish and Shane had faced in their marriage. What better way to do that than to ask Tish herself?

Plus, Shane had never talked about his ex-wife. This was certainly one way to get him to open up and face his feelings about her and resolve them once and for all. This way, she and Shane could have a fresh start.

It might be rocky for a bit, until Tish and Shane ironed out their differences, but in the long run, Elysee was convinced hiring Tish to video their wedding was the best thing for all concerned.

"Hi," Shane said, but didn't meet Elysee's gaze. Was he feeling guilty, too?

A momentary panic gripped Elysee. What if Shane still cared about Tish? *If he still cared about her, he wouldn't have left her. Shane's a loyal guy.*

That idea made her wonder what Tish had done to chase him away. Had she cheated on him? She seemed to be a very adventuresome and passionate woman, with her snapping green eyes and sassy red hair.

Elysee's heartstrings tugged, and she smiled sympathetically at Shane. Poor baby. She was going to make everything all right in his world again. She glanced from Shane to Tish and back again.

"Did you two have a nice chat?"

Tish cleared her throat. "We've . . . er . . . *I've*, got something to tell you."

"Oh?"

"Shane's my ex-husband." Tish cringed as if waiting for a bomb to detonate.

"I know." Elysee grinned. "Isn't it great?"

"You knew?" Tish sounded stunned.

"You knew?" Shane echoed, looking bushwhacked.

Elysee shook her head at Shane. "You know that I

don't hire anyone without doing a thorough background check. Of course I knew."

"And you hired me anyway?" A suspicious frown furrowed Tish's brow. "What's this all about?"

"I want us all to get along. Like Demi and Bruce and Ashton," she said. "Wouldn't that be great?"

Tish looked at her as if she was seriously delusional. Elysee supposed it might appear that way to her. She winnowed into the bathroom with them, threw one arm around Shane's neck and the other around Tish's.

"Call me naïve," she said, "but I think this is the emotionally healthiest thing we can do. So, are you still on board, Tish? Please know that we both want you here. Don't we, Shane?"

"We do?" Shane said it more as a question than a confirmation, but she pretended he was one hundred percent behind her.

Elysee operated on the assumption if you believed the best about people they usually lived up to your expectations. Well, except in the case of her three ex-fiancés—but those relationships hadn't worked out because they hadn't been The One. Elysee was a firm believer that everything happened for a reason.

"See." She beamed at Tish. "We're all in agreement. You're going to videotape our wedding and it's going to be fabulous. Now let's get out of the bathroom and go have dinner. I'm starving!"

Chapter 8

"I'm in serious need of an intervention," Tish wailed to Delaney over the telephone.

It was after ten o'clock at night and it was really too late to call, especially since her best friend was a newly-wed and it was a Monday. But Tish was drowning deep in emotional quicksand and Delaney was the only one who would know how to pull her out of it.

"What's wrong?"

"There's a half-gallon of Blue Bell mint chocolate chip in my refrigerator and a very big spoon in my hand and I'm afraid of what will happen next."

"Don't do anything drastic. I'll zip right over."

Ten minutes later her doorbell rang. Dressed in one of Shane's old T-shirts, fuzzy yellow Tweety Bird slippers, and a purple chenille bathrobe, Tish shuffled to the door, the half-gallon of mint-chocolate-chip Blue Bell tucked in the crook of one arm. She flung open the door without even checking the peephole first, something she never did. *That's how depressed I am.*

"I brought reinforcements," Delaney said, "and they've all got spoons."

Tish had to smile at the sight of her two other close friends, Jillian Samuels and Rachael Henderson, standing on the porch beside Delaney. All three held up white plastic spoons.

Swinging the door wide, Tish sighed with relief at the cavalry and said, "Move your fannies in here now. I need all the help I can get."

They ended up piled in the middle of the king-sized bed she had once shared with Shane. Tish sat cross-legged in the center, with Rachael on her left, Jillian to her right, and Delaney right in front of her. Tish held the Blue Bell in her lap while everyone dug in. What good friends they were! They weren't about to let her get fat alone.

"So let me get this straight." Delaney licked a dab of mint-green ice cream dotted with chocolate off her upper lip. "Elysee Benedict hired you specifically because you *were* Shane's ex-wife?"

Tish nodded. "No kidding, you guys, the first daughter is a nutcase. She's impossibly nice. When I had to tell her who I was, it felt like I was a rabbit hunter looking down the barrel of a rifle at Flopsy Cottontail."

"I still can't believe your Shane is engaged to marry the President's daughter." Delaney shook her head. "How did that happen?"

"He was on her protective detail and he saved her life."

"Ah," Jillian said. "She's got him up on a pedestal. He's her hero."

"Which is perfect," Tish said, "because Shane has a desperate need to be a hero. It bodes well for their marriage. I'm happy for them."

"You don't have to lie to us," Delaney said. "Go ahead, dis the President's daughter. We won't tell."

"Do you think they could have your bedroom bugged?" Jillian, who was a bit on the paranoid side, asked and eyed the corners of the room as if she were going to spy a radio transmitter recording their conversation and sending it along to the FBI.

"I'm confused. Why would the President's daughter want her fiancé's ex-wife to videotape their wedding?" Rachael interjected. Rachael was a sweet-natured kindergarten teacher, with dazzling green eyes, long-flowing blond hair, and creamy porcelain skin. She was the starry-eyed romantic of the group. If she couldn't understand Elysee's motives, no one could.

"Apparently, Shane would never talk about me to her." Inwardly Tish winced. It hurt to think that he disliked her so much he wouldn't even discuss her with his fiancée. "So Elysee had someone do a little digging into his background, learned my name, and found out I was a wedding videographer. She believes this will help me and Shane 'confront our baggage' as she put it over dinner, help us 'assimilate the trauma' of our marriage."

"Is she for real?" asked Jillian, an ebony-haired, black-eyed, street-savvy lawyer.

"Exactly," Tish said. "De-lu-sion-al."

"Maybe she's just trying to be very adult about the whole thing," Delaney said.

"Yeah? Like you would have hired Nick's ex-wife to videotape your wedding?"

"Oh, hell, no."

"See? That's what a normal woman would say. You know what else Elysee wants from me?"

Her three friends leaned in closer, spoons dangling above the mint chocolate chip.

"What?" they breathed in unison.

"Bedroom secrets."

"What!" her friends shrieked.

"Yep. She wants me to tell her what Shane likes." Tish took a deep breath. "She said they're waiting for the wedding night to consummate their relationship and she doesn't want Shane to be disappointed. Can you believe she's asking me for sex tips?"

Clearly scandalized, Rachael slapped a hand over her mouth and her eyes widened.

"It's always the mousy ones." Jillian shook her head. "Never trust the mousy ones."

"I used to be a mousy one," Delaney said.

"Case in point." Jillian raised a finger. "Who staged their own wedding day abduction, hmmm?"

"You've got me there," Delaney admitted with a big grin.

Last year, before she'd married Nick Vinetti, Delaney had been engaged to an old childhood friend. Because of the pressure of family expectations, she hadn't known how to get out of the wedding. In desperation, she'd ended up hiring someone to kidnap her. It had turned into a big media drama, but also into a spectacular happily ever after.

"That's gotta hurt," Rachael said, looking at Tish with sympathy. "Your replacement expecting you to pave the road for her that you had to stumble down."

Trust Rachael to ferret out the real meat of her emotions. Tish bit down on her bottom lip and thrust the mint chocolate chip away from her. "You guys do something with this, please, before I end up with ice cream intoxication and ten pounds of extra blubber on my butt."

Delaney whisked the ice cream away to the kitchen and Tish glanced around at her remaining friends.

"The thing of it is," she said, "I like Elysee. It's impossible not to like her. And she and Shane just seem to go together. Far better than he and I ever did. They're both so calm and steady and they look so comfortable around each other. Like an old married couple. I can definitely see them making it to their golden wedding anniversary."

"Comfortable." Jillian snorted. "Like a sweater."

"Like wool socks," Rachael added. "Who wants to marry wool socks?"

"Being around them made me feel like a total disaster. I mean, Shane's not only moved on but he's going to be the President's son-in-law. It doesn't get any bigger than that, and meanwhile I'm still this stupid loser who can't manage her finances or hold on to the best thing that ever happened to her." Tish's voice caught.

"The reason you and Shane broke up runs much deeper than money problems and you know it," Delaney murmured as she stepped back into the room. "Don't keep beating yourself up for something that couldn't be prevented."

"You'll land on your feet. You always do," Jillian said.

Rachael rested a hand on Tish's shoulder. "You're still in love with him, aren't you?"

Tish nodded and instantly tears sprang to her eyes. Savagely she swiped them away. She didn't break down like this. She was tough. She'd survived her nomadic childhood. She should be able to skip blithely through a broken heart, particularly one two years in the making.

"What am I going to do, you guys? If I do a good job on this wedding, the dream I've been struggling to achieve for so long will finally come true. Plus, it will solve all my money problems. I don't see how I can turn it down. But I don't know how I can survive it emotionally."

"We'll stand by you, whatever decision you make," Delaney said. "We're always here for you."

Rachael shook her head. "You can't take this job. It would be pure mental torture. Seeing Shane happy with the first daughter, feeling his hand on yours every time he touches *her*."

"I think you have to take the job." Jillian was so tough and strong. She was Tish's hero. "It's the only way to prove you're over him."

"But I'm not over him."

"Then this will help you get over him. It's time to move on, Tish. It's been two years. Shane's found someone else. Let him go so you can be free." Jillian's words might be stark, but they were exactly what Tish needed to hear.

It was way past time to move on. And she could only do that by accepting reality. She had to experience the pain and allow herself to fall through it to the other side in order to be free.

Tish looked around at her three friends gazing at her with supportive sympathy. She was so lucky to have them in her life. "I'm going to accept the job," she said. "I'm going to see this thing through, make the best damned wedding video I've ever made, clear up my finances, and end up on top of the world."

"You go." Jillian grinned. "Don't let any man keep you down."

But even as she was declaring it, Tish wondered if she truly had the courage to make it happen. "Enough about me," she said. "I'm through whining. What have you guys been up to lately?"

Jillian had a cryptic smile on her face. "I'm moving to San Francisco for six months."

"What?" Delaney arched an eyebrow.

"Why?" Rachael asked.

"We'll be bereft without you," Tish said.

"I've got a golden opportunity I just couldn't turn down," Jillian rushed on excitedly. "I've been selected to be on the team of co-counsel with Belton Melville on the Nob Hill murder trial."

"No way!" Delaney leaped off the bed and gave a hoot of joy. "*The* Belton Melville?"

"It's going to be an amazing education for me, although I'm sure I'll just be doing research." Jillian beamed.

"This is that case where the ex–NFL football star stabbed his estranged wife to death in her boyfriend's backyard?" Rachael asked.

"Allegedly," Jillian said.

"Spoken like a true defense attorney," Tish said, and hugged her friend. "I'm so happy for you, but what are you going to do with your condo?"

"I've already leased it out."

"This is happening so fast," Tish wailed.

"When the time is right to move on, the time is right to move on," Jillian said and shot Tish a meaningful glance.

"I've got a little news of my own," Rachael said shyly.

"Oh?" Everyone turned to look at Rachael.

A grin spread across her cherubic face. "I've met someone."

"That's so wonderful," Tish exclaimed, and meant it. Rachael was a loving person, but she had such a Cinderella outlook on love. She was always getting her bubble burst when reality met fantasy. Her friend deserved someone nice.

"So tell us about him."

"It's too soon to say much," Rachael said. "Except he's sent me flowers every day since we met."

"How long ago was that?" Jillian asked.

"Just last week. See, I told you that it was too soon to say anything, but you guys, he's so gorgeous." Rachael swooned. "Blond and broad-shouldered and with the most amazingly rippled washboard stomach."

"You've seen his stomach already?" Jillian teased.

"Don't jump to conclusions. He was washing his car," Rachael said. "But I have a very good feeling about this relationship."

"Then you're going to be needing this." Tish got up off the bed, went to the closet, and retrieved the antique wedding veil. She took it to Rachael and laid it in her arms.

"Oh," Rachael exhaled. "Don't you want to hang on to it?"

Tish shook her head, remembering the day she'd tried it on and made her wish. "I've no use for it."

"Thank you." Rachael held the veil to her chest. "I'll treasure it."

"Just remember what they say about making a wish on it," Jillian warned. "Be careful what you wish for—"

"Because you just might get it," they all finished in unison.

"Well, I think that's great," Delaney said. "We're all

getting what we wanted. I got Nick, Jillian's got a fabulous job opportunity. Rachael's got a new man, and Tish is videotaping the President's daughter's wedding. Are we on top of the world or what?"

Yeah, Tish thought. *Or what?*

All her friends were slowly drifting away and she was facing the next several weeks, helping to make Shane's new marriage wonderful. That was the funny thing about being on top of the world. Nobody clued you in to the sacrifices it takes to get there.

Long after her friends had left, Tish lay in bed trying to sleep, but the past wouldn't let her be. Finally, at midnight, she threw back her covers and got dressed.

The past was a tombstone weighing on her chest, to the point where she could scarcely breathe. She had to find some release. Picking up her purse, she hurried out to the car Delaney had loaned her. Not even knowing where she was going or why, Tish began to drive.

Meanwhile, on the President's ranch in Katy, Texas, Shane couldn't sleep either. Dinner had been as surreal as a Fellini film. He'd sat sandwiched between his bride-to-be and his ex-wife, saying as little as possible while they made small talk about the wedding.

Tish looked so damned good. Every time his gaze landed on her, he felt a familiar tightness in his chest. It had taken everything he had in him not to ask Tish to leave. If she was courageous enough to stick it out, then he had to be courageous enough to let her stay. She needed this assignment.

As painful as it was going to be to have her around, he owed her this much. He also owed it to Elysee to uphold the promise he'd made to her. They were engaged. He had no business having feelings for his ex.

Not long after midnight, edgy, restless, and conflicted, he left his bed, got dressed and drove into Houston. He cruised past the house he and Tish used to own. A family lived there now. He hoped they were as happy in the place as he and Tish had been before the worst had happened.

A trip down memory lane; this was what he needed. A good review of what had gone right and what had gone wrong with his first marriage before he embarked upon the second. He didn't know where Tish lived now. That was good. The last thing he needed was to end up on her doorstep.

Instead, he found himself at Louie's Blues Bar on Second Street near the edge of downtown Houston, just before the neighborhood turned seedy. Yuppies loved this place, with its mysterious atmosphere and top-notch musical fare. A flight of gray stone stairs descended into the belly of the club. Wailing notes from a woeful saxophone lured him down.

He'd been here before with Cal, when they were on assignment. With one long deep breath, Shane stepped over the threshold and was transported back three years.

He and Cal had been undercover in polo shirts and jeans, but Shane had felt strangely naked without his black suit and tie. At the time, they had been junior field agents bucking for the same promotion.

They'd had a serious competition going and Shane was determined to win. More than anything in the world, he wanted in on protective detail at the White House and the new promotion was another step toward that goal. He'd dreamed of it since he'd been an Eagle Scout.

To avoid getting clipped by a low-hanging entryway, they were forced to duck their heads as they entered a room lit only by blue neon lights. Both of them were big men, Cal just a shade taller at six-three to Shane's six-two. Although, at two hundred and three pounds, they weighed the same. Shane was twenty-six, Cal twenty-seven.

They'd traced a credit card identity theft ring to Louie's weekend bartender, a slender, rat-faced man known as Cool Chill. Cool Chill liked to pretend he was a young, urban gangsta. In reality he was thirty-three-year-old Euell Hotchkiss, who perpetually smelled of high-grade marijuana and still lived in his parents' converted garage.

But they didn't find Cool Chill behind the bar. Cool Chill, one of the waitresses had told them, was on supper break. They took a corner table and sat with their backs against the wall, assessing the situation and waiting it out until Cool Chill returned.

Cal ordered gin and tonic. Shane got a seltzer. He didn't drink on the job, didn't drink alcohol much at all. He leaned back in his chair, getting the lay of the land.

Shane knew the curvy redhead was trouble the second he spotted her.

She was everything he shouldn't want. But as he watched her undulate alone on the dance floor, swaying to a sultry rendition of an old Muddy Waters tune, his body ached for her.

This was bad.

"Check out the redhead," Cal said.

"Where?" Shane said, pretending he hadn't noticed.

"On the dance floor. By herself. God, she's a stunner."

He was obligated to take another look. After all, Cal had pointed her out.

What was her story? Who was she? Where was she from? Why was a gorgeous chick like her alone in a blues club on a Saturday night?

Shane was intrigued. Here was a woman who packed a sexual punch and every man in the vicinity knew it.

Cal nudged him in the ribs. "Is she a hottie or what?"

Or what. Hottie didn't begin to cover it.

"She's attractive," he said and took a sip of his seltzer.

Cal snorted. "You dead from the neck down, Tremont?"

Not hardly.

The guys in the band were watching her with the same horny expression in their eyes, particularly the long-haired trumpet player striving for the Chuck Mangione look with his cool cat hat and hip daddy beard. The musicians' lust for the redhead reflected exactly what Shane was experiencing. But then he felt a new emotion.

Jealousy.

It fisted inside him, hard and petulant.

How the hell could he be jealous over a woman he didn't even know? This wasn't like him. He wasn't usually easily distracted from his goal. In fact, he had received commendations for his ability to focus and get the job done under pressure.

Purposefully, he forced his eyes off the dance floor and scanned the rest of the smoky bar. It was still early in the evening and the place was fairly empty. He speculated that most of Louie's regular patrons were still out to dinner, and they wouldn't be wandering over to the nightclub for another hour or two.

That suited Shane just fine. The smaller the crowd, the easier they would be to handle if something went wonky. And with Cal for backup there shouldn't be any problems. The only fly in the ointment was Cool Chill's MIA status.

The band left Muddy Waters behind and slid into Beyoncé's "Crazy in Love." The tune drew a few more couples onto the dance floor. The redhead never stopped dancing, just changed tempo in time to the rhythm.

Shane's peripheral gaze locked on Red, even though he was fighting not to notice. Something about her ease with her own body, the way she danced all alone and didn't care that everyone was watching, stirred his admiration along with his spirit. He would never have been able to let go like that, shed his inhibitions. He was envious and lustful and jealous and deferential. He didn't like this mix of feelings one damned bit.

Head in the job, man, head in the job.

Great advice, but then he spied a thick-shouldered, shaved-bald man treading across the dance floor toward Red. He was bigger than the bouncer lounging against the wall by the front door. Bigger even than he and Cal.

Shane forgot why he was in the bar. He rotated in his seat, eyes narrowing, alert for trouble.

Baldo said something to Red.

Asking her to dance?

She shook her head, stepped away from the bald man and kept boogying all by herself.

It's her prerogative to reject you, Baldo. Take the hint and keep moving.

But apparently Baldo wasn't going to take no for an answer. The massive man grabbed hold of Red's arm and spun her around.

There was no fear on Red's face, only spitfire anger. She snapped at Baldo, warning him off.

He didn't budge. Instead, he started arguing with her. She tried to jerk her arm away from him, but he held on tight. She was not a small woman, but next to Baldo she looked delicate as a porcelain doll.

That was all the provocation Shane needed to get involved, which wasn't like him. Not at all. He was the rational partner, the one slow to anger. The good cop to Cal's bad cop. He jumped up from his chair, pushing aside tables, knocking over beer bottles in his rush to the dance floor.

"Tremont," Cal called out sharply, but he didn't listen.

Shane knew better. He shouldn't be getting into a bar fight. Cool Chill could walk in any minute. He could blow his cover. And for all he knew Baldo could be Red's old man come to drag her home.

But he couldn't seem to stop himself. He slapped a hand on Baldo's shoulder. Up close the guy was the size of a tugboat. "Let go of the lady."

Baldo pivoted, snarling, "Fuck off."

Big the guy might be, but he was slow. Shane saw the punch coming long before the larger man finished making a fist.

Baldo took a swing.

Shane ducked just in time to hear air whoosh above his head. The swing would have knocked him out cold if it had made contact.

"Fight!" someone yelled.

Couples scattered from the dance floor like chickens fleeing a coyote. The trumpet player blew a sour note.

A woman screamed, but he didn't think it was Red. She didn't seem like a screamer. At least not in a bar fight.

Fist cocked, Shane popped up and smacked Baldo dead on his jaw.

Turned out the dude had a glass chin.

Baldo's eyes glazed. His knees wobbled. He made a noise like a strangled bull and toppled face-first onto the concrete floor.

Shane figured he just might get away scot-free.

But he didn't count on Baldo being a pal of the band. Next thing he knew horns were flying and the microphone was screeching tortured feedback as it got knocked off the stage onto an amp. The lead singer came out of no-where and punched Shane squarely in the eye.

He wasn't thinking of himself. He'd been in worse fights than this. Red was on his mind.

Where was she? He had to make sure she was safe.

He swiveled his head, but didn't see her. Good, maybe she got out of the building unscathed.

Someone grabbed him around the neck, locked him in a choke hold. Someone with deeply muscled arms. Some-one very strong.

The bouncer?

The grip around his neck tightened. Where the hell was Cal? Some partner he'd turned out to be.

Shane couldn't catch his breath and his head throbbed. In his worry over the redhead he'd made a classic mis-take. He'd forgotten to protect his flank.

"Let him go, you jackass!" Shane heard a woman holler.

Was it her? Was it Red?

He tried to turn his head to look for her, but between the pressure on his carotid and the smoke in the air, it was pretty nigh impossible to see anything more than the guy in the Chuck Mangione hat coming at him.

The trumpet player punched him in the breadbasket while the bouncer squeezed his neck so hard Shane feared his head was coming off. He gasped. Soon he was going to pass out.

Shit, where was Red?

That was the last thing he remembered until he came to a few minutes later. He was propped up beside the Dumpster in the back alley behind the nightclub. His lungs burned and his brain felt as if he'd had nails hammered through it.

Way to go, Tremont. No more undercover at Louie's for you.

His boss was going to be steamed and Cal was going to get his promotion. All over a woman he'd never even met. He drew in an aching breath trying to rouse the energy to get to his feet. Then he heard the crisp snap-snap of stiletto heels clicking on asphalt. Gingerly, he raised his head and looked around.

There was Red.

Standing in front of him, her gorgeous legs positioned shoulder-width apart. The skirt she wore was extremely short, revealing a mile of coltish legs and creamy thighs. The stretchy material molded tight against her generous hips.

He was overwhelmed by the sight.

She met his stare openly, took his measure even as he took hers. No shrinking violet, this one.

Looking at her, he felt a sappy sloppy feeling light up his heart for no fathomable reason at all.

"Hey, there," she said and squatted beside him in the alley. She smelled like a spice shop, hot and zesty. She *made him think of a brownie he'd once had that was made with smoked jalapeño peppers. Tasty, but fiery.*

"Hey there yourself," *he surprised himself by answering. By nature, he was not a flirtatious man, but something about her spurred changes in him. He was getting his first real eyeful of her up close and personal and definitely enjoying the experience.*

"You make a habit out of this Sir Galahad thing?" *That voice, vivacious and sultry as a tropical night, was as flat-out erotic as the rest of her.*

Shane tried to shrug and ended up just wincing. So much for macho cool. "I hate to see women get pushed around by drunken jerk offs."

"I could have handled the situation, but thank you anyway. It was sweet."

Sweet. Hmph. He didn't want her to think of him as sweet. He wanted her to see him as her own personal Hercules.

Hercules. Right.

"I'm afraid," *she said and tenderly ran a fingernail down his cheek,* "you got the worst end of the deal."

He nodded. "Forgive the line, but what's a nice girl like you doing in a place like this?"

"Who says I'm nice?" *She winked.*

"You're out here with me. If you weren't nice, you would have ditched me."

"And leave Sir Galahad all alone? Not even a naughty girl is that cruel."

"So you're naughty? Is that the reason you come down to Louie's and dance by yourself?"

She touched the tip of her tongue to her upper lip. "Usually it's a safe place to come blow off steam."

"Safe's not exactly the word that leaps to mind." *He*

jacked himself up higher against the Dumpster and held a hand over an aching rib, praying it was bruised and not broken. He flicked an apple peel from the cuff of his pants.

"The bald guy was new. A roadie for the band. Normally no one bothers me."

"Ah. That explains it."

"Lucky for you, Louie is my ex-stepfather."

"Ex-stepfather?"

"My mother's second husband."

"How many husbands has she had?"

Red shrugged. "I lost count after three. Anyway, I convinced Louie not to call the cops."

"Kind of you," he mumbled.

She laughed and the sound of it lit him up inside. He was not a particularly humorous guy, but he had a sudden urge to spend the rest of his life trying to make her laugh.

"One small detail," she said. "I promised Louie you'd pay for the damages."

"Didja now?"

"It was that or the cops."

"Smart call."

"I thought it a fair exchange."

His cheek was cut and one eye was swelled shut, but he felt like the king of the universe because she was safe and here with him and her long red hair was trailing across his bare arm as she leaned forward. And kissed him.

Gently, on the forehead, but it was still the most erotic kiss he'd ever had. Then she held out her hand and tugged him to his feet. She led him to her car. Took him to her apartment. Tended his wounds.

She let him sleep in her bed with the condition that he

promised to keep his hands to himself. Even with bruised knuckles Shane had found it a challenge to honor that promise, because no woman had ever turned him on the way she did.

All night he lay awake, watching her sleep. By morning, he had decided she was the woman he was going to marry.

And he didn't even know her name.

Chapter 9

"W hat'll you have?" The smooth voice of the woman behind the bar at Louie's jerked Shane out of the past and back to the present. He blinked, reorienting himself to place and time.

"Club soda," he said.

"Heavy drinker," she commented dryly.

"Okay, add a splash of cranberry juice."

She laughed and turned to get his drink.

Shane pivoted on his barstool. The place hadn't changed much in three years. On a Monday night, without a band and this close to last call, the bar was empty except for hard-core drinkers. The bartender passed him the club soda and cranberry juice. Shane took a sip.

A hand clamped down on his shoulder. "Well, hell, look what the cat dragged in."

Shane turned his head to see Louie Browning grinning at him. They shook hands. "Hey, you old sonofabitch, you haven't aged a bit."

Louie plunked down on the stool beside him and

waved a hand at their surroundings. "This place keeps me young. How you been?"

"Good, good."

Louie's gaze dropped to Shane's damaged hand. "Looks like things could be better. On-the-job injury?"

Shane resisted the urge to tuck his hand out of sight. He hadn't expected Louie to be here this late. A strained awkwardness quickly replaced his delight at seeing a familiar face. Louie was Tish's ally. Shane was on her turf. Why had he come here? What was he searching for?

"You talked to Tish."

"No." Louie shook his head. "Not lately. I just took a wild guess about the hand."

He hoped Louie wouldn't ask him any more questions. He didn't want to explain about this injury, about his job, about his engagement to Elysee, about what had happened between him and Tish. He drained his club soda and cranberry juice, put a ten-dollar bill on the bar, and got to his feet.

"You leaving already? What? I forget the deodorant or something?" Louie pantomimed sniffing his armpits.

Crap. How was he going to get out of having this conversation? "I just gotta go." He jerked his thumb in the direction of the men's restroom.

Louie nodded.

Shane hightailed it to the restroom. The place was empty. He sank his shoulder against the wall and took a deep breath. Briefly, he closed his eyes and thought again of the first time he'd come into this bar. The first time he'd laid eyes on Tish.

Coming to Louie's had been a bad idea. Why had he come here? He had to get out. He spun on his heel, pushed through the door, and stepped back into the bar.

Just in time to see Tish come skipping down the stairs, calling out, "Louie, I've come to pay back the two hundred dollars I owe you."

Shane blinked, froze in mid-stride, unable to believe what he was seeing.

No, no, she couldn't be here.

Tish stopped in the dead center of the bar as her gaze landed on him. "Shane," she whispered on an exhaled breath.

"Tish." He fisted his good hand.

Louie's Blues Bar on Second Street filled with loss and pain and Tish. Shane felt as if he was fighting for his very soul. Three years ago, on this same spot, they'd first met and started their inevitable dance toward destruction. Why had wretched fate drawn them together again? Both back to this place, on the same night, at the same time.

He looked at her and she looked at him and time shifted under their feet, the past and present morphing together in keen weirdness.

"Are you really here?" she asked.

"I'm here."

"But why?"

"I don't know."

Tish gave him a long searching look. A dozen different emotions flitted across her face like a slideshow from the past. For one brief second, he could have sworn he saw a tear in her eye, but no, it had to be a trick of the lighting. "Why aren't you at the ranch?" she asked.

"Couldn't sleep."

"Me either. Unless I fell asleep and I'm dreaming this. Am I dreaming you?"

"Maybe." He shrugged as if he wasn't unnerved. "You always were uncanny."

"Maybe we're both dreaming."

"Just a dream," he murmured.

Shane sensed rather than saw Louie, the sly old fox, as he slipped around behind them and dropped two quarters in the jukebox. A couple of seconds later, Beyoncé began to sing "Crazy in Love."

Their song.

Was he just dreaming? Only one way to tell.

He stalked the short distance between them, reached out to her with his good hand. "Dance?"

Her eyes rounded, but she didn't take his hand.

"For old time's sake?"

"For old time's sake," she echoed and sank her palm into his.

He guided her toward the dance floor, knowing this was insanity, but once in motion, he was unable to stop.

One last spin around the dance floor. That's all it is.

But once he had her there, he didn't know how to proceed with his damaged hand. He slipped his good arm around her waist, but felt off balance with his right arm cradled against his side.

Why had he started this?

She read him, obviously sensed his anxiety. Gently, Tish took his right hand in her left, interlaced their fingers and raised their joined arms.

Her eyes met his. The mood between them burned intensely.

"It's our last dance," she said.

"Yes."

"So we should enjoy it." Her eyes were like daggers, sharp and glistening, stabbing him deep.

"Yeah." His throat was so tight he could barely force the word out.

They swayed to the beat, gazes welded. She sighed and the sound of her sigh, sweet and forlorn, seeped through him, unhinging coherent thought. And then she did something that unraveled him completely. Tish laid her head on his shoulder, buried her face against his neck.

His heart thumped. He tightened his grip around her waist. In that moment, she had him. He felt it. The deep pulse of sexual energy they'd always shared. The music hummed, vibrating the air, vibrating their bodies moving in faultless harmony.

"Shane," she whispered, her lips touching the bare skin over his collarbone.

Her vulnerable voice cut him quick. Chill bumps slipped down his spine. He dipped his chin, pressed his nose against the top of her head, breathed deeply of her distinctive fragrance.

They swayed past a revolving beer sign. It cast blue fingers of neon over them, bathing the moment in pathos. Her hot body was pressed against him. He could feel every line, every curve, causing him to think things he should not be thinking. Her cheek lay pressed against his chest, inciting in him an old desire that should best be ignored.

"Tish." Her name rolled from his tongue on a groan.

She pulled back and stared at him, studying his face, seeking answers to unspoken questions.

He met her gaze. He was sorry he had no answers to give.

She had eyes that were at once both sultry and mystical, eyes that held no slight amount of sorrow, tucked behind her brave smile. Her thick cascade of curly auburn hair tumbled down her shoulders like an angel's mane.

The look she gave him shot straight through his heart and made it hard to breathe.

He blinked, dazed, even as a small part of him buzzed with the magic of holding her in his arms again. He stared into her eyes and she stared into his, and Shane just felt lost.

Around them in the almost empty nightclub stretched rows of tables, and the staff turned chairs upside down in a higgledy-piggledy thrust of legs. The yeasty smell of spilled beer rode the air. On his tongue, in his mouth, was the taste of everything he'd lost.

Tish splayed her palm over his chest. Her eyes went wide as his heart rate quickened. It shook him up.

The song ended. The jukebox fell silent. The bartender announced last call.

And just like that, the dream was over.

The next morning, Tish was out running errands, struggling not to think about what had happened at Louie's the night before or the significance of she and Shane both showing up at the bar at the same time, when her cell phone rang.

She pulled it out of her purse and flipped it open. "Capture the Moment Videos."

"Tish, it's Elysee."

Guilt, immediate and ruthless, squeezed her stomach. "Um . . . hi."

"Hi," Elysee bubbled. "There's a WorldFem luncheon today and I want to go. Shane's rattling around the house all by himself. I think he's a little down in the dumps because his physical therapy sessions aren't going well. If you're not otherwise engaged, I think this might be a prime time to start putting together the *Our Love Story* video for the wedding reception. You could get a head start on it and Shane wouldn't have to be by himself when he's feeling so low. But don't tell him that I told you he's bummed out. You know how proud he is."

That she did. "You want me to go to the ranch right now?"

"Please."

Aw, hell, she still hadn't sorted out her feelings from last night. The last thing she wanted right now was to come face-to-face with Shane. "Um, I'm in line at the drive-through at the bank."

"Well, after you finish that, of course."

"Okay," Tish agreed, because she didn't know what else to say. This check had to go into the bank today or she was screwed in a hundred different ways. She had no real choice. But once the check was cashed, there was no turning back.

The car in front of her moved on and she drove up to the teller window.

"Great," Elysee said. "Oh and by the way, we want you to come to DC next weekend to film our engagement party. Are you available?"

"Washington DC?"

"The one and only."

Tish Gallagher in Washington DC, filming the first daughter's engagement party? It was simultaneously a dream come true and a living nightmare.

Be careful what you wish for, Tish remembered Claire Kelley telling Delaney when she'd bought the veil. *Or you just might get it.*

"Um . . ."

"We'll pay to fly you there, of course. Put you up at the Ritz-Carlton."

Tish Gallagher from South Houston living it up at the Ritz in Washington DC? Just yesterday she'd been eating Ramen noodles and dodging bill collectors.

"And we're granting you exclusive video rights. Yours will be the only movie camera allowed into the party."

"Really? An exclusive of the first daughter's engagement? I don't know what to say, Elysee."

"Say yes. The party's on Saturday. Please don't tell me you have another wedding scheduled for next Saturday."

"No."

"Great, so you can do it?"

"Yes."

She thought of having to spend the afternoon at the Benedict ranch with Shane, looking through old photo albums, and felt sick to her stomach. *This is how Julia Roberts's character must have felt in* My Best Friend's Wedding. *Trapped into being nice to a woman she wanted to despise, but couldn't because she was just so darned nice.*

She stared at the phone, stared at the check, stared at the teller who was raising her eyebrow, waiting for Tish to make a move.

Taking a deep breath, she rolled down the window and did the irreversible. She handed the teller her deposit slip and the check.

It was official. Like it or not, she was committed to seeing this thing through.

"You're out of your mind, you know that," Elysee's secretary, Lola, told her as they entered the WorldFem meeting, Secret Service escorts leading the way. "Leaving your man alone with his ex-wife. It's insanity."

"They won't be alone. The ranch is crawling with people."

"Yes, but you won't be there to put a stop to any hanky-panky."

"There's not going to be any hanky-panky. Trust me, I know what I'm doing."

"Do you?"

Elysee wasn't going to let Lola's opinion rattle her. She trusted Shane implicitly and odd as it might sound to someone else, she also trusted Tish. Whatever her faults, whatever the reason she and Shane had broken up, Elysee couldn't help feeling Tish had integrity.

"They need time alone to heal the old wounds without me peeking over their shoulders."

"If you say so."

Elysee chose to ignore Lola and any niggling doubts she might have of her own. She was very excited that the WorldFem conference was right here in Houston. When the organizers had learned she wanted to attend, they instantly made her a guest speaker. It was a last-minute invitation, so she hadn't prepared a speech. She intended to speak from her heart.

Being in the presence of like-minded women fired her up. There were several celebrities on the panel—including a famous actress, a cable news anchorwoman, and a late night talk show host's wife who'd been instrumental in drawing attention to the plight of women in Afghanistan long before the second Gulf War.

Toward the end of the conference, Agent Ackerman came over to whisper to Elysee. "There's a woman who wants to speak with you. She says it's urgent. A matter of life or death, but I don't advise you to see her."

"What woman?" Elysee asked.

Cal Ackerman pointed her out. She was waiting near the exit, dressed in a sari with a veil cloaking her face.

"I'll speak to her."

"For security reasons . . . ," Agent Ackerman began, but Elysee cut him off.

"I'll speak with her in the limo. You can secure that easily enough and check her out before bringing her to me."

"Yes, Miss Benedict." He didn't seem happy about it, but a few minutes later Elysee and Lola were waiting in the back of the limousine. He brought the woman over, opened the car door, and she slid in.

Agent Ackerman started to get in as well but Elysee raised her hand. "You can wait out there."

His body stiffened in response and his eyes narrowed. He did as she asked, but he didn't look pleased.

"Hello," Elysee said to the veiled woman sitting across from her. "Do you speak English?"

The woman dropped the veil. "It is me, E-lee. Your Nana Rana."

"Rana!" Elysee threw her arms around Rana's neck and hugged her tightly. "Thank God you're alive. I saw your picture in *People* magazine and that's when I knew I had to get involved with WorldFem."

"I am so proud you are here." Tears streamed down Rana's face. "This is such a happy moment for me. To see you all grown up and passionate about human rights. Your mother would be so proud."

They both swiped at tears then. Lola extracted tissues from her purse and passed them around.

"Agent Ackerman said you needed to see me on a matter of life and death. Do you need me to hide you?"

"It is not my own safety that concerns me," Rana said. "I come to you on behalf of another."

"Yes?" Elysee leaned forward, eager not to miss a single word.

"The young woman's name is Alma Reddy. Her father is a cabinet minister in India. He was very distressed when she dishonored her family by secretly marrying an American student attending university in Bombay. The young man's visa was revoked and he was thrown out of India. Alma's father demanded she renounce the young man and have the marriage annulled. Alma refused and her family has hired attackers to kill her. WorldFem managed to hide her, but we need to get her out of India. Her beloved husband lives in Texas, but we don't have the funds or proper entrance visa to get her into the U.S. Can you help?"

"How much money do you need?"

"One hundred thousand dollars."

Elysee sat back against the seat. "That's a lot of money."

"We must bribe many people. Pay hush money. Plus the route to smuggle her out of the country is an arduous one. There are many planes, trains, and boats she must take. She must change transportation modes often to ensure she is not followed. We must also hire a decoy and send her on a similar journey. Alma's father is ruthless. He has put a price on my head. This all must be kept as secret as possible. He has many spies, many eyes."

"I don't have access to that kind of money here, Rana. Since I'm not yet twenty-five I can't withdraw funds without my father's permission. I do have a safety-deposit box with antique coins left to me by my grandmother. They are worth at least that, but the safety-deposit box is in DC. I'm headed there this coming weekend for my engagement party. If you can meet me there, I'll give you the money on Saturday."

"Thank you, thank you." Rana kissed Elysee's hands. "You are an angel."

"I'll make sure you get an invitation to the engagement party. We can make the transfer there."

"She's playing you," Lola said after Rana exited the limo. "Want to bet you never see her or your money again?"

"Shame on you, Lola," Elysee scolded. "Rana was my nanny."

"And that precludes her from being a con artist?"

"You always think the worst of people."

"That's why your father hired me as your secretary. You need a counterbalance."

"Well, I don't care what you say. I'm giving her the money and I forbid you from discussing the matter with my father."

Lola shrugged. "Don't say I didn't warn you."

"Squeeze it. Push. Go for the burn."

Shane grunted against the grapefruit-sized rubber ball the physical therapist, Pete Larkin, had dropped into the open palm of his right hand.

Once upon a time, he could hurl a fastball sixty miles an hour. Those days were gone. Sweat beaded on his brow as he struggled to contract his fingers around the spongy ball.

I'm half the man I used to be, he thought, and tried not to feel bitter. He'd been doing his job for his President and his country. He couldn't complain when injury and painful rehab came with the territory.

What was he going to do if, no matter how hard he pushed, it didn't work? Would he be happy with Marshal Vega's job, running the Secret Service? Did he even want it? What in the hell did he want? He'd never had this kind of self-doubt in his life and it was troubling.

After ten measly squeezes, his throbbing hand forced him to drop the ball. Shane swore loudly.

"Don't get discouraged," Pete said. "You're making steady progress."

"Doesn't feel like it."

"You're distracted, dude. You're not focusing on the squeeze. You gotta focus."

Shane shook his head. He already knew that. After driving back from Louie's, he'd spent the remainder of the night tossing and turning, unable to get Tish and the impromptu dance he'd instigated off his mind. Hiring her as their wedding videographer had been a huge mistake.

Elysee was convinced working with Tish was the only way he was going to get her out of his system. Shane was determined to prove to Elysee that he had let go of the past and was ready to embrace the future with her.

But his fiancée was naïve. She didn't understand the complexities of marriage, how emotions lingered long after the legal bonds had been severed.

Shane remembered how it had felt being locked in the bathroom with Tish. The hairs raised on his arms just thinking about how close he'd come to kissing her. Even after being away from her for two years, she still affected him like no woman on earth. Hell, to be honest, the powerful pull she held over him was scary.

If you're so hot for Tish, why are you marrying Elysee?

Because he'd been down that road before with Tish

and he knew exactly where it led. They were oil and water. No matter how hot the chemistry between them. Passion was a very dangerous thing and after Tish, he'd sworn to avoid it at all costs. The thing he had going with Elysee was much safer.

Since when have you opted for safe?

Shane stared down at his hand.

"You wanna talk about it?" Pete asked, casually curling twenty-pound dumbbells, making it look as easy as kneading bread.

"Talk about what?"

"What's got you tied up in knots?"

"Who are you?" Shane growled, wiping sweat from his brow with a gym towel. "Oprah Winfrey? Dr. Phil?"

"I'm just saying. If you need to talk, I got two ears and a quiet mouth. I know how to keep secrets."

"Nothing to talk about." Shane didn't like dissecting his feelings. He wasn't about to open up to a stranger.

"Still, it can't be easy. Going from the Secret Service agent in the background to center stage as the President's son-in-law-to-be. I can't imagine it. But things are just going to get worse, you know, when the media get wind of the engagement."

"Yeah," Shane mumbled. He'd already considered that.

And it would happen soon. The wife of the Speaker of the House was throwing a party for him and Elysee this upcoming weekend in DC to officially announce their engagement.

"Elysee hired my ex-wife to videotape our wedding," Shane confessed.

"No shit." Pete gave him a grin that said *you poor dumb bastard*. "Weird coincidence."

"No coincidence. Elysee hired her on purpose. She wants us to get along. Be friends."

"Dude"—Pete shook his head—"that's so screwed up. No wonder you can't concentrate on physical therapy. Your mental lifting is a helluva lot heavier."

Shane sank down on the weight bench. His knees seemed suddenly to be made of paper. His nerves poked like sharp spikes, sticking him all over.

His injuries had brought him close to death. Closer than he'd ever been. Was his mortality the problem? Was that what had him questioning everything? Was that what had him missing Tish? Was that what had him fearing that divorcing her was the biggest mistake he'd ever made?

Ah, there it was. The thought he'd been running from all night long. It felt like a dash of ice-cold water in the face. Frigid and sobering.

"Forgive me, Tish," he muttered. "I was such a damn fool."

"You talkin' to me?" Pete racked the dumbbell.

"Yeah." Shane shoved his thoughts away. The damage was done. He couldn't turn back the clock. All he could do was make damn sure he didn't commit the same mistake with Elysee. He couldn't allow his relationship with his ex-wife to get in the way of their wedding. "Hand me those three-pound weights. It's time I moved on."

Chapter 10

Tish arrived at the ranch to find Shane behind a push mower with his shirt stripped off. She didn't know which was more unexpected. Seeing Shane mowing the President's lawn, or catching a glimpse of his incredible bare body.

She pulled to a stop in the driveway, slung the backpack that served as her camera bag over her shoulder and got out of the car, bumping the door closed with her hip as she went. Tish shaded her eyes and a rivulet of sweat slid down between her breasts—not because the weather was hot, but because Shane was.

Every chest muscle was perfectly honed and defined, ripped and rock hard beneath the silk of his skin. Her gaze slid over him, her mind remembering how firm and thick his skin had felt beneath her fingers. She remembered and ached to touch him again. His denim jeans hugged his hips, molded to his thighs. His dark hair glistened in the sunlight

She swallowed hard and felt the movement of her gulp

track all the way down her throat, leaving her feeling dry and breathless. She'd never been so aware of his body.

Or of her own.

Her heart knocked against her rib cage. She moistened her lips, tasted cinnamon-flavored gloss.

This had to stop. She couldn't keep lusting after him, not if she was going to make it through the wedding in one piece.

Shane's left hand guided the lawn mower. His right hand balanced awkwardly against the handle.

Her gaze fixed on that damaged hand. Sadness for him, for them both, swelled inside her on equal par with her regret.

He saw her then, watching him. He killed the mower engine. His gaze lasered into her, sharp as a razor, burning right through her, causing her nipples to tighten underneath her shirt.

His expression was inscrutable, the cool countenance of a protector—a man who always needed someone to look after. That was why he was marrying Elysee; ultimately, it was the same reason he'd left *her*. She hadn't let herself need him. At least not in the way that he needed to be needed.

"What are you doing here?" he asked.

"What are you doing mowing the lawn?" She forced herself not to watch as a bead of sweat trickled down his bare bicep.

At first it seemed as if he might not answer; his mouth drew tight into a straight line. But then, as if forcing the words from his mouth, he said, "Bored out of my skull with rehab. I figured I'd have a go at the last mow of the season. There's something satisfying about putting in an honest day's work."

A hint of a smile quirked one side of his upper lip, and drew her attention to the fact that he hadn't yet shaved today. The sight of his beard growth made her shiver. She recalled exactly how it had scratched and tickled. Involuntarily, she arched her back; her breasts rose.

He sank his hand onto his hip, looking arrogant and dangerous. His grin widened.

No, no, she thought as her knees quivered, *not that damnable lopsided grin*. She thought of last night in Louie's bar, the dance they'd shared, the feelings that touching him again had conjured. Feelings she'd hoped she'd laid to rest.

Her lips craved to caress his mouth, to brush against his stubbled cheek; to lick the salt off his skin. But she couldn't. Shane no longer belonged to her. He was Elysee's man now, and she was just their wedding videographer. He was taboo and this feeling was forbidden.

Yet it thrilled her to the very core of her soul.

"You haven't answered my question."

The smile disappeared. His eyes darkened as his gaze flicked from her face to her body. She was wearing the same clothes she'd run errands in—a snug pair of jeans and a shirt that conformed to her breasts. He was definitely noticing.

"Elysee sent me." She held up her camera bag. "She thought it would be a good idea to start on the *Our Love Story* video for the reception."

"*Our Love Story*?"

"Well, your story. Yours and Elysee's."

"I'm not following."

"You know. I take photographs from both of your pasts, mix them together with pictures of you two dating, add your favorite love songs, headlines of the times, and meld all of it into a pictorial video of the story of your romance."

"Um . . . Elysee and I never really dated."

"What do you mean? You're getting married. How could you not have dated?"

"I was her bodyguard for over a year and then I saved her life. That's our love story."

It made perfect sense. Shane loved to save people and Elysee had needed saving. "Yeah, so when did you fall in love with her?"

"I don't recall you and me having all that many dates before we decided to get married."

"Look how that turned out."

"Tish," he said. An odd expression crossed his face.

"Shane." She tossed her head.

"I've known Elysee longer than we were married."

"Ouch." Tish pantomimed pulling a sword from her heart. "Want your blade back, Zorro?"

"You started it." He raked his gaze over her, his dark eyes narrowing.

They used to enjoy teasing each other with lighthearted banter. It had been the cornerstone of their relationship, back when things were good. Back before the very worst had happened. Tish caught her breath and forcefully shoved away the dark memory from her mind.

"I don't have time to stand here bickering with you," she snapped. She nodded toward the veranda where a row of heavy mesquite rocking chairs sat. "Get cleaned up and I'll meet you on the front porch and we'll go through your old photo albums."

"I don't have any old photo albums."

"I do," she said. "That's what's in my camera bag."

"Where did you get old photos of me?"

"Your mother gave me copies of your childhood pictures when we were married, remember? Plus, I did take a few of you myself. I'm a photographer, you know. That's what I do. Take pictures, make videos."

"As if that's something I could forget." His voice cracked. With sarcasm? Or another kind of emotion altogether? "And you kept photographs of me?"

"Yeah."

"Why?" He looked amused. It was not a reaction she'd anticipated. "I would have expected you to scissor my head off."

She shrugged, keeping it light. Trying to deny her heart had fallen forward against her chest. Trying not to think about all the other things she remembered about him. "Like it or not, Shane, you were a big part of my life. I'm allowed to keep your photographs if I want. You didn't get sole custody of the photos."

They stood staring at each other, only a few feet apart, both breathing in the heavy, still air thick with the scent of freshly mown grass. She knew they were being watched. Knew there were security cameras hidden all over the ranch and that there were servants and Secret Service agents within eavesdropping distance.

The knowledge only heightened her arousal. Tish desperately wanted to ask him if he'd kept any pictures of her, but she was too afraid of his answer to ask. If Shane said no, it would hurt her feelings and if he said yes, well, that might hurt even more. To think that he still cared. Even just a little bit.

Resolutely, she turned her back and picked her way across the lawn in her sandals, blades of damp St. Augustine clinging to her toes. She could feel the heat of Shane's gaze on her back and it was all she could do to keep from turning around, running right back to him, and flinging herself into his arms.

She sat down in one of the rocking chairs on the front porch.

A maid appeared from seemingly out of nowhere. "Would you like some lemonade to drink while you wait, miss?"

"Um, yeah, sure. Thanks."

It was weird, this presidential life, being waited on hand and foot. Living in a fishbowl. She wondered how Shane was going to like it.

Doesn't matter if he likes it or not. It's no concern of yours.

The maid returned with two glasses of lemonade and a plate of homemade sugar cookies. She set the refreshments on the round patio table positioned between the two rocking chairs and disappeared as silently as she'd come.

Tish sat sipping lemonade and gazing out at the red-and-white Hereford cattle grazing on the other side of the fence until Shane appeared ten minutes later smelling of sandalwood soap and shaving cream. He loomed over her, blocking out the sunlight.

Suddenly she felt a tiny splash of fear.

Calm down. It's all right. You've got absolutely nothing to lose. You've already lost it all.

The thought was strangely freeing. She took a deep breath, smiled up at him, and patted the rocking chair beside her. "Sit."

He sat down awkwardly.

"Lean over."

"Why?"

"Just do it."

"Why?"

"Why not?"

"What is it?"

"Some things never change. I see you're as argumentative as always."

"Me? You're the feisty one."

"Stop being difficult. You've got a smudge of shaving cream on your earlobe."

He didn't lean over, but she did, reaching out to wipe the spot of white shaving cream away. It dissolved against the heat of her thumb.

Shane sat back in his chair, angling his body away from hers, then picked up the lemonade and took a long swallow. She watched his throat muscles work and realized he was more nervous than she was, but he'd carefully arranged his features not to give himself away.

The Secret Service had taught him a lot of tricks, but she'd been intimate with this man. She knew him inside and out. The clues to his emotional landscape were easy for her to read.

He held his shoulders like a razor, stiff and sharp. He sat leaning away from her as if an accidental brushing of their skin would unravel him completely. A sweet sense of power rippled over her. This man was four inches taller than her and seventy pounds heavier, yet he was afraid of her. Tish almost laughed. Instead, she reached for the top album on the stack. "Let's see what we've got here."

"I don't . . ."

She pulled the album into her lap, cocked her head, and slanted him a sideways glance. "Yes?"

His gaze met hers and she felt it. That click. That lock. That old black magic.

One look in his eyes and she was jettisoned back in time to the moment that had sealed their fate.

Tish had never intended for him to be more than a fling. They were simply too different and she'd known it the minute she met him.

It was about sex.

Or that's what she told herself. That was how it started out.

The morning after she'd taken him home from Louie's was his day off. She asked him if he wanted to go to Galveston Island for the day and he'd surprised her by saying yes. They enjoyed the island, and neither of them wanted to go home. It was almost midnight when Tish suggested they walk onto the ferry and take a late night cruise.

"I don't know about that," he'd said, eyeing the sky. "Looks like rain."

She touched the tip of her tongue to her upper lip and gave him a wicked grin. "I don't melt. Do you?"

He smiled back. They were the only foot passengers on the ferry and there weren't even many cars. They climbed the stairs to the open-air deck. The wind was whipping and the waves were rocking and thick black rain clouds obscured the stars.

They found a little alcove between a support beam and the railing. Shane pulled her into his arms and crushed her mouth with his. It was the first time he'd kissed her, even though they'd been touching all day. And it was the most savagely wonderful kiss of her life. Full of sex and promise.

He pulled back from the kiss and shoved his fingers

through her curls. "I love your hair," he murmured huskily. "Autumn on display."

She tasted rain on his lips, and that was the first time she realized it was sprinkling. She tasted her own desperate hunger for him. The intensity of her hunger was stark and startling. She yearned to be joined with him. Nothing less than full body contact would do.

Tish had never possessed much self-control, but around Shane, her willpower was nonexistent. The hold he had on her was mysterious and strong. He was not her usual type. Too darkly handsome. Too straitlaced.

But how she longed to undo those laces!

This whole thing was turning into a big game. Could she seduce him without losing her heart? It would be fun to try. And dangerous.

What if she fell for him? What then?

I won't fall for him, she promised herself, but secretly, deep inside where she kept the truth well hidden from herself, she was halfway there already.

His arms were around her and he pressed her spine into the side of the ferry. The rain picked up speed, falling warm and spiky against their skin. The wind caught the skirt of her short dress, whipping it around her legs. Brilliant lightning so white it hurt her eyes split the churning black sky with a single perfect hot-fingered fork.

In the stab of lightning, lash of rain, bluster of wind, there was no resistance, no logic, no regret. There was only pleasure. Great waves of sweet, intense pleasure.

"I've never done anything like this," Shane rasped after he pulled his mouth from hers and stared deeply into her eyes.

"Neither have I," she whispered back.

He looked like he didn't believe her. That sort of hurt her feelings.

"I haven't," she insisted.

"I'm not saying that you have."

"You think I'm easy. Because I like to have fun. Because I'm not interested in commitment." They'd already spent the day talking about those things.

"No," he'd said. "You're wrong. That's not it."

"What is it then?"

"Every time I look at you, I can't help but ask myself why me? Why would a stunning woman like you bother with a guy like me?"

No man had ever talked this way to her. He made her feel special. "What are you talking about? You're handsome."

He shrugged. "Not in a traditional way. I've been told I can be pretty scary-looking."

His eyes were deep-set, almost black. His eyebrows were thick and dark. His chin was strong and determined. He could look a little scary to the timid sort.

"I'm not a traditional girl."

"So I've noticed."

She smiled.

"Why are you here with me?" he asked.

Tish didn't have an answer. She couldn't say why she was attracted to him. She simply was. He stirred her blood in a way no man ever had. Couldn't that just be enough? Why did he need to analyze it?

If there was one thing that troubled her about him, it was that. His need to dissect everything.

"Just shut up and kiss me again." She slid her arms around his neck as the next crack of thunder shook the

small ferry. The waves rocked against the boat in sensuous, rhythmic motions.

Raindrops splattered the deck, patterned their skin. Tish's T-shirt had stuck wetly to her chest, clearly outlining the contours of her bra.

"This is insanity," he said.

"Yes," she agreed, laughing loud enough to be heard above the wind.

The next charge of lightning was hotter than ever and mind-jarringly close. The chance they could be struck by lightning was very real and very thrilling. This was the most erotic thing that had ever happened to her. She had a feeling the same was true for him.

He pulled her up tight against his chest, pressing her to his hard angles that promised so much enjoyment. She tilted her head to plant a kiss on his masculine chin.

Cupping a palm behind her head, he trapped her to him. He kissed her, thrusting his tongue deep inside her mouth, ironing his body flat against hers. She could feel him everywhere—her breasts, her pelvis, her knees. His taste was in her mouth. His smell, mingling with the rain, was in her nostrils. His breathing, rough and rapid, resonated in her ears.

Awareness sparked off them, sharp as the lightning decorating the sky. She gripped his hard-muscled back. His hips locked hers against the boat, holding her safe. He wasn't going to let her slip into the churning black waters.

But she couldn't trust him completely, no matter how tightly he squeezed her. For her whole life, there had never been anyone to catch her when she fell. Her father had taken off when she was a kid. Her mother, while well-intentioned, bounced from man to man, always looking *for the one great true love that Tish had decided never to believe in.*

She might not be able to trust him, but she wanted him right now more than anything else in the world.

Desire rolled like liquid fire through her veins, tugged her down on an upsurge of sexual need. Tossed her heedlessly, mindlessly toward a destiny she couldn't fathom but lusted after.

He was a stranger. She barely knew him. Maybe that was the reason she wanted him so badly. Attraction to a stranger was always more exciting than the familiar.

The waves rocked the ship, rocked her pelvis into his. Tish moaned soft and low. She swayed into him. She had no self-control. She couldn't stop her hips from rubbing against his; not even if the ship were sinking could she stop.

Their clothes hung heavily from their bodies, sodden with rain. The weighted sensation added to the intrigue.

Tish wanted out of her clothing. Wanted to feel his naked body against hers. Wanted to feel the rain sluicing off of them. Wanted to feel everything all at once. She'd always been greedy that way. Hungry for experience, thirsting for excitement, desperately seeking to hide her pain through pleasurable sensations.

His hips kept moving against her. He was measured, slow, taking his time. He wasn't as desperate as she. Either that or he was much better at hiding his need. Maybe it was just that he liked to draw things out. Liked how he was torturing her.

He possessed a lot of control. Here was the kind of man you could spend a whole weekend in bed with and never grow tired of making love. Sore, yes, tired, no.

Shane kissed the length of her neck, nibbling and nip-

ping as he went. She thrilled to the vibration of his lips on her throat.

"I want you naked," he said, although she could barely hear him above the noise of the rain and her steadily pounding pulse. "I need to touch you."

Yes! It was exactly what she wanted, too!

Sighing happily, she burrowed her face against his chest, shielded her eyes from the pelting storm. She slid two fingers down the column of his throat. He swallowed as she stroked his Adam's apple.

They nuzzled and kissed. Tasted and teased. He treated her with tender licks. His tongue was an instrument of delicious delight. Somewhere along the way, his hand had inched up beneath her shirt, easing aside the cotton material, skating up to unhook her bra.

The feel of his rough, masculine fingertips against the soft, gentle skin of her breasts was highly arousing. Her nipples hardened tight as diamonds.

Then he dipped his head and began unbuttoning her shirt with his teeth. One by one, they popped open.

Her knees weakened. If he hadn't been holding her pinned to the wall, she would have melted straight into the floor. They were going to get naked right here on the top level of the ferry. Right here in the rain, hidden from view by a support pillar, but standing underneath a full flowing sky.

She shoved her hands underneath his shirt, as eager to get at him as he was to get at her. Her hunger escalated his need. Frantically, he stripped off his own shirt and tossed it, sopping wet, to the ground.

Lightning flashed, illuminating him.

He was magnificent.

Her breath left her body at the sight of his muscular

bare chest. He was exquisite. Not an ounce of flab on his hard-honed frame. This was indeed a man.

And she couldn't wait to get him out of his pants.

Thunder growled, low and sexy.

Her shirt hung open. Her bra was unhooked. He pulled both garments off her shoulders in two forceful moves and then he dropped to his knees in front of her. His eyes stared at her bare breasts with awe and reverence.

His caresses grew frenzied. She realized she was just as frantic as he was, maybe even more so.

Their breathing grew ragged, husky. It all seemed so urgent. She must have him or she felt as if she would literally die. Things were totally out of control and she loved it. This was the way she lived her life, acting on impulse, obeying her gut instincts.

She told herself he was nothing more than a way to take her mind off her problems. A diversion she would soon tire of. That was okay. She wasn't going to fall into the trap her mother had fallen into so many times. She was not going to lose herself in a man. Sex, yes, but with just one particular man, hell no.

But this man seemed to have other plans.

He twisted away from her and her body throbbed to have the contact back. In the darkness, his gaze collided into hers. The expression on his face was feral, primal.

She was vulnerable. Alone with a stranger. She acknowledged this. She shrank back into the shadows, suddenly realizing how vulnerable she truly was. This crazy foolishness was beyond comprehension.

Yet, in spite of the passion, in spite of her out-of-control urges, in spite of her raw vulnerability, something told her she could trust him. That he would keep her safe. And that scared her more than anything else. She had an urge to bolt over the side of the ferry, plunge straight down into the inky water and swim away.

"God, Tish," he said with a catch in his voice. "You are so beautiful."

She'd been told she was beautiful before, but never with such heartfelt rendering.

Tish found herself pressed hard against him. They were chest to breasts, skin against skin. He wrapped his arms around her, seized her mouth with his, tipped her backward until her hair trailed the ground.

She exhaled sharply and he swallowed up the sound.

He read her need and his hands explored unfamiliar territory, slipping past the waistband of her skirt, firmly grasping her zipper, jerking it down with rough, demanding movements.

The next thing she knew his hand was inside her panties and she was on fire. Burning up inside, shoving her pelvis hard against his.

"Finger me," she demanded.

But he didn't have to be told. He was already doing it. He pushed his thick middle finger inside her, stroking her ache.

"Devil," she growled.

"Wench," he growled back.

She nipped his shoulder, sank her teeth into him.

He touched her in places that ignited thoughts of what it would feel like when he was between her thighs, pushing deep enough inside her to soothe that throbbing ache.

He lowered his head, made love to her breasts with his wily tongue. He zeroed in, plucking a straining nipple into his mouth.

Tish wobbled in his arms. He braced his hand against her spine.

"I'm going to make love to you now," he said.

"Yes."

It was that simple. Her acquiescence. He had her. She would do anything he wanted. God, she was lost. And it felt wonderful.

His mouth caught hers again in a possessive kiss that made her quiver. Caught her, arrested her. She wasn't going anywhere until he'd branded her as his own. They were in a whirlwind, swept up by a maelstrom of chemistry and passion and need. Shane unzipped his pants, wrestled himself out of them and his underwear.

She shimmied out of her skirt, shucking her panties, and then shifted her gaze back to the magnificent man in front of her.

They stood completely naked on the upper deck of the ferry, in the middle of the night, in the crescendo of a thunderstorm, completely vulnerable to each other.

It was, quite honestly, the most exciting moment of Tish's life. She let her eyes drop from his. Allowed her gaze to travel over the length of his bare chest, down his taut belly to his very impressive package.

She lifted her eyes to meet his again and saw he was assessing her as avidly as she'd been assessing him. The corner of his mouth quirked upward in approval. That lopsided grin shot an arrow straight to her heart.

The emotions playing across his face riveted her.

A strange feeling overcame her, a combination of fear and excitement and danger and trust. Yes, trust. In spite of their wild circumstances she trusted this man.

That she trusted him scared her. A lot.

The impulse to back out was suddenly overwhelming.

But then he clamped a hand around her bottom and drew her up tight against his hardness and she just melted. Into him, into the rain, into the darkness of the steamy night.

He braced her back against the support column. He took her right leg and guided it around his waist. She understood what he wanted and pulled her left leg up as well, until she was pinned against the pillar, totally supported by the strength in his body.

And she trusted him to support her. That was the miracle.

He leveled into her, slipping in with surprisingly gentle movements considering how fired up they both were.

She hissed in a breath. The minute Shane was snugged inside, her muscles contracted around him.

"Oh, no ma'am, don't start that yet," he said, "or I won't last a minute."

But he felt so good. So big and thick inside her that she couldn't resist squeezing.

"Ah, Tish, I can see I'm going to have to distract you if I want to satisfy you."

His mouth sought hers, kissing her thoroughly, imprinting her with his taste. She could hear the rasp of his breathing through the sound of the slowing storm.

"That's it," he whispered. "Settle down. Enjoy the ride."

And then he began to move.

Their bodies fit. Hand in glove.

She felt every manly inch of him as he slid in and out of her warm moist folds, his movements languid and pointed, clearly designed to drive her quite mad. She could feel it coming.

The storm.

Not the one lashing them against the ferry. But the one gathering in her womb.

Legs braced wide, penis sliding in and out of her, Shane anchored her to the wall, his strong arms holding her in place. Like a dedicated explorer, he took his time, getting to know the feel of her.

She slid the fingers of one hand down his back, feeling the bumps in his spine, grateful for him, for this moment, for this delicious pleasure.

His thrusts quickened. She egged him on with hot little gasps and soft, hungry moans.

Tension mounted.

Shane drove into her. Forceful now, demanding. His early gentleness evaporated in the face of urgent need.

Fearing she was going to slip, she tightened her legs around his waist. He cupped her buttocks in his hand, spearing her hard, banging into her until she was shaking all over.

The inside of her thighs rode his hips. He was pounding her, driving as hard as the pelting rain, his penis a searing sword of pleasure so intense it almost hurt.

"That's right," she cried. "Make me come."

She could feel his legs quivering, knew he was on the verge of climax. Oh God, it was gonna be big.

They exploded.

Shattering into pieces. Blasting apart. The orgasm tore through them simultaneously. She felt it ripple through her womb. Felt the hot shot of his heat flood through her.

In that quivering second in time, everything changed forever.

Chapter 11

"Tish. Tish?" Shane's voice tore her from the past. "Where did you go?"

"Huh?' She blinked and found herself back on the porch at the Benedict ranch, staring deeply into her ex-husband's eyes.

The sizzle was still there. Deadly as ever. Tish gulped. The chemistry might linger, but she'd accepted the fact that Shane no longer belonged to her. The expression in his eyes was just the caress of a memory and the passion that had once defined them. But they'd gone beyond that.

They had, she realized with a start, grown up.

They could feel this passion and not act on it. She could let the sensation of want and need wash over her and then move on. She liked the cleanness of what was left behind. She'd never thought she could find physical restraint appealing, but there it was.

"You zoned out on me."

"Did I? I'm sorry. What were you saying?" she asked

in a rush, praying her heated memories didn't show on her face.

"I'm proud of you," Shane said.

"What?"

"You're one tough cookie."

"Since when did you admire toughness in a woman?"

He looked bewildered by the question. "I've always admired your toughness."

"Ya coulda fooled me. I thought my toughness was the thing that broke us."

He didn't say anything else, just pressed his lips together, reached over with his scarred hand, and flipped open the photo album. He was so close she could smell the scent of his soap, feel his body heat. The memory of their lovemaking on the Galveston ferry was burned into her brain for eternity.

Their gazes were welded. The sound of the autumn breeze sweeping through the oak trees filled the silence between them, the wind whispering as it rustled and danced around tree branches burdened with acorns.

They both knew what had really broken them. The tension rose, curling around him and around her, ensnaring them in the hurts of the past. She dropped her gaze, stared at his hand. Shane caught her staring. She longed to bring his damaged hand to her mouth, press her lips to his scars, healing him with her kisses. But of course she could not, did not.

Hurriedly, she shifted her gaze from his hand to the book between them. There was a picture of five-year-old Shane, cocking that lopsided grin that would later become a ladykiller. He had a bottom tooth missing and his eyes were sparkling mischief. He was sitting on a back porch stoop, a black and white spotted puppy in his arms, licking his chin.

"This is definitely going into the *Our Love Story* video." Tish peeled back the plastic covering and slipped the photograph from the album. "Along with a quote about what little boys are made of."

"I never really liked that picture," Shane muttered.

"Why not? It's adorable."

"My ears stick out like cup handles."

"All little boys' ears stick out like cup handles. Elysee is going to love it."

"Find another picture," he said gruffly.

Something Shane had once told her occurred to Tish out of the blue. "The cup-handle ears aren't the reason you don't like that picture, is it?"

"Huh?"

"That's your dog Bandit."

He nodded.

"You told me you saw Bandit get hit by a car and it hurt you so much you refused to get another dog. Remember when I wanted to get a collie?"

"Yeah."

"You lost Bandit not long after that picture was taken, am I right?"

Shane made a noise of surprise that she'd guessed. "It was the same day."

She studied him and the look in his eyes made her glance away before she started tearing up. She couldn't very well tarnish her reputation for toughness. Tish slipped the photograph of Shane and Bandit back between the plastic and quickly flipped the page.

Next was a snapshot of Shane and his sister with their parents on an amusement park ride. Shane looked to be eight or nine, his sister, Amy, about four or five. All of them were waving for the camera—a happy nuclear family on vacation. Tish felt jealous.

"How's Amy?" she asked, battling back her feelings.

"Finishing her graduate degree in journalism at Columbia this year. She's had a great job offer from the *New York Times,* although she's still weighing her options. She has a serious boyfriend. Everyone's expecting an engagement announcement from them soon."

"How are Charlotte and Ben?" Tish asked, referring to his parents.

"Dad retired this fall and they've taken off on that around-the-world cruise they've been dreaming of for years."

"That's wonderful," she said and meant it. She'd always adored Shane's mom, and while she'd been a little scared of his stern Vietnam veteran dad, she respected and admired Ben Tremont.

"How's Dixie Ann?" he asked.

"What can I say? She's Dixie Ann."

"Married? Dating?"

"In between men right now."

"Where's she living?" Shane propped his long, lean legs up on the porch railing.

"San Diego."

"Nice place. You visit her much?"

"Not much. You know my relationship with Dixie Ann. I bet your parents were thrilled when you told them you and Elysee were getting married. I know your dad shares Nathan Benedict's politics."

"I haven't told them yet."

Tish's eyes flew to his face and her heart gave a strange little bump. Why didn't they know about his engagement to Elysee? He and his parents had always been close. She figured they would be the first people he would tell.

"Hmm."

"Hmm, what?"

"Hmm, nothing."

"Don't read anything into it."

"What? I didn't say anything."

"You said *hmm*."

"That's a sound, not a word."

"It's hard getting through on those ship-to-shore calls," he said defensively. "I phoned them after I got out of the hospital, to let them know I was doing okay and staying at the ranch to recuperate, but that was before—"

"You asked Elysee to marry you," she interrupted.

He ran his good hand through his hair, ruffling the damp locks, and angled her an exasperated look. "Yeah."

"Are you just going to let Charlotte and Ben read about your engagement in the papers?"

"No, no." He shook his head. "Of course not. I'll call them before the engagement party next weekend."

"So this photo is okay to use?" She tapped the picture of Shane and his family.

"Sure."

"Oh . . . I forgot all about this picture." She pointed to the photograph below it. "I absolutely love how adorable you look in it."

It was a snapshot she'd taken of Shane not long after they'd started dating. He was lounging in the middle of her bed in his underwear, his back propped against the headboard, hands cradling the back of his head, elbows jutting outward, looking like a thoroughly bad boy.

A trickle of sweat slid down the back of her neck in spite of the balmy temperature. Her pulse quickened, as it always had when she was near him. She felt a rush of sexual awareness so potent she had to bite down on her bottom lip. Thank God they weren't alone on this ranch. If they had been, Tish didn't know if she could have stopped herself from kissing him.

She heard his breathing speed up. Bravely, she tilted her head and peeked over at him. He was staring at her intently, at the bead of sweat that had tracked from her neck and was now sliding slowly toward her cleavage.

"Remember," he murmured, his breath fanning coolly against her skin, "what you were wearing when you took this picture?"

She caught the wicked gleam in his eyes.

His gaze held hers captive.

"What?" she breathed.

"Absolutely nothing."

She could not look away. Not that she wanted to. His finger crept up to touch a curl at her shoulder.

"You looked glorious, with all that red hair tumbling over your bare skin."

"That was a long time ago."

"Not that long ago."

"So much has happened since then." She inhaled. His hand was still at her shoulder. "Too much."

Quickly, Tish thumbed the next page, and what she saw made the breath catch in her lungs. She'd forgotten about this picture. Hadn't looked at the album in over two years.

It was a Polaroid of her and Shane on their honeymoon at Galveston Island. They were coming out of the Gulf of Mexico, soaking wet, Tish riding on Shane's shoulders. The afternoon sun was glinting off their sun-burnished skins; his hands were locked around her ankles to keep her from falling off. But there was no need, for she was perfectly balanced on the broad platform of his shoulders. They were laughing with their eyes shut and water rolling down their faces. They looked like they were in perfect harmony. Sharing one mind. One thought.

Yin and Yang.

Whole.

A beachgoer had snapped the photograph of that perfect moment in time. The man had told them he'd been so captivated by their unity, their pure joy, that he'd taken the picture because special moments like that didn't happen often. After they'd come ashore and dried off, he handed them the Polaroid and walked away. Leaving them with a visual of one precious second in time.

They did look happy. Poor lovestruck fools. They had no idea what they were in for.

A knot formed in Tish's throat. "We *were* happy once, weren't we?"

"Yeah," Shane said. "But that was before . . ."

His words trailed off, and the name neither one of them had the courage to say lay in the air between them.

As she stared at the photograph, the earth tilted and it felt as if she were being catapulted into outer space, flung far from sense and reason. Her loss was now a physical thing in her hands. Something she could touch and see. A thousand flashes of memory formed in her head. Formed and coalesced, melded and changed, jumbled and shifted. His kisses, their bodies, the taste of cake, the fizz of champagne.

Everything burned bright and clear and oh so painful—Tish's dreams, her hopes, her regrets.

Shane didn't move.

She could hear him breathing huskily beside her and

she knew he felt it, too. This loss, this hurt she'd been trying so hard to bury for two long years. She started to flip the page, to run from those naïve newlyweds, but Shane's hand, raw and pink with scars, anchored the corner.

Tish couldn't turn the page. Not without his permission. Not without wrestling the book from him. How long was he going to make her sit here looking at her biggest failure, her greatest mistake?

No, no, not a mistake. Marrying Shane had never been the mistake.

"Tish." He spoke her name softly, but the sound was sharp, intense.

She couldn't look at him.

Instead, she turned her head, peered at a cow scratching her polled head against a fencepost. Brought her arms up, crossed them over her chest, futilely thinking the gesture would protect her. That it would hold in all these feelings she didn't want to feel.

What the hell am I doing here?

"I don't think Elysee would be too keen on having this picture in her video," she said. "In fact, I don't know why I'm hanging on to it. Why don't we destroy it together? A symbolic letting go so you can start your new life with Elysee fresh and free of me."

"No!"

They both heard the sudden heat of the word as it exploded from his lips. What did it mean? His abrupt rejection of her suggestion to destroy their honeymoon photo?

Don't read anything into this. Don't get your hopes up. You're only asking for more pain.

"Shane?"

Immediately, he backpedaled from the impact of that

single reverberating "no." He pulled away from her, let go of the page. "What I mean is, there's already been enough destruction between us. There's not going to be any harm in you keeping the photograph."

"You know," she said, "I think this was what Elysee wanted from us. To take a look at the past and let go of it. To realize that while we've had some good times, we weren't necessarily good for each other."

"We were good for each other," he said gruffly.

She met his eyes. *So then why did you leave?* But she didn't ask the question that was in her head. She knew the answer, but didn't want to make him say it.

"Not good enough," she said instead. "But you and Elysee, you guys *are* good together. She needs you and you need to be needed. That was something I just couldn't give you."

"Wouldn't give me."

"Couldn't, wouldn't, the end results were the same."

"Tish." He gave her that "you've-disappointed-me" look that used to send her heart sinking to her shoes. Whether it was true or not, she'd often felt like she fell short in his eyes.

"It's okay, Shane, really. And I think Elysee Benedict is a very wise person. I like her. She's great. I don't know how she had the courage to hire me as her videographer, but this . . ." She toggled her index finger in the air between them. "She was right. This is clearing up a lot of old baggage between us."

"Is it?"

"I think so." She canted her head. "Don't you?"

He surprised her by giving her one of his signature lopsided grins. "Yeah."

"Everything's going to be okay, isn't it?"

He nodded.

"We can be friends." She touched his wounded hand.

"Friends." He repeated the word like he'd never heard it before, pushing it tentatively around on his tongue.

"Friends," she echoed.

Her hopes lifted. Could they really be friends? The thought was enticing. To have him in her life in some small way would be a gift beyond measure.

Friends?

Shane watched her walk toward her car, the alien concept stomping around in his brain. His gaze landed on her swaying behind. Immediately guilt had him by the short hairs. Was it even possible that he and Tish could be friends, considering their sexual chemistry? And if they could, would it be fair to Elysee?

Anger fisted inside him. Anger at Elysee for bringing Tish here. Anger at Tish for trying to be his friend. Anger at himself for being so damned conflicted about what he wanted.

What was the matter with him? Ever since the accident he'd been acting like a pansy, letting circumstances push him around rather than taking action. The only purposeful thing he'd done since leaving the hospital was ask Elysee to marry him, and he'd been second-guessing that decision from the moment he'd made it. What had happened to the old Shane? The man who took a stand and never wavered from his course of action?

Shane stalked back inside the ranch house and headed for the gym. He knew of no other way to dissipate this mishmash of regret, anger, sadness, guilt, helplessness, and longing. He ground his teeth, marched down the hallway, and pushed through the doorway into the gym.

"When you want to hit something, son, take it out on a punching bag," his father had instructed him. "Whale away until your anger is gone."

He strode to the box where they stowed the gym gear, pried it open, and rummaged around for a pair of boxing gloves. He put one glove on his bad hand, but then fumbled with the other glove, failing repeatedly to get it on.

In frustration, he slung the glove to the ground, and muttering a dark curse laid into the punching bag with his bare-knuckled left hand and his ineffective right hand.

He slammed into the heavy punching bag. Jarring pain shot up through his arm.

Again and again he punched, harder and harder, punishing himself, accepting the physical pain, inviting it in to gratefully crowd out his emotional turmoil.

His muscles bunched. Sweat slicked his brow. He grunted in ragged breaths.

Throughout his entire life, Shane had been all about self-control. His father had drilled it into this head. He was from a military family. A Tremont. He had a reputation, a code of honor to measure up to.

Even as a kid, he'd tried to do the right thing, to uphold his legacy. He could hear his father's voice, the echo of platitudes in his head. "You make a decision, you stick with it. Doubt is weakness. Don't ever show weakness. No second-guessing. It's better to make a mistake and fail than to be a wishy-washy girl of a man."

Whenever he thought back on his childhood, all he could remember craving was his father's admiration and respect, two things not easily earned from Ben Tremont.

"Dad, watch me go off the diving board."

"Don't whine for my attention, boy, just jump."

He'd stood at the end of the diving board, six years

old and staring down into the swimming pool, unable to jump now that his father was watching.

Ben stood on the sideline, hands on his hips, scowl on his face. "Don't be a pussy. Jump."

His toes had curled over the end of the board. Paralyzed by his father's expectations, he couldn't do it.

In disgust, Ben had climbed up the ladder, grabbed him by the seat of his swim trunks, and threw him into the water. "Hesitate and you're dead."

Shane smacked the punching bag. The pain was strong, but his anger was stronger. Punch, punch, punch.

Why was he so mad?

Punch, punch, punch.

He pounded the bag, beating back not only his frustration but the sexual desire he still felt for Tish that he was so ashamed to acknowledge.

Shane recalled another childhood memory. He had been twelve years old this time and eager to go on his first hunting trip with Ben and his cronies. Crouching in the deer blind, shivering cold, rifle clutched in his hand, pulse pounding with fear and adrenaline.

The big antlered mule deer walked into the clearing nibbling corn from the deer feeder they'd set up to lure him in.

Ben's mouth was pressed against Shane's ear as he whispered, "Look down the sight. Take aim at his heart."

Shane raised the gun, peered down the barrel, the buck in his crosshairs.

"Commit," his father commanded.

Shane's finger curled around the trigger, his breath fogged frigid air. The deer turned, lifted his head, staring through the small rectangular window of the blind and straight into Shane's eyes.

"Fire!" Ben's demanding whisper sounded like a shout in Shane's ear.

He pulled the trigger just as impulse telegraphed this thought to his brain: *I don't want to kill the deer.*

His arm moved in response to his thoughts, throwing off his aim. The gun blasted, the noise reverberated in the small enclosure, inside his head. The air filled with the acrid smell of gunpowder. Shane flung the gun away from him, closed his eyes.

His father cursed, grabbed him by the scruff of his neck and shook him. "Come on, boy. You're going to finish what you started."

Ben dragged him through the underbrush, tracking the blood drops spattered over the fallen autumn leaves. They walked for half an hour before they found him, lying against a cedar tree.

The buck thrashed on the ground, eyes glassy, breath raspy—dying. Slowly, painfully.

Bile rose in his throat and he dropped to his knees to retch in the weeds. He'd caused this.

Ben laid a heavy hand on Shane's shoulder. "The animal is suffering, son. Suffering because you second-guessed yourself. Now get up and finish what you started. Put this animal out of his misery."

Shane had learned an ugly but important lesson that day. He'd made up his mind. No more second-guessing. From now on he would not hesitate. He would do his duty. He would finish what he started.

And except for his marriage to Tish, he'd lived by that vow.

Wham, wham, wham. He pummeled the punching bag.

His right hand was past pain now. It was numb. Dulled by the repeated punches.

He'd failed with Tish. Failed his marriage. Failed himself. He hadn't stood by his commitment and they'd both suffered.

She pushed you away.

But that was no excuse. She'd needed him and he hadn't been there. Not sticking with Tish was the biggest mistake he'd ever made. But it was over and done with now. He had a new commitment. He was engaged to another woman. A good, kind, trusting woman. And not just any woman, but the daughter of the President of the United States.

Exhausted, he dropped his aching arms to his sides, stepped back from the punching bag, rested his back against the wall and slowly sank to the floor.

He'd made promises. To Elysee. To Nathan Benedict. To himself. Promises he intended to keep.

Elysee needed him in a way Tish never had. He was determined to take care of her, especially since he'd messed things up so spectacularly with Tish.

So what if the sexual chemistry between him and Tish still lingered? It didn't change the fact that he'd made a commitment to Elysee. She trusted him and he would not betray her.

No matter how much he might long to make love to his ex-wife, he'd do whatever it took to eliminate those desires. Slam a punching bag into oblivion, take cold showers and stay as far away from Tish as he could get.

It wasn't going to be easy to accomplish with her underfoot as their wedding videographer. But this time he was determined. He was not going back on his promise. There'd been too much hurt already.

Chapter 12

When Elysee had told Tish she was going to fly her to Washington DC to video the engagement party, she'd assumed they would give her a coach ticket on a commercial airline. What she hadn't counted on was traveling via *Air Force One*.

When the stretch limo pulled up to the private airfield in Houston with Tish sitting in the backseat, her mouth dropped open at the sight of the presidential airplane parked on the tarmac. Just looking at the 747 with the emblem of the United States flag painted on its tail made her want to put her hand over her heart and recite the Pledge of Allegiance. For the first time she fully understood the sense of pride Shane felt working for the Secret Service.

It *was* awe-inspiring.

As the limo driver held open the door and she alighted in blue jeans and a flowing, amber-colored tunic top, she felt even more out of place than she had in the limousine.

She'd ridden in limos before, at her senior prom and

a couple of times when her mother was dating men with lavish expense accounts. In comparison to this sleek, polished piece of equipment, those limousines had seemed old and shabby.

A no-nonsense-looking woman dressed all in black and holding a clipboard asked for her name and identity before she got within ten feet of the plane. Tish fumbled for her wallet, overwhelmed by what was happening and pulled out her driver's license. She explained who she was and why she was there. The woman took Tish's suitcase and passed it to a cohort for inspection before they stowed it in the plane.

When the woman reached for her camera bag, Tish clamped a hand around the strap. "This stays with me."

"Fine." The woman nodded curtly. "But it must be examined first."

Tish nodded, pulled out her expensive digital camera and accessories. She cringed while the woman turned on the camera, flipped settings, played with the focus.

After she made it past that gatekeeper, a Secret Service agent frisked her. The frisking put Tish in mind of the favorite sex game she used to play with Shane. Where he was the Secret Service agent and she pretended to be a foreign spy out to seduce him for state secrets. Her face heated at the memory.

"You may proceed," the agent said, sounding stern and not smiling.

She remembered that, too. How Shane could look at her sometimes so coldly and unemotionally. She hadn't really realized until now it was something he'd learned in training.

The revelation startled her.

Maybe all those times he had seemed to be stonewalling, he was actually struggling hard not to show his feelings, thinking it would make him seem weak somehow. She bit down on her bottom lip and followed the female staff member who ushered her inside the plane.

Ascending the retractable stairs at the rear of the plane was a mythic experience. She was being granted entry where few had ever gone.

Once inside *Air Force One*, the staffer led her immediately up another staircase to the middle level. It looked more like a hotel or an executive office than a jetliner, except for the seat belts on the chairs.

"The lower level on the plane serves as a cargo hold," the woman said, acting as tour guide. "Most of the passenger room is here on the middle level. The upper level is largely dedicated to communications equipment and the cockpit. The president has onboard living quarters, with his own bedroom, washroom, workout gym, and office space."

The woman paused, letting Tish catch up. She'd been lingering, looking around at the masterfully handcrafted furniture with a photographer's admiring eye.

"All in all," the woman continued, "*Air Force One* can comfortably carry seventy passengers and twenty-six crew members. Passengers are not allowed to move forward within the plane. If the President should wish to speak with you, he'll walk back here to see you."

Staff members were moving to and fro. Security, military men and women, and members of the press were all dressed in either uniforms or suits. Tish felt out of place and extremely underdressed.

Why hadn't she realized what a big deal this was? Feeling like the proverbial local yokel, she stood in the middle of the aisle, confused and fighting the urge to turn around and run right out the way she'd come. She even turned her head toward the exit, checking the escape route.

She spied Shane's physical therapist, Pete Larkin, coming up the ramp with Shane bringing up the rear. At the sight of her ex-husband, Tish's breath slipped from her lungs, falling like mercury through a thermometer during a Blue Norther. Even before their tête-à-tête on the porch at the Benedict ranch house, Tish had been battling old memories and feelings she thought she'd put to rest.

He looked like Sir Galahad with a beam of sunlight streaming in through the window from over his shoulders, as if he were a mythological god bringing illumination to those inside. He wore the ubiquitous Secret Service sunglasses, even though he was no longer Elysee's bodyguard.

Old habits died hard.

For some strange reason that thought lifted her spirits. Like what? Was she subconsciously thinking of herself as one of Shane's old habits?

Stop it. Stop it right now.

He spotted Elysee sitting in the corner, but apparently he hadn't seen Tish. His face softened into a gentle smile as he went toward the President's daughter.

Elysee smiled back and tilted her face up to him. He leaned down and pressed a kiss to her cheek. Elysee looked at him as if he'd singlehandedly created the world.

It was a sweet, romantic moment that knocked the breath from Tish's lungs. She felt mean and petty and hurt. Jealousy was an ugly thing.

Panic spread through her veins like a firestorm.

It's all a mistake. Coming here today. Going to Washington. Agreeing to be the videographer for their wedding.

Not fighting harder to keep Shane.

What made her so self-destructive? Why couldn't she latch on to what was wrong with her and fix it? Why wasn't she able to control her spending? How come she swept her finances under the rug? Why had she just given up on their marriage?

He gave up on me first!

Misery had her jonesing for Ben and Jerry's Cherry Garcia. Either that or a double shot of really strong tequila. Unexpected hysteria clamped down on her mind.

I can't do this. I can't stand by and watch while Shane marries another woman.

Her knees trembled and her heart was in free fall, tumbling out of her chest and into her feet.

Elysee noticed her, waved, and called out, "Tish, come sit with us."

I'd rather stick a hot poker in my eye, thank you very much. "Okay."

Pasting on a fake smile worthy of a politician, Tish ambled over to a quartet of plush leather chairs arranged so they faced each other. Elysee and her secretary, Lola, sat on the forward-facing chairs, while Shane and Tish sat side by side on the backward-facing chairs.

If she were to reach out her right hand she could trail her fingers along the left sleeve of Shane's dark jacket. Instead, she made sure that both hands were tightly clutching her camera bag.

"Something to drink?" asked an attendant.

"V-8 juice, please, if you have it."

"Certainly, miss." The flight attendant departed.

Silence descended. Tish was aware that Elysee was studying Shane, who was looking over at her, an enigmatic expression in his eyes. He'd taken off the sunglasses and tucked them in the front pocket of his jacket. Lola was discreetly staring out the window.

Tish inhaled sharply. Oh God, this trip was going to be horrible.

"So what do you think about *Air Force One*?" Elysee asked. Tish could tell she was struggling to make pleasant conversation.

"Impressive. Photographs don't do it justice."

"It is difficult, catching the atmosphere of something on camera." Elysee gave a forced laugh. "But of course you know that. You spend your life trying to breathe dimension into a one-dimensional medium."

It sounded like a criticism, even though Tish knew Elysee hadn't meant it that way.

"Oh," Elysee said and brought two fingers to her lips. "That sounded stupid, didn't it? It's just that Shane told me how hard you work to capture the core emotional content of a moment with your camera. He said you focus in on the small details. An untied shoelace on a two-year-old ring bearer, a single bead of perspiration on the upper lip of the father of the bride, a bridesmaid fondling her own bare ring finger."

"He said that?" Tish slid her gaze in Shane's direction.

"Don't sound so surprised," he said gruffly.

"I never realized you ever paid much attention to my work." She studied him with fresh eyes.

"I was proud of you; of course I paid attention."

"Really? When was that? Before or after you bitched at me for buying this camera?" She clutched her camera bag to her chest.

"Tish." He leveled a warning glance. "You're distorting things."

"You're right." She held up her palms. "Ancient history."

"I didn't mean to stir up controversy between you two," Elysee apologized.

"You didn't," Tish and Shane said in unison and glared at each other. The undercurrent of tension was still there, strong as ever.

The flight attendant returned with the V-8 juice she'd ordered and Tish set it in the cup holder nestled in the arm of her chair and rested her camera bag at her feet.

A commotion at the door drew Tish's attention to the entrance. A knot of Secret Service surrounded the President as he entered the plane. Awestruck, she stared open-mouthed as the Commander-in-Chief made his way over to Elysee.

Nathan Benedict's presence was palpable. Not only because of everyone's reaction to him, but from the aura emanating from him. He had steel gray hair and a no-nonsense stride. He slipped out of his suit jacket, handed it to an underling, and rolled up the sleeves of his starched white shirt. He hugged Elysee, shook Shane's hand, nodded hello to Lola, and then turned to her.

"You must be Tish," he said warmly. "My daughter speaks very highly of you and your work as a videographer."

"It's a great honor to meet you, sir."

"Likewise."

"Please, take my seat, Mr. President; sit with your daughter."

She was up and moving, desperate to get away from the sudden claustrophobia squeezing her lungs. This was too much. She was ill-prepared for such a momentous encounter. She couldn't look the President in the eye. Not when she was still aching for Shane, who was about to marry his daughter. She was terrified that this perceptive man would see her secret etched upon her face.

"No, young lady, sit, sit." The President gestured toward the chair she'd vacated.

"I'm more comfortable standing."

"We're about to take off," he said, a bemused smile playing across his lips. "You have to sit down."

Tish pointed over her shoulder at vacant seating in the rear corner. "I'll be more comfortable over there."

He studied her a moment, obviously reading her nervousness.

"As you wish."

She snatched up her camera bag and grabbed her V-8 juice from the cup holder on the chair. She moved to the right. The President went in the same direction.

"Oh, sorry," she mumbled and stepped left at the very instant he did the same.

"Hold still, young lady, and let me get around you." Nathan Benedict chuckled and reached out with both hands to grab her shoulders.

Call it a subconscious response. Call it extreme nervousness. Or call it what it really was—her self-destructive mode kicking into high gear. Either way, it was a major snafu.

The second he reached for her, Tish raised her arm in a protective gesture, forgetting she was clutching a glass of viscous V-8 juice.

Her hand went up.

The glass came down.

Thick red juice splashed, blooming like blood in the center of Nathan Benedict's pristine white shirt.

The President made a startled sound.

Tish gasped.

"She stabbed the President!" someone shouted.

The Secret Service converged in a swarm.

The next thing Tish knew she was pinned to the floor by six burly bodyguards.

People were shouting. Hard knees jammed into her back, pressing down on her lungs, making it hard for her to breathe. Someone sat on her legs. Her knees dug into the carpeting. Both of her hands were staked to the ground by thick wrists heavier than iron shackles and her camera bag had disappeared.

Panic seized her. Her camera was her most valuable possession. It had cost her fifteen thousand dollars and her marriage.

"My camera!" she cried. "Where's my camera?"

Above all the hubbub she heard Shane calmly explaining that they could let her go, because while his ex-wife was a monumental klutz, she'd hardly intended to assassinate the leader of the free world with a glass of V-8 juice.

"Get off my wife." The words were on the tip of his tongue. Shane almost spoke them, but just in the nick of time, he managed to bite them back. Instead he said, "All clear, suspect no threat to the eagle."

"I'm fine," Nathan Benedict reiterated as another agent whisked him away. "It's nothing more than spilled tomato juice."

"I can't breathe," Tish mumbled, her face pressed against the floor.

A shock of concern passed through him. "Get off," he snapped at the bodyguards. "You're hurting her."

Slowly, the Secret Service agents let her up and backed away, holstering their drawn weapons as they went. Shane understood why they'd done what they'd done, but he couldn't help feeling as if they'd acted overzealously.

He reached down to take Tish's arm. "You okay?"

She raised her head, pushed up on her knees, and threw him a scathing glance. Reluctantly she took his proffered hand, but once on her feet she immediately twisted from his grasp and glowered at him darkly.

"Are you pissed off at me?"

"Why on earth would I be pissed off at you?" Her voice was laden with sarcasm.

"I don't know. That's why I'm asking."

She just glared and leaned over to dust off the knees of her jeans. When she did the gauzy top she was wearing fell forward, giving him a clear view of her cleavage.

Tish's skin was so creamy and soft. He remembered exactly what it felt like to press his face into the delicious scoop of her cleavage. He could smell her scent—an intoxicating cinnamon, ginger, and licorice mix. His heart did a weird somersault.

It had been a very long time since he'd been privy to that amazing view and he hadn't realized exactly how much he missed it. Shane blinked and just stood there for the few seconds it took to remember where he was and what he was supposed to be doing.

You're an adult, he scolded himself. *Not a randy teenager. Knock it off. Remember what you promised yourself. Remember, you're engaged to Elysee.*

Tish raised her head and her eyes met his. For that

split second in time it was just him and Tish and the way things used to be.

Once upon a time, when it came to sex, they'd been insatiable for each other. Even in the rockiest moments of their marriage, their lovemaking had been monumental. She could turn him on with just one sultry, well-placed glance. Fortunately for Shane, she was scowling at him as if he had leprosy.

"Where's my camera?" she demanded.

"Hang on."

"I want my camera."

Shane glanced around and saw that Cal had it slung over his shoulder. He also saw his old partner had noticed Tish's cleavage. Shane had the sudden urge to smack him right in the kisser.

"Cal?" He stepped closer and held out his hand. "May I have the camera?"

"You sure that's a good idea?"

"She's not a security threat," Shane growled. *And stop looking at her like that.*

"Maybe not intentionally," Cal muttered low enough where only Shane could hear. "But she's got 'walking disaster' written all over her. Remember the first time you met her?"

"Give me that." He snatched the camera from him. "And mind your own damned business."

Cal arched an eyebrow. "Guarding the first daughter is my business. What's yours, Tremont?"

Shane glared. He knew where Cal was coming from, but he also knew Tish was mentally browbeating herself for having caused such a scene. She took things so personally.

"I feel so humiliated," Tish moaned softly when Shane brought the camera back to her.

"Don't be. It happens."

"What about the President?" She worried her bottom lip with her teeth. "Is he okay?"

"He's gone to change his clothes. Don't worry about it. No damage done. President Benedict knows you were just nervous."

"I don't get how you do it." Tish shook her head.

"Do what?"

"Move in these circles and act so cool."

"Practice," he said. "FYI, whenever you bend forward, that blouse shows off a lot more than it should."

Tish splayed a hand to her cleavage. "Really?"

"Really. Why do you think Cal was staring?"

"Oh, no, and I leaned over the President to pick up my camera. Do you suppose he—"

"Saw your ta-tas? Probably."

"I flashed the President?" Tish groaned and covered her face with a hand. "God, kill me now. Thanks for telling me. I'll be extra careful until I get a chance to pin it up."

Sympathy stirred inside him. Shane reached out to touch her, wanting to reassure her that everything was going to be all right. The minute his fingers brushed her skin, he knew it was a grave mistake. Immediately, he drew back his hand.

Madness.

The heat was back again, hotter than ever. A maze of emotions rushed through his blood. Shane steeled himself. He had no right to feel this way. He was grateful that his back was to Elysee. He'd hate for her to read in his eyes what he struggled so hard to hide.

The pilot's voice came over the loudspeaker. "If everyone could take their seats, we'll be on our way."

Everyone was already sitting down except for Tish and Shane. And everyone was staring at them.

"Shane?"

He turned to take his seat beside Elysee. She crooked her finger at him. He leaned in.

"Why don't you take Tish to the back and get her settled in? I think she'll feel more comfortable back there. Go ahead and sit with her until we're airborne. She's probably feeling very embarrassed and could use some moral support from a familiar face."

Elysee's thoughtfulness was the thing he admired most about her. Honestly, he didn't deserve her. Not with the way these contradictory emotions were running through him.

"You're one hell of an understanding woman, Elysee Benedict," he said and gently chucked her under the chin. "You know that?"

She smiled sweetly. "I try. Now, shoo. Go on, so we can take off."

He escorted Tish to the back of *Air Force One*, found two empty seats side by side, stowed her camera in an overhead bin and then plunked down beside her.

Tish raised an eyebrow. "You're staying back here with me?"

"Elysee thought you could use the company."

"Hey," she said, "don't do me any favors. I don't need you. Go sit with your bride-to-be."

"You *are* pissed off at me."

"Oh please, stow your ego. I have better things to think about than you."

"Look, you've got a right to be upset. I know it's disconcerting to be tackled by six Secret Service agents."

"It was V-8 juice, for God's sake. What's the potential crime? Assault with a deadly beverage?"

"You've got to understand the Secret Service's position."

"If I could do that, we'd still be married."

She had a point. "You've got to understand. We're always waiting for an attack. On constant alert. Our adrenaline switch is always ramped to high. We're trained to react to danger with a hair-trigger response. They overreacted, sure. But they live and breathe for the President."

"And while you were guarding Elysee, you did all that for her?"

"Yes."

"I'm glad you weren't on protective detail when we were married."

"How come?"

"Heady stuff. I would have been fiercely jealous. No wonder Elysee is head over heels for you. All the macho, save-the-day stuff makes a girl feel tingly."

"I never made you feel tingly?"

Her eyes met his. "You seriously underestimate yourself, Tremont."

"So I do make you tingly?"

"Stop fishing for a compliment."

He grinned.

The plane taxied down the runway.

"Besides," she muttered under her breath, "it doesn't matter whether you make me feel tingly or not. You're with Elysee. There's no more tingly feelings allowed between you and me."

Now *he* was feeling tingly.

Think about something else.

But that was a hard to do considering how good she smelled and how her quick-witted teasing was bringing back fond memories.

Take a deep breath. The feeling will pass.

"How's your friend Delaney?" he asked, desperate for something neutral to talk about, something that wouldn't stir unwanted feelings.

"She's fine. Got married."

"She and Evan?"

"Actually no, she married a cop."

"No kidding."

"He's very sexy."

"Sexier than me?"

"There you go again, fishing for a compliment. You'd think we were still married or something."

"We're not," he said hurriedly.

"No."

The plane thrust forward, leaving the runway. Glancing down, Shane noticed Tish was gripping the armrests with white-knuckled intensity as they became airborne. He remembered she hated flying.

"Do something to distract me from takeoff, will you?" She had her eyes squeezed shut.

He put a hand on her forearm and she let out a tight sigh. "We were such total opposites. It's little wonder our marriage didn't work."

"But the sex was good." She opened one eye to peer at him and looked so damned adorable his pulse skipped a beat. "Right?"

"It was great." God, why was he doing this to himself?

"Best you ever had?" Tish smirked.

"Now who's fishing for compliments?"

"I just want a ballpark figure. On a scale from one to ten, ten being the best you ever had. Where did I fall?"

"Eleven," he said without hesitation.

Tish lowered her voice. "Where does Elysee fall?"

Shane shot a guilty glance toward the front of the plane. Elysee was dictating something to Lola, who was taking notes on her BlackBerry. The airplane noises drowned out the sound of their conversation. "We haven't—"

"Done the deed?" Tish's grin turned impish.

"We're waiting. You know. To consummate."

"I find that hard to believe."

"Why's that?"

"I'm just saying celibate Shane doesn't sound like the Shane I knew."

"Things change. She's the President's daughter."

"And I was raised by Dixie Ann."

"That's not what I meant."

"I was really an eleven?" Her voice turned husky.

"No," he said. "I lied."

"Huh?"

"You were at least a twelve." He was getting in deep here. He should stop this and he knew it, but the smile on her face lit him up like hot chocolate on a cold winter day.

"Twelve is not on the scale."

"My point exactly. When it comes to sex, you're off the charts. No one can hold a candle to you."

"But when it comes to my money management skills, I've got a feeling I'm off the charts in the opposite direction. Say negative fifteen?"

"Let's not get into it. We've been down that road before with no resolution."

"Come on, admit it," she said. "Sex is the only reason we hooked up in the first place."

"You don't really believe that."

She cocked her head. "No? Then why were we together? If it was more than just sex, why didn't we fight harder for each other?"

Shane shifted in his seat and met her gaze. He felt a heavy, hollow feeling deep inside him. "What do you want me to say? Just tell me and I'll say it."

"I don't want you to say what I tell you to say. I want you to say what you really feel."

"I'm way past the point of understanding anything about what I feel where you're concerned," he admitted.

"At last, honesty. This is nice," she said. "That we can still tease each other, but it doesn't have to mean anything."

Her quick wit had always made him feel inadequate. She could out-quip him every time.

"Shane?" she said.

"Uh-huh?"

"You can let go of my hand now. We're at cruising altitude. That scared feeling I get on takeoff has passed."

He moved his hand away. His palm was hot and damp from holding hers.

"In fact," she murmured, "why don't you go back to Elysee? I'm sure she's wondering what's keeping you. What is keeping you?"

Her eyes met his and made him long for all the things he'd forgotten. How it felt to soap up her body when they showered together. How she could almost keep up with him when they ran in the park. How she was a terrible cook and how all her recipes had something to do with Ramen noodles.

There was so much he wanted to tell her. Express his regret over the way things ended. Apologize, maybe, somehow. But how could he do that? They were surrounded by Secret Service and generals and a senator.

And there were just no words. If words could fix what had gone wrong, he would have spoken them two years ago.

He would have saved his marriage.

Elysee Benedict felt sorry for Tish. She was such a nice person, but she seemed to make a habit out of doing the wrong thing. For instance, beyond the V-8 juice incident with her father, she had let a wonderful man like Shane slip through her fingers.

Not the ploy of a brilliant woman.

Elysee glanced over her shoulder at Shane and her heart swelled with pride. He was so handsome and strong and brave. He'd laid his life on the line for her, taken a tremendous hit and she would be forever grateful.

Poor Tish.

Her gaze shifted to the other woman. Her color was pale and she looked to be on the verge of airsickness.

Poor, poor Tish.

She was proud of herself for sending Shane back to sit with her. She could afford to be generous. Shane belonged to her now. She felt a sense of pride and gave herself a mental pat on the back. It was the same way she felt after hosting a charity event or visiting sick children in the hospital. Or deciding to get involved with WorldFem and helping Rana get Alma Reddy out of India.

Poor, poor, poor Tish.

It had to be tough. Watching while her ex-husband married the President's daughter.

Had hiring Tish for the job actually been a cruel thing to do? She hadn't intended it that way. She'd just thought it was time she found out about Tish, time to force Shane to deal with any leftover baggage from his first marriage before he took fresh vows with her. Her plan had seemed simple enough at the time, but now she found herself questioning her wisdom.

Too late now. Tish is already here.

Doubt nibbled at her. She looked over her shoulder again—searching for reassurance that Tish was okay. Elysee hated seeing anyone in pain. But she didn't have to worry. Tish was leaning back in the seat with her eyes closed and Shane was making his way back toward her, a big, strapping smile on his face. He settled into his seat across from her, taking his rightful place, and all her fears vanished.

Everything was right in Elysee Benedict's world.

Chapter 13

"Why don't you take Tish sightseeing around DC?" Elysee suggested to Shane after they'd arrived at the White House. She'd come into Shane's bedroom on the pretext of helping him unpack. She hung up the suits from his garment bag and turned back to look at him.

The truth was she was anxious to get to the bank, take the antique coins out of her safety-deposit box, and liquidate them without anyone finding out what she was doing. If Shane knew what she was up to Elysee feared he might try to talk her out of it.

Or worse, tell her father she'd gotten deeply involved in WorldFem.

Rana had called her before she left Texas and begged her to keep their endeavor as quiet as possible for Alma Reddy's safety. She would have to take Agent Ackerman to the bank with her of course, but she hoped she could convince him they didn't need a full entourage. Plus, she didn't have to let him know exactly why she was going to the bank.

"Is there a particular reason you keep throwing me together with my ex-wife?" Shane asked.

"Come on, being with her isn't that bad, is it?"

Shane swallowed. "No."

She could tell this was hard on him. Elysee crossed the room to slip both arms around his waist and looked up into his dark brown eyes. "I feel sorry for Tish. She's alone here, except for us, and far out of her element."

"Why don't we all three go sightseeing?" He smiled down at her, ran his finger over her forehead to push away an errant strand of hair.

"You know what a production that would be if I came along," Elysee said, worrying she might not be able to talk him into this.

"I'd rather just stay here with you."

"Come on, please? Do it for me."

"What are you going to do while we're gone?"

"You forget my aunt Jackie and uncle Felix are arriving soon. We're having dinner with them tonight. You want to be stuck with them all day, too?"

"Aunt Jackie with the purse dogs?"

"And Uncle Felix the draft-dodging hypochondriac."

"Gotcha. Sightseeing with Tish it is, then."

"You'll thank me later," she teased, glad she'd found an angle.

"We'll see about that."

"It's a kind thing you're doing. Good karma and all that. I know Tish will appreciate the company." Elysee went up on tiptoes to brush her lips against his. "Dinner's at seven; see you guys then."

She hurried out of the room, glad she'd gotten Shane squared away. Now to find Agent Ackerman and get on over to the bank before her relatives showed up.

Her pulse rate quickened and her palms grew slick with anticipation as she thought about helping Alma Reddy escape her assassins. She felt like a spy.

And for a quiet woman who never rocked the boat, it was an exhilarating sensation indeed.

The last thing Shane wanted was to take Tish sightseeing. Not because he didn't enjoy her company, but precisely because he did. He knocked at the door of the Lincoln bedroom where Tish was staying.

Tish flung the door open. She grabbed him by the lapel and tugged him over the threshold. "Look at this room. Look at this furniture. Presidents have touched it. Celebrities have slept in this bed. How can I sleep in this bed with so much history surrounding me?"

"You probably won't."

She took his hand and pulled him over to the stately desk. "Look, look, a copy of the Emancipation Proclamation under glass. It makes me feel so American!"

He chuckled at her wide-eyed enthusiasm, but he fully understood. He remembered the first day he'd come to the White House, wide-eyed, overwhelmed, and trying his damnedest to look cool.

"Omigosh, Shane, can you believe it? We're here! In the White House. In the infamous Lincoln bedroom. Pinch me. I must be dreaming."

"You're not dreaming, sweetheart. You're here. You held on to what you wanted, never giving up, even when I wasn't very supportive of your dreams, and now you've made it."

She looked at him with sudden sadness in her eyes. "You've made it, too."

"Yeah."

"Too bad we couldn't have made it together," she said.

"Too bad," he echoed. They looked at each other and his heart lurched sideways.

"Do you ever get used to it?" she asked.

"Get used to what?"

She waved her hands. "Being under the microscope. Being watched."

"I'm one of the ones doing the watching," he said. "Or at least I used to be."

"How's the role reversal working for you?"

"It's an adjustment," he admitted. "You get used to the feeling of being watched, but you never forget you're under scrutiny."

"It restricts you," she said. "Limits your freedom, your choices."

"Yes."

"Kind of ironic, huh?"

"Kind of," he agreed.

"We're being watched right now, aren't we?"

"Uh-huh."

She rubbed her upper arms with her hands as if she'd gotten a chill. He realized to his dismay she was still wearing that peepshow blouse of hers.

He tried not to look, but he couldn't help himself. His gaze tracked down the length of her long neck to lodge firmly in her cleavage.

God, she was stunning. Hot, sensuous, and curvy.

Stop thinking like this.

He cleared his throat. "I came to see if you'd like to go sightseeing."

"With you?" She arched an eyebrow.

"Yes. It's Elysee's idea. You've never been to DC and

she's entertaining relatives from out of town. She thought you might be feeling out of place."

"Sure," she said. "I'd love to take a breather from the fishbowl. Just let me get my coat."

Shane had called her sweetheart.

Tish could think of little else, which was a bit surprising considering they were at the Smithsonian. It was probably just a slip of the tongue, she told herself. He didn't mean anything by it. She knew that, but it didn't matter. *Shane had called her "sweetheart."*

The museum was crowded and they found themselves jostled together. Shane's arm would brush against her shoulder or her hip would collide with his. It shouldn't have been any big deal, but she was acutely aware of every tiny bump and touch.

She kept sneaking glances over at him, trying to gauge whether their contact was having any effect on him, but the guy was a regular Mount Rushmore. Stoic self-control. At least when it came to his emotions.

Nothing rattled him.

In profile, in the museum lighting, he was as ruggedly handsome as ever. Maybe even more so. His craggy features had always appealed to her more than classic good looks. His chin jutted out in determination, his cheeks were high slabs of masculine dominance.

Delight shivered over her spine. *Stop it.*

"I would so have loved to come here with you when we were married. Think of all the dark alcoves we could have explored." She wriggled her eyebrows suggestively.

"There's security cameras everywhere."

"Oh yeah, like you're not a bit of an exhibitionist, Mr.

Get-Naked-on-the-Galveston-Island-Ferry-in-a-Rain-storm."

He grinned. "That was a helluva night."

"Incredible," she agreed.

Then they both fell silent. She could tell that he was thinking about the consequences of that night, just as she was.

She had to distract herself. "Let's check out the photography exhibits."

"It's where I was headed all along." He held up a map of the floor plans. "We're almost there."

A warm, sappy sensation settled in her bones. He'd been thinking of what she'd like to see. *Stop it, stop it.*

"Oops, watch out." He reached out, grabbed her elbow, and tucked her against his side, pulling her clear of a pack of unruly preteens in school uniforms.

This close she could smell him. She halfway expected for his scent to have changed—gone all highbrow like his new lifestyle. But he smelled like he did when she was married to him. Soapy clean and serious.

The kids passed by.

Head reeling, Tish stepped away from him and darted toward a display of architectural photographs. "Look, pictures."

Shane came to stand behind her. She was acutely aware of the heat of his presence.

"I love this one." She cocked her head to study the black-and-white photo of an old village church resting pastorally on a bluff overlooking a turbulent sea.

"Explain to me why it's so special," he said.

"The composition is magnificent."

"I just see an old church."

Tish clicked her tongue and shook her head. "Look

closer. The photographer has perfectly captured the peace of the church and contrasted it with the churning waters below, suggesting underlying turmoil."

"Hmm."

"You still don't get it."

"The church represents faith?"

"And the sea?"

"Rebirth?" he guessed.

She shook her head.

"What then?"

"Temptation."

He inhaled sharply. "If you say so."

"Here, look at the clouds." She pointed. "See, in this part of the sky they're white, fluffy, safe."

"Safe," he echoed.

"Exactly. While over here in this corner we have the dark, brooding clouds, gathering quickly, promising trouble."

"So what does it mean?"

"I'm not going to spoon-feed you. Come on, you can think this through."

"I had no idea pictures were so complicated," Shane groaned.

"Regular pictures aren't, but photographs good enough to hang on the wall of the Smithsonian? You bet-cha they're complicated."

"I'm beginning to understand you now."

"Me?" She swiveled to look at him. "What do you mean?"

"Why you're attracted to photography. What it is that you see when you look through the viewfinder of your camera." He placed a palm against the back of his neck.

"You're saying I'm complicated?"

"Understatement of the century."

She felt a pleased little flush run up her neck, but swiftly turned back to the picture so Shane couldn't read the telltale signs in her face. "Examine the colors."

"What colors? It's in black and white."

"I know, but pay attention to the grays. The gradations between light and dark."

"Uh-huh."

"Can you see the complementary play of brightness against shadows?"

He squinted, his gaze following her fingers as she traced the air in front of the framed photograph. "I think so."

"Is it making more sense to you now?"

"Not really," he confessed. "Over my head. I'm too literal."

She sighed. What could she do to get through to him, to make him see? "Let's try a different approach. What do you feel when you look at the picture?"

He stared for a moment, and then straightened. "This is too much pressure. Feels like the art appreciation class I took as a gimme credit in college and almost failed."

"It's not rocket science. Look at the picture and tell me what you feel."

"I feel stuck."

"Interesting. So what is it in this picture that makes you feel stuck?"

He chuffed in exasperation. "I dunno. Let's see. No roads, no cars, no people. There's nothing going on. Stuck."

"Oh no, no, no. That's where you're dead wrong. There's something very important going on."

"What's that?" He cocked his head, trying to look at it from a different angle.

"In this serene, bucolic scene, a fierce battle is being waged."

"Between good and evil?" he ventured. "That light and the dark, faith and temptation stuff?"

"Nope."

He threw his hands into the air. "I give up."

"Between balance and chaos."

"Ookay, if you say so."

She laughed. "Maybe you are too literal."

He stepped closer to the photograph. "The sea is wild, untamable, shrouded in mystery. The church is stable, grounded, rooted in tradition. Together they're balanced. But one without the other, apart, it's chaos."

Her pulse skipped for no discernible reason. "Yes."

"Why do I feel a sudden need to pray?"

"That's something for you to figure out." Her hands were quivering and she clasped them together to keep him from noticing. He was standing over her, his breath warm against the nape of her neck. He wasn't touching her, but she could feel him like a brand on her skin. She inhaled the honest, masculine scent of him and her heart pounded.

How easy it would be to turn around, frame his face in her palms, and kiss him. How easy to fall blindly into chaos.

Do it. Touch him. Kiss him. Hold on to him.

Tish clutched her hands into fists, fighting off her impulses. *No, you can't.*

Donning every ounce of emotional armor she could muster, Tish bit down on her lip, tossed her head, and gathered all her willpower to slip weak-kneed away from him. She wasn't going to trust what felt easy when it came to Shane.

Not ever again.

While Shane and Tish were wandering around the Smithsonian, Cal Ackerman and Elysee were in the safety-deposit vault at Citibank.

"You want to explain to me what we're doing here?" Cal asked.

"I do not." Elysee tossed her hair. She couldn't put her finger on what it was, but something about Ackerman rubbed her the wrong way. He made her bristle in a way no one else ever had.

"If it concerns your security," he said, "I have a right to know."

"It doesn't." Elysee sent him a scathing look. Agent Ackerman was going to take some getting used to. He wasn't at all like Shane. He was bigger for one thing and he made her feel unsettled instead of safe the way Shane did. "Now mind your own business."

He glowered. "FYI, your safety is my only business."

"Do you have a problem with me, Agent Ackerman?" she said in the most haughty first daughter tone she could muster. "I could have you reassigned."

"Who, me?" He held up his palms.

"That's what I thought," she muttered and turned to the safety-deposit box the bank officer had carried over to the table for her.

She turned the key in the lock and flipped open the lid, revealing the box full of valuable coins.

"Holy shit, what'd you do? Rob Captain Jack Sparrow?" Ackerman breathed.

Elysee narrowed her eyes at him. "Not a word of this to anyone."

"What's the big deal?" Ackerman shrugged. "It's your money."

"Exactly."

"How much is there?"

"Again, none of your business."

"How come you're sassier with me than you are with other people?" he asked.

"You have a way of bringing out the worst in me."

"Looks like the best to me."

Elysee felt her face flush.

Ackerman was standing over her, eyes assessing the coins. "That's some valuable change you've got stowed there. Collector's items."

"How would you know?"

"I collected coins as a kid."

"You?" She arched an eyebrow.

"That so hard to believe?"

"Yes. You look like the guy who beat up the kids who collected coins."

"I didn't get my growth spurt until my senior year. Before that I was president of the geek squad."

"Charming story, I'm sure." She dumped the coins into the black leather bag she'd brought with her.

"Whoa," Ackerman said. "You're not just going to waltz out of here with over a hundred grand worth of change in your carryall."

"Why not? I've got a badass Secret Service agent as a bodyguard. Who'd be dumb enough to try to snatch it?"

He looked pleased that she'd called him a badass. "Thank you."

"I didn't mean it as a compliment." She wrinkled her nose at him. "Come on."

"Where are we going?"

She shot him a look. "Where would you guess?"

"Coin dealer?"

"Bravo. He's got an I.Q. Who knew?"

"And who knew you had such a smart mouth?"

I don't, Elysee thought. *Not normally.* But this swaggering tough guy set her teeth on edge. She was definitely going to have to talk to her father about having him reassigned.

Elysee stood up with the carryall. It was so heavy she couldn't hold her shoulder straight.

"Here." Ackerman reached for the bag. "Give it to me."

"I can carry it," she protested.

"Not without signaling to everyone who sees you walking out of the bank toting a black bag you can barely carry that you're a target."

"Please, I spend my life as a target." She reached for the bag.

He held it over his head where she couldn't get to it. The thing had to weigh at least thirty pounds and he was holding it like it was a bag of popcorn.

"Give it up," he said and pushed the buzzer for the bank officer to let them out of the vault.

Elysee seethed at his high-handedness. "You're a very infuriating man, you know that?"

"So I've been told."

"And arrogant."

"Been told that, too. If you're planning on insulting me you're going to have to do better than that."

"Ass."

"Princess."

"Jerk."

"Sweetheart."

"If I wasn't a lady . . ." She broke off her threat.

"Ah, but you are." He winked, took her elbow, and escorted her out of the vault.

Chapter 14

The engagement party held at the Ritz-Carlton was unlike anything Tish had ever attended. Lavish far beyond normal standards. Elaborate ice sculptures. Exotic flowers in leaded crystal vases on every table. Extraordinary cakes constructed by world-renowned bakers. The opulence stole Tish's breath away. She felt as if she'd stepped into a fairy tale.

If this was just the engagement party, what in the world would the wedding be like? The notion spun her head.

Elysee's secretary, Lola, escorted Tish into the room just ahead of the guests so she could find a prime spot for filming. No other video cameras were allowed in. After the party, Nathan Benedict planned to hold a press conference, officially announcing his daughter's engagement to the world.

Tish had an exclusive.

You got the exclusive only because you used to be married to the groom.

It didn't matter, she told herself. However she got the

gig, she had it and her career was going to be made because of it. She owed Elysee a debt of gratitude.

I'm living my dream.

This was more than she could ever hope for. Yet, in spite of her excitement, an exquisite sadness seeped into her limbs, weighing her down, making the camera feel impossibly heavy. Yes, she was on top of the world careerwise. It didn't get any higher than this. After the wedding was over she would be one of the most renowned wedding videographers in the world.

Why, then, did she feel so blue?

A string quartet played chamber music as the guests filtered in. She thought of her mother and wished Dixie Ann was here to see this. After settling her camera on its tripod, she dug out her cell phone, found an unobtrusive spot in the corner, and placed a call.

"Dixie Ann," she whispered as soon as her mother answered the phone. Her mother didn't like to be called Mom. She always said it made her feel old. "You'll never guess where I'm calling you from."

"Tish, honey, is that you? I can hardly hear. What's that noise?"

"I'm at Elysee Benedict's engagement party."

"Elysee who?"

"Elysee Benedict. You know, the daughter of the President of the United States."

"No!"

"Yes."

"You're pulling my leg. Stop teasing me right now, Patricia Rhianne Gallagher."

"Swear to God, I'm not."

"How?"

"Elysee hired me to videotape both her engagement party and the wedding."

Dixie Ann squealed. "I'm so proud of you! That's wonderful. You deserve something good in your life."

"Thanks, Dixie Ann."

"Have you seen the President? He's nice-looking for an older man. And he's single. You're a pretty girl, Tish. You've got just as good a chance to hook him as the next gal. Are you wearing something nice? 'Cause you know nothing attracts—"

"Affluence like affluence, yes," Tish interrupted. "I know. You've told me over and over."

Dixie Ann said longingly, "Oh, I wish I could be there with you."

"I know. That's why I called."

"So who's there? What are they wearing? What food's being served? What's the music? Are any movie stars there?"

"Oops, sorry, Dixie Ann, I've gotta go. Shane just came in. I'll fill you in on all the details later."

"Shane? He's there?" The excitement in her mother's voice hit top pitch.

"He's here." Tish looked across the room at him and her heart was in her throat. He wore a black tuxedo, and when he entered the room, he took stock of his surroundings, surveying the entrances and exits, eyeing the crowd. Secret Service to the bone. Even with his damaged right hand tucked in his pocket, he looked imposing and dangerous. James Bond had nothing on him.

Seriously, you gotta stop drooling over your ex.

"Tish, this is wonderful, wonderful news. You're videotaping Elysee Benedict's engagement party and you and Shane are getting back together and—" Her mother's excited voice jerked her back to the cell phone conversation.

"No, Dixie Ann, you've got it all wrong. Shane and I are not getting back together."

"Oh." The sound of Dixie Ann's disappointment grabbed hold of Tish's gut and twisted. "Then what's he doing there?"

"He's getting engaged to Elysee Benedict."

A long silence ensued. Tish could hear the sound of her own heart beating in her ears.

"What did you say? There must be something wrong with your cell phone reception because I thought you said your Shane was marrying the President's daughter."

"I did. He is."

"Oh."

"Don't sound so surprised. We've been divorced for two years."

"But the President's daughter? How did that happen?"

"Long story. I gotta let you go. I have to catch all this on camera."

"Call me back later. I want to hear everything."

Tish hung up, pocketed her cell phone, and then picked up her camera from the tripod and started moving around the room, filming as she went.

Shane sauntered across the ballroom to where Elysee stood chatting with the Prime Minister of Israel. The human sea of tuxedos, designer labels, and expensive haircuts parted before him.

Tish raised the camera and zoomed in on his face. Something deep inside the most feminine part of her tightened.

Lust.

Pure and raw and wild.

And from the looks in the eyes of half the women in the room as they tracked Shane's journey toward Elysee, Tish wasn't the only one having lusty thoughts.

They all wanted him.

This man who had once belonged to her.

Misery winnowed inside her. Her feelings jerked her in two directions at once. Ecstatic one minute, despair the next. She shuttled back and forth so quickly she feared emotional whiplash.

Just do your job. Focus on your work. It's the only thing that will save you.

She knew the truth of it. Tish took a deep breath, calmed her mind, and became one with the camera.

Elysee smiled at Shane. He took her hand.

Tish moved in closer.

By the time the President entered the room a few minutes later she was nothing more than a camera lens. Seeing without feeling, capturing what was before her. A fly-on-the-wall view. Detached and professional. Using her camera to tell the story, her aim to bewitch the viewers. But she would not fall under the spell. She'd learned the hard way you couldn't trust happily ever after.

Elysee's hair was piled atop her head in an elegant, old-fashioned style and she wore a floor-length dress of lemon chiffon. The color made her appear prettier than usual, less washed out. She was a plain girl but a sweet one, and Tish did the best she could to capture Elysee's better features—her smile, her graceful walk, her straight white teeth.

She changed lenses, looking for the best filter, the right focus for the President's daughter. How ironic was this, presenting the competition in her best light?

But there was no competition.

Elysee, with her chaste innocence, had won. She'd known how to play a man like Shane. A valiant knight. A staunch defender who proved his worth by slaying the mightiest of all dragons—his independence, sexual hunger, and pride.

Tish had lost because she'd held nothing in reserve. She loved too messily, gave too much of herself too soon only to have it all end wrongly. Her stomach took a nosedive.

Back behind the camera. Close off your mind. Just capture the moment. Don't think.

She recorded everything—waiters moving through the crowd with champagne on silver serving trays. The press secretary calling for everyone's attention. Then Shane presenting Elysee with a beautiful marquis-cut three-carat diamond engagement ring.

The camera couldn't blunt Tish's jealousy, but she swallowed it back and kept filming.

She captured the President making the announcement to the room of friends and supporters. His beautiful daughter was marrying her stalwart bodyguard. Nathan Benedict welcomed Shane into the family with a warm embrace and a hearty pat on the back.

Everything was committed to the camera.

The crowd lifted their glasses in unison and toasted the happy couple. Everyone loved a good fairytale romance.

Shane and Elysee kissed. Sweetly, romantically. The crowd applauded politely. So civilized.

"When's the wedding?" someone asked.

"Christmas Eve," Elysee sang out.

"Who's designing your gown?" asked someone else.

"Top secret." Elysee blushed prettily.

"How did you two hook up?"

Elysee slipped her arm around Shane's waist and gazed up at him. "He was my bodyguard."

"Shane, is your family here tonight?"

From across the room, his gaze met Tish's. His dark, familiar eyes were all she could focus on. "Unfortunately my parents couldn't be here. They're on a worldwide cruise for their fortieth anniversary."

That answer drew a collective "ah" from the crowd.

"Where will you honeymoon?"

"Fiji." Elysee beamed.

Tish filmed without evaluating, without filtering content. *Get everything on camera. You can worry about the effects when you edit.*

She circled the couple. Shane watched her from his peripheral vision. She was glad her eye was pressed to the lens of the camera. She preferred that view to looking at the monitor. With the monitor, you couldn't hide behind the equipment. The last thing she wanted was for Shane to catch a glimpse of her eyes and read something in her face that she couldn't disguise.

Tish filmed him watching her. Zeroing in on his inscrutable brown eyes, his expression revealed nothing.

When he saw what she was doing, he winked boldly for the camera. She recalled that when they were married, she had loved to take his picture, how he would protest and then just finally give in because she wouldn't stop pestering him until he did.

He was even more attractive now than he'd been when she'd met him three years ago. And he'd been pretty darned cute then. But now, he was heartbreakingly, impossibly handsome as the corner of his lips tipped up in his lopsided smile.

Something low and hot fluttered inside her. Something

dangerous and subversive. It felt as if she were climbing
a rickety ladder in a hurricane, destined for a fall. Enough
pictures of the happy couple for now, she decided. It was
time to scope out the crowd for interesting reactions to
the engagement announcement.

Tish honed in on the dignitaries. Capturing VIPs from
various countries all over the world—fraternizing together at the bar. Whispering gossip in corners. Kowtow-
ing to the President with compliments and flattery. It was
the photo-op of a lifetime.

The string quartet was playing a waltz and people
started dancing. The French Ambassador spun the Vice
President's wife across the ballroom. A Democratic senator from California cozied up with an NRA gun lobby-
ist. The prince of a small European country dazzled an
up-and-coming starlet. Tish wasn't very political herself,
but she knew good content when she saw it.

Elysee danced with Shane. His arm was around her
waist. Tish thought of the dance they'd shared at Louie's
and her throat went dry.

Halfway through the waltz, Elysee saw Rana Singh walk
into the ballroom, an anxious frown furrowing her brow.
She was dressed in an exquisite ruby red sari, but she
looked decidedly out of place and uncomfortable with
her surroundings. Elysee's former nanny kept casting
nervous glances over her shoulder at the male foreign
dignitaries in the room.

Elysee's pulse skipped. Could one of these men be
responsible for putting the price on Rana's head? She
stopped dancing.

"Is something wrong?" Shane asked.

She looked up at her husband-to-be and briefly thought

about telling him what was going on. But Rana had sworn her to secrecy and she wasn't about to do anything that could jeopardize Alma Reddy's life.

"These shoes are killing my feet," she said. That wasn't a lie. Her feet did hurt. "Do you mind if we sit this one out?"

"Not at all. Where would you like to sit?"

Elysee peeked around his elbow to see Rana edging toward the back corner of the room. Their gazes met. The expression in Rana's eyes was urgent.

Hurry.

"Um, I'll find a spot." She smiled at him. "Could you get me some water?"

"Certainly."

The second Shane turned away, Elysee hurried over to Rana. "This way."

She led Rana to a shadowy corner of the outside patio where earlier, she'd stashed the cash she'd gotten from liquidating her grandmother's antique coin collection inside a safe made to look like a rock. After lifting the safe from a flowerbed filled with chrysanthemums, she spun the tumblers on the combination.

Rana kept glancing over her shoulder. "I'm so worried. The last thing I want is to put your life in jeopardy."

"Please, don't worry about me. I have around-the-clock bodyguards. See, Cal is standing right over there watching me as we speak."

"Anyone can be bribed for the right amount of money."

Elysee's eyes met Rana's. "They're that desperate to kill you?"

"You don't understand how much I threaten those small-minded tyrants."

"What you're doing is very brave and dangerous," Elysee said.

"No more than you." Rana's smile was tight, slight.

The combination to the rock safe yielded and Elysee took out the money. Furtively, she slipped it to Rana. The woman quickly stowed the cash into the folds of her sari.

"Bless you," Rana said and kissed Elysee on the cheek. "With this gift, you may very well have saved Alma Reddy's life."

Suddenly, Tish felt hot and dizzy, claustrophobic. The camera weighed heavy in her arms. She had to get out of this room. Without even thinking to turn off her camera, she hurried from the room. She passed a Secret Service agent posted at the doorway and went in search of the ladies' room.

She swung the camera up onto her shoulder and opened a door where she believed the bathroom was located, but ended up outside on a patio. A few guests were there, taking in the fresh air, enjoying a quiet moment away from the crowd.

Rounding a cluster of potted ficus trees, she spied Lola talking in hushed tones to a man Tish didn't recognize. The setting looked intimate. Glasses of champagne rested on the table in front of them and they were leaning in toward each other. Lola's shoulder touched the stranger's.

That's when Tish saw the red Record light and realized the camera was still on.

Lola looked up at her, saw the camera, and frowned darkly. "Is that thing on? Turn that camera off. Right now."

Jeez, what was she getting so fired up about? Was the guy beside her married or something?

"No, no," Tish said. "It's not on."

"Don't video me, Tish. I don't like to be filmed." Lola prickled.

"I'm not filming you. I was looking for the bathroom and got lost."

"Go back inside the ballroom and out the second exit. The ladies' room is the first door on your right."

"Thanks, thanks." Tish nodded at the man, but he had his face turned away from her. Hmm, she was getting the feeling the guy was definitely married.

For shame, Lola.

As Tish turned and hurried away, she heard Lola mutter to her paramour, "What a pathetic woman."

Shane couldn't find Elysee. Perhaps she'd gone upstairs to change her shoes. He stood in the middle of the room, water glass clutched in his hand, trying to spot his fiancée. Instead he saw Tish rush into the ballroom from the adjoining garden courtyard. He noticed as the Secret Service agent positioned at the door touched his earpiece and mouthed a coded message into the microphone.

Tish was under surveillance.

Shane sighed. What had she done now?

He set the glass of water down on a table and went after Tish. He saw Cal cruise by a bowl filled with matches engraved with the date of Shane and Elysee's engagement and stuff them in his pocket.

Shane stepped through the doorway, peered down the empty hall, and then stepped back to speak to Cal.

"I thought you stopped smoking," Shane said.

Cal shrugged. "Hard habit to break."

"Did you see which way my wife went?"

Cal arched an eyebrow, but otherwise kept his face noncommittal as he'd been trained. Grace under pressure was part of the Secret Service agents' code. "Your *wife*?"

It was only then Shane realized his Freudian slip. "I meant my ex-wife. Which way did she go?"

"Ladies' room."

"Thanks." Shane went down the corridor to the ladies' room and knocked on the door.

The attendant who'd been hired for the evening's event poked her head from the lounge. "Yes, sir?"

"There's a redhead in there with a camera." He handed the woman a ten-dollar bill. "Will you tell her I want to see her, please?"

"Just a minute, sir." She shut the door.

Feeling awkward, Shane waited in the hall. Cal stood at the other end of the hallway, watching him. Shane stuffed his hands in his pockets, turned his back, and tried to appear nonchalant.

What the hell was he doing out here anyway? So Tish was upset about something. What did he care? It was no longer his job to look out for her. This was Elysee's big night. He should be at her side.

But he couldn't shake Tish off his mind. She'd been upset about something. He'd seen it in her face. And no matter how he might wish things were otherwise, he still cared about her. Probably more than he should.

The door to the ladies' lounge opened again and Shane straightened.

It wasn't Tish, but the attendant. "She doesn't want to talk to you."

"Tell her I'm not going away until she does."

The attendant sighed, rolled her eyes, and let the door close between them.

A couple of seconds passed. The attendant returned. "Actually, I'm cleaning this up a bit, but she said for you to buzz off back to your fiancée."

That made him mad. He knew what word Tish had used in place of "buzz." Shane glanced down at the woman's nametag. "Stand aside, Mattie, I'm going in."

"You can't do that." Mattie moved to block the door. "It's the ladies' room."

"I'm aware of that, but I'm going in anyway," he growled and glowered, giving her his full burly tough guy routine. "I'm Secret Service. Now step aside."

The look on his face must have said it all, because Mattie hurriedly stepped aside.

Shane stalked past the mirrored sitting room where a handful of women were applying makeup, brushing their hair, and gossiping. They gaped when they saw him. He blew past them, his shoes trodding heavily on the tile as he walked down the row of stalls. He was pissed off. "Tish," he said sternly. "Where are you?"

"Go away!" she hollered from the last stall on the left. In spite of the command, her voice sounded shaky.

"Come out here," he said. "We need to talk."

"Go back to Elysee. It's her big day."

"Exactly. So get out here. Let's get this over with so I can get back to her."

"Just leave me alone."

What in the hell was wrong with the woman? He turned slightly, glanced back the way he'd come and spied a clutch of women standing in the doorway, craning their necks, looking for a show.

"That's it," he said and pointed for the door. "Out, out,

everyone out." He marched toward them, scowling and shooing them out with extravagant hand gestures. "You, too, Mattie. Go on, everybody mind your own business."

"Ooh, he's so manly." One woman giggled. "He could boss me around anytime."

"But this is his engagement party to Elysee and he's come into the bathroom after another woman." One of the women glared at him. "What's that all about?"

"It's the wedding videographer," interjected a third woman.

"I heard she's his ex-wife."

"Out!" Shane rumbled, pointing at the door.

Tittering, they left.

Once he made sure the ladies' lounge was empty, Shane dragged one of the heavy sitting room chairs in front of the door to block further interruptions. Then he went back after Tish.

"Open the door," he demanded.

"No."

"Tish, don't make me bust the door down. I'm not in the best shape of my life here."

"Please, Shane, just go away." Her voice sounded so vulnerable, it sliced him like a blade. Emotion clotted inside him—a dark viscous knot of anger and regret, helplessness and concern.

"Tish, open the door."

"What is with you and following me into bathrooms? Can't a girl get a little privacy when she needs it?"

"If you don't come out here and talk to me, I swear I'm kicking down this damned door."

"You wouldn't."

"I sure as hell would." No one could irritate him as much as Tish when she was being stubborn.

"What would Elysee think? Directing so much passion toward me when you're marrying her?"

"It's not passion, dammit!" he yelled.

"You're yelling and threatening to break down doors. Sounds like passion to me."

"Okay, if that's the way you want to play it. Who cares what upset you? I'm leaving."

"Good."

"Fine."

"Good-bye."

"So long."

"I don't hear your feet carrying you off in the opposite direction," she said.

Shane fisted his good hand, shifted his weight. This was idiotic. He was arguing with a bathroom stall door.

"Patricia Rhianne"—he almost said *Tremont*, but managed to bite off the word before it came out of his mouth—"Gallagher, get out here this minute."

What was he going to do if she didn't come out? Shane had made such a big deal out of this he couldn't just walk away, although it was the sensible thing to do. Just walk away, go back to the party, back to his sweet-tempered Elysee, back to the new life he was forging for himself. But when it came to Tish, when had he ever taken the sensible route?

To his amazement, the stall door swung slowly inward and Tish peeked out at him, her eyes red-rimmed.

Tish? Crying?

Shane had only seen her cry once, and that was when . . . He bit down on the inside of his cheek at the rush of raw, hot emotion that suddenly filled the back of his throat.

"Have you been crying?"

"No," she denied viciously. "I had something in my eye. That's why I rushed into the bathroom. Happy now?"

"Sweetheart." Instinctively he reached for her, with his raw, scarred hand. "Tell me the truth. What's really wrong?"

Tish shrank back from him. "Don't you dare touch me, Shane Tremont. And don't you dare call me 'sweetheart.'"

He retracted his hand. Understanding he'd started across a line that he couldn't cross. "I just want to help," he said, and helplessly let his arm drop to his side.

"Why?" She glared at him and her lungs rose sharply as she drew in a deep breath of air.

Tish had always asked hard questions of him. She made him think, often goading him into reconsidering his positions. She challenged him to examine his values and beliefs.

In the beginning of their relationship, he'd loved that about her. Toward the end, it had driven him crazy. She could never leave well enough alone. Always prodding, digging, wanting more answers than he had to give.

"Because I care."

"If you cared, why did you leave me?"

"You know why I left."

"I needed you and you abandoned me, you asshole."

Shane winced as her words struck him like a stunning blow. She was right and his failure ate at him. She didn't deserve this.

"What can I do to make it better, if you won't tell me why you were crying? Is it me? Is it Elysee? Is it the engagement? Is it too much for you to handle? Do you want out of the job?"

"I was *not* crying." She enunciated the words slowly, injecting her sarcasm. "I don't cry. It's not something I do. Got it?"

He watched the emotions play across her face. Anger sparked in her eyes, tightened her jaw. Frustration furrowed her brow, sadness dragged down the corners of her mouth.

She looked haunted.

"So what is it? Just tell me."

"Johnny," she said. "I was thinking about Johnny. Happy now?"

He couldn't believe she said it. He stared at her, his heart constricting in his chest, unable to believe she'd uttered their dead baby's name.

Until that very moment, Tish hadn't been thinking about Johnny. She'd spent the last two years learning how to bury that hurt so deep she couldn't find it. Hiding it under clothes she didn't need and shoes that were criminally expensive, disguising it with ice cream, locking it away in the attic of her mind along with those tiny little baby things.

But then Shane had insinuated she was pining over him, that she was jealous of Elysee, that she couldn't handle the stress of videotaping their precious wedding. And she'd just gotten mad. She was determined not to let him know she'd been tearing up over him and their shattered marriage. So she said what she knew would stop him in his tracks.

Once the name of their dead son had been uttered, the past jumped up and slapped hard against her.

Chapter 15

*T*ish was in labor, but it was too soon. Two and a half months early. Something was very wrong. She knew it deep inside her. Her baby was in serious trouble and there was nothing she could do about it.

And she was all alone. Shane, the bold, strong Secret Service agent who she'd thought would always protect her, no matter what, was out of town on an undercover assignment.

"Help me," she cried to the doctor. "You've got to help me. Help my baby. Something's wrong with my baby."

Please, God, don't let the baby die.

The doctor, with his green scrubs, chubby cheeks, and coffee-colored skin, stared at the monitor. Then he looked at her. He was a professional. He knew how to hide his feelings, but for one brief second, she saw both fear and pity in his eyes.

And in that awful moment, Tish knew the dream was over. Nothing would ever be the same again.

The wonderful, romantic fantasy that began that night in Louie's nightclub, the night Shane sauntered into her *life and swept her off her feet, was shattered. The magic vanished. Shane couldn't protect her from this. She didn't believe in miracles anymore.*

It was over.

"Is there someone I can call for you?" the doctor asked.

"My husband," she said. "Call Shane." When he got there everything would be all right. He would make it all right. Shane had that kind of power.

Dread, more powerful than anything she'd ever experienced before, took hold of her as a disabling contraction twisted through her body, mangling her womb.

"The baby," she gasped and grabbed the doctor's arm. "What's happening to my baby?"

The doctor didn't answer. He pulled away from her. Called to the nurses. The room filled with medical personnel. They were doing things to her, prepping her, hustling her down the hallway to the operating room.

C-section.

Before, she'd feared the word. Terrified at the thought of being cut open. Thinking she would be less of a woman if she couldn't give birth the "real" way. But now, all she could think was Yes, yes, yes. Cut me open, get him out. Save my son.

They placed a mask over her face. Told her to count backward from a hundred. The room was cold, sterile, lonely. She was scared. So scared.

Shane, where are you when I need you most? Shane. Shane!

"We've lost the fetal heartbeat," she heard a tense-voiced nurse call out.

Save my baby!

Where's Shane? She needed Shane. She could not do this alone.

"Shane!"

Then the world blurred, her eyelids sank closed, and she was gone.

Shane laid a hand on Tish's forearm. A gesture of sympathy. She stiffened beneath the weight of it. She didn't want his pity. Didn't want to see the regret in his eyes. He'd screwed up. She wasn't going to make it easy for him.

"I don't need you," she said. "Not anymore. You belong to Elysee. Leave me alone."

He looked hurt. Good. He'd hurt her plenty; now it was his turn.

Tish shrugged off his hand, turned and headed for the exit. Stepping carefully so that she didn't falter. Didn't stumble and give away what she was truly feeling.

But when she reached the door, she found a chair blocking her exit. She leaned over to push it aside, but Shane was already there. His hand brushed against hers as he shoved the chair away from the door.

Adrenaline rushed through her blood, strummed her nerve endings, shoved her senses into overdrive. The familiar feeling of heat and excitement she'd always associated with Shane filled her.

But there was more. She felt something different. Something starkly fresh and unexpected.

Danger.

The hairs on her arms lifted.

What was this? How could being with Shane suddenly feel dangerous and new?

She knew him so well. The texture of his hair. The

sound of his throaty voice. The smell of his Shane-y scent. The way he phrased his sentences. How he preferred his eggs sunnyside up and liked the crust cut off his bread. She knew what motivated him. What thrilled him. What turned him off. She knew how to push his buttons, how to provoke his anger. She also knew what words soothed him. How to appeal to his highly honed sense of honor and integrity.

So why this sense of danger?

Because it was taboo. Being alone in the ladies' room with a man who was engaged to someone else. And not just any someone else, but the President's daughter.

She wasn't the only one feeling this forbidden sensation.

Shane's Secret Service training might have taught him how to hide what he was thinking, but he couldn't fool her. His arousal strained at the zipper of his tuxedo pants.

For a breath-stealing second, she had an almost irresistible urge to reach out and touch him where it would affect him the most. She ached to feel the hard outlines of his male body pressed against hers just one more time.

Heat swamped her.

A purely physical response. She had an overwhelming urge to kiss him. Never mind that he was engaged to Elysee. *She* was the one who did this to his body.

Chemistry.

They still had it. Apparently, not even divorce could destroy it.

Tish raised her eyes to meet his.

They stared at each other.

From the chagrined expression on his face, she recognized that he knew she'd seen his acute reaction to the simple brushing of their hands.

"Don't worry," she whispered. "Your secret's safe with me."

Then without giving him an opportunity to respond, she pushed through the door and rushed out into the corridor. Her heart pounded erratically, her palms sweaty.

Shane wanted her!

It doesn't mean anything. He's engaged to Elysee. He's not the kind of guy who cheats. His body just reacted. History, chemistry. It doesn't mean anything.

But she could still make him hard.

Tish suppressed a grin and forced herself to amble back into the ballroom, past the stern-faced Secret Service agents.

"Tish!" She glanced over to see Elysee waving at her from across the room.

Ho, boy. Feeling like a traitor, Tish hitched in her breath and went over.

"Have you seen Shane?" Elysee asked.

"He was in the hallway earlier."

Not a lie. Okay, so it wasn't the complete truth either, but there was no sense hurting Elysee with the details of what had transpired in the ladies' lounge.

"Where's your camera?"

Instinctively, Tish's hand went to her shoulder, but she'd already realized the familiar weight was missing. Oh gosh, she must have left it in the bathroom stall, forgotten because she was too preoccupied with Shane. Leaving her camera behind was equivalent to a first-time mother forgetting her newborn infant in the backseat of a car.

Panic smacked against her rib cage. She spun away, running back toward the bathroom.

Please let it still be there.

She crashed into Shane's chest just as he was coming into the ballroom.

His hands went up to grasp both her shoulders. "Whoa. Slow down."

"Let go." She tried to pull away from him but he held on.

Anxiety mingled with attraction. Fear dueled it out with chemistry. He was the reason she'd forgotten her camera in the first place. His fault.

"What is wrong with you, woman?" he growled.

"My camera."

"What about it?"

"I left it in the bathroom."

He let go of her then, followed her back into the hallway. Tish was barely aware that Elysee was behind them. There were several people in the corridor and they were all staring at her.

Tish clambered through into the bathroom, heels snapping against the tile as she hurried to the last stall on the left, shoved the door open and stuck her head inside. Her eyes went to the purse hook where she'd hung her camera bag.

When she saw the empty space, her heart dropped into her shoes.

While she'd been foolishly getting sexually charged up over her ex-husband, her camera—the most precious thing she owned—had been stolen.

The look on Tish's face was a knife to Shane's gut. He knew how important the camera was to her. Not only because it was the tool of her trade, but because behind it was the only place she felt truly safe in the world.

On the outside she presented a bubbly, optimistic, free-spirited front. She even had herself convinced she was an outgoing extravert who loved fast-paced activities.

But Shane knew better.

When things got too rough and the world got too fast, she would retreat behind her camera. Even during their marriage, when he would try to pull her into his arms and give her the safety and security she'd never had growing up, she hadn't really been able to accept it. Oftentimes in the middle of cuddling, she would slide off the bed, pick up her camera, and start filming him. As if what she saw through the viewfinder was her only avenue to real intimacy.

It had irritated him to no end. During their marriage, what she hadn't seemed to understand was that for Shane, the camera was a barrier to their intimacy, not a conduit. She always had a camera with her, no matter where they went. She had never really let him into her life at all, he realized with a start. She always kept him a camera's width away.

"Oh, Tish," Elysee exclaimed. "This is awful."

It was only when she spoke that Shane even remembered his fiancée was standing behind him. He turned his head toward Elysee, saw four Secret Service agents clumped up in the ladies' lounge beside her. A group of curious onlookers craned their necks behind Elysee's wall of bodyguards.

Tish started humming.

Uh-oh.

Shane flashed a glance at his ex-wife and her pallor confirmed his fear. He understood her, and that understanding scared the hell out of him. Tish was teetering on the verge of cracking up. She'd been under tremendous stress and having her expensive camera stolen was the last straw.

And he was at fault.

He had followed her into the ladies' room earlier, pressured her into talking to him, stirred the old sexual chemistry between them, and caused her to forget her camera.

A memory flashed in Shane's mind.

He remembered coming home one day to find Tish in the nursery. Surrounded by sacks and packages and boxes of brand-new baby things—clothing and bassinets, diapers and bibs, stuffed animals and picture books. She was humming a lullaby and putting away the things she'd bought, a dreamy smile on her face as she swayed gracefully.

A mother getting ready for her new infant.

Just one problem. It was after they'd lost Johnny.

Whenever she hummed like that it scared the living shit out of Shane and he knew of only one way to stop it. He had to get that camera back.

Sir Galahad to the rescue again, eh? It didn't work before, what makes you think it'll work now?

He didn't have an answer. He just didn't know what else to do. It had only been a few minutes. Whoever had stolen the camera couldn't have gotten far.

"Get to the exits," he barked to the Secret Service agents. "Don't let anyone leave the floor until we've found that camera."

"Shane?" Elysee raised a hand to her throat. "We've got guests. VIPs. Dignitaries. We can't ruffle political feathers, but we can buy Tish a new camera."

Elysee didn't get it and he didn't have time to explain.

"Come with me," he said to Cal. "We're searching the rooms in this wing. Elysee, go back to the ballroom and make some politically correct excuse why the guests can't leave yet."

Everyone jumped to obey him.

Tish stopped humming. A good sign.

He and Cal tore down the corridor. Cal took the rooms on the left side of the hall, Shane the ones to the right. He wrenched open the door to a conference room, did a quick search. Nothing seemed disturbed.

He tried the next room, then the next.

In the fourth room, he found what he was looking for. The French doors leading out into the courtyard stood ajar.

Shane rushed into the courtyard just in time to see a shadowy figure sprint across the lawn. Instinctively, his wounded hand reached for the shoulder holster that wasn't there. God, he wished he had his gun. He felt naked without it. Just as Tish must feel without her camera.

"Stop!" he called out. The thief didn't know he didn't have a weapon. "Secret Service!"

The culprit kept running.

Shane swore under his breath and took off at a dead sprint. But the thief had too much of a head start and Shane just couldn't keep up. His lungs throbbed, sending sharp pulses of pain shooting through his chest. He'd become sadly out of shape since his accident.

The thief broke through the privacy hedges to the street beyond. By the time Shane got there, he was out of breath. He stood a moment in the darkness, heaving in air, body quivering, wondering how he was going to break the news to Tish that her camera was gone.

Then he spied the camera bag lying in the dirt underneath the Japanese boxwoods.

Feeling like a conquering hero, he shrugged off the pain and made his way back to the party with the bag. He slipped inside to find Elysee holding court, Tish sitting quietly beside her.

The minute Tish spotted him she was on her feet, her eyes wide, overjoyed to see her bag.

"You found it!" she breathed and reached out to take the camera bag like it was her long-lost baby. She clutched it to her chest for a moment, then unzipped it and took the camera out.

"Is it okay?" Shane asked.

Elysee came over and slipped an arm around his waist. "Are you all right, Tish?"

Tish shook her head. "I'm fine," she said. "But whoever stole the camera took the disk."

Thanks to Shane, Tish had her camera back. Everything was going to be okay.

"I don't understand. Why would the thief leave an expensive camera like this, but steal the disk?" Elysee asked.

"They weren't after the camera," Shane said.

"Who'd go to such lengths for a disk of our engagement party?" Elysee wrinkled her nose in confusion.

"Tabloids," Tish said. "They'll pay millions for exclusive shots of the first daughter's engagement party."

"Oh, no." Elysee groaned, crossed her palms and pressed them against her heart. "I hadn't thought about that."

Tish felt instantly protective of her. "It's okay."

"No it's not." Elysee shook her head. "It's going to be a nightmare for security and . . ."

"Fear not." Tish grinned and dipped her hand into the pocket of her dress, pulling out a compact camera disk.

"Is that what I think it is?" Elysee breathed.

"Yep. I'd just changed out the disk before the camera went missing. I've got your engagement party pictures right here. You're safe."

"I'm not sure I trust her," Lola Zachary said to Elysee after the engagement party, when they were alone in Elysee's bedroom at the White House.

Elysee wasn't really listening to Lola. She was thinking about Shane. She'd wanted to spend some quiet time with him after the party—maybe kissing in the garden under the full moon. They hadn't spent nearly enough time kissing, but protocol and circumstances had reared their heads. All she'd gotten from him that night was a chaste kiss.

While she liked the excitement of waiting until their wedding night to have sex, the lack of physical contact with him was starting to get to her. They were engaged, after all. Nothing wrong with letting him get to third base. She imagined Shane's hand sliding up her thigh, disappearing under the hem of her skirt, and her face heated.

"Did you hear me?" Lola asked.

"Huh?" Elysee blinked.

"You shouldn't trust her."

"Trust who?" Elysee unzipped her dress and stepped out of it.

"Tish Gallagher." Lola held out her hand for the garment. Elysee scooped it off the floor and passed it to her.

"What do you mean? Tish is great. She saved the engagement party. If she hadn't changed that disk when she did the photographs could be all over the Internet by now."

"Please, Elysee, you are so naïve." Shaking her head, Lola went to the closet, plucked a wooden hanger from the rack and hung up Elysee's dress. "Sometimes I can't believe you're really Nathan's daughter. Your father has been in politics all of your life. Hasn't that taught you anything about human nature?"

Lola was always so serious. Sometimes, Elysee wished she'd either lighten up or shut up.

"What are you saying?"

"Tish is Shane's ex-wife."

"And?"

"There's a possibility she could be trying to sabotage you. I mean, think about it: what professional photographer leaves her camera bag in the bathroom? Those cameras are heavy. Wouldn't you notice there's no big heavy camera bag hanging off your shoulder when you left the ladies' room?" Lola relished being the voice of doom and gloom. She was an excellent personal assistant, but sometimes her negativity grated on Elysee's nerves.

"Don't you think if Tish were trying to sabotage my engagement to Shane that she wouldn't have told me she'd changed the disk? That she would have sold them to the tabloids herself and probably made a lot more money than what she's getting paid to put together the wedding video?" Elysee asked.

"Not if she felt guilty and decided at the last minute not to go through with her scheme."

"You make her sound so Machiavellian."

Lola arched an eyebrow. "Maybe she is."

"You have a tendency to look on the dark side of life," Elysee chided, plunking down at the vanity and reaching for the cold cream to remove her makeup.

"Sometimes you're such a child."

Elysee bristled and sat up straight. It took a lot to ruffle her feathers, but calling her childish was one way to do it. She worked so hard to be grown-up, especially since she'd been thrust into the role of her father's companion on the political trail after her mother passed away. To be thought childish was her Achilles' heel and Lola knew it.

"I'll thank you to leave me for the night," she said coldly. "And I don't want to hear another word against Tish."

"But . . ."

"Not another word." Elysee raised a cold-cream slathered hand. "Understand?" Her assistant gritted her teeth so loudly she could hear her from across the room.

"As you wish." Lola hurried for the door, head down. As she passed by the vanity, Elysee heard her mutter, "It's your funeral."

Lola's words ended up poisoning Elysee's sleep.

Could her assistant be right? Was she being foolish by assuming that Tish cared only about producing a great video and launching her career? Did Shane's ex-wife still have romantic feelings for him?

More important, did Shane still have feelings for Tish?

The thought struck terror in her heart. Damn Lola anyway, for making her doubt the only man, other than her father, that Elysee had never doubted.

Disturbed by the direction of her thoughts, Elysee forced her mind onto other things. She thought about

Rana Singh and what Rana had told her about Alma Reddy's journey to America. Alma would arrive in Houston via a cargo freighter through the gulf shipping channel. Elysee had promised to offer safe harbor at the ranch until Alma and her husband could be reunited.

Ah, romantic love.

She sighed, the thought bringing her restless mind back to Shane. She tossed the covers aside and crept out of bed. She knew of only one way to put a stop to these gnawing concerns. She needed to have a serious talk with him. He was her fiancé. They shouldn't keep secrets from each other.

After donning her bathrobe over her pajamas, Elysee stepped from the bedroom and padded past the sentinel posted at her door. Cal Ackerman was reading a J.D. Robb novel.

Elysee missed having Shane as her bodyguard. She recalled other nights when she'd had trouble falling asleep. How he would play chess or watch a silly movie with her until she got drowsy. She thought about how he'd listened while she chattered on and on about her trivial concerns. How he'd often gone down to the White House kitchen and brought back warm milk and chocolate chip cookies for her, just like her mother used to do when she was a little girl.

Sometimes, if she begged him long enough, he would show her things he'd learned in the military and Secret Service training. Self-defense techniques and methods of disabling opponents. She liked those lessons most of all, and yet those had been the ones he'd been most reluctant to teach her.

Affection for Shane rushed through her, filling her chest with a warm tightness of emotion. He was such a good man. A real hero. A great friend. Could anyone really blame Tish for still being in love with him?

The thought brought a stab of fear, draining the joy from her heart. Had she indeed made a grave mistake in hiring Tish? Was she, as Lola contended, ridiculously naïve?

"Need something?" Cal asked, resting his open paperback on his knee. His sharp eyes met hers.

Elysee shook her head. "Go back to your book."

"Where you headed?" He closed the novel, set it on the small hallway table beside him, and got to his feet.

She hated this part of being the President's daughter. Zero privacy. She jerked a thumb in the direction of the room where Shane was staying.

"Shane's not in his room," Cal said. She noticed then that his gaze had strayed to where her breasts curved beneath her pajama top. A strange thrill of excitement raced through her. Shane had never looked at her with such frank sexual interest.

Doubt squeezed her hard. Suddenly, her stomach rolled queasily. Elysee raised a hand to her mouth. Could he be with Tish? "He's not?"

"No."

"Do you know where he is?"

"I think he and your father are discussing security for your wedding." Cal's gaze locked on hers, he settled his hands on his hips. He was not a particularly handsome man, but he was potently male. He was taller even than Shane and a few pounds heavier. All muscle and edge.

Nervously, Elysee looked away and wet her lips with her tongue. "But he shouldn't be up this late. It's after midnight. He's still recovering from his injury."

"Once a bodyguard, always a bodyguard." Cal shrugged as if it explained everything.

That notion made her feel better. Of course Shane was talking to her father about security matters. Nothing meant more to him than her safety. He was her hero. She had absolutely nothing to worry about, unless she wanted to fret about the bizarre warmth that suddenly heated her stomach whenever she met Cal's eyes.

This was ridiculous. She was imagining things. She was engaged to Shane. She wouldn't attach a meaning to a momentary exchange of meaningful glances with her new bodyguard. She was engaged to Shane and he would take care of her, no matter what. He was the man her mother had promised would come into her life. Elysee was certain he was The One.

But how can you be absolutely sure?

Especially when Cal kept staring at her like she was a birthday cake. *He's not. You're reading something into his look that isn't there. You're just getting cold feet, like you did with the other three guys. The problem isn't Shane, or the way Cal is looking at you, or even Tish. It's your own fear that you've made the wrong choice.*

Again.

"You want me to call Shane?" Cal reached for the two-way radio clipped to his belt. She noticed how his large fingers skimmed over the smooth, black leather. "Tell him you're looking for him?"

Elysee could go find Shane and ask him about his feelings for Tish. Or she could accept things at face value and go back to bed. Shane had asked her to marry him. They'd officially announced their engagement. She twirled his engagement ring on her finger. It was the prettiest engagement ring she'd ever gotten.

He loved her.

She loved him.

There was no need to talk about the past. It was over. The future lay ahead of them. What was the point of cornering him for an answer? Did she really want to know the truth? What would she do if Shane told her he still had feelings for Tish? Would she fire Tish? Would she let Shane out of the engagement? Elysee nibbled a fingernail.

And then there was the flip side. If Shane assured her that he felt nothing for his ex-wife, could she believe him?

There was a catch-22 between truth and ignorance.

Elysee shook her head at Cal. "No, no, don't call him."

Turning, she went back to bed, making the conscious decision to embrace ignorance.

And forget all about the sultry look she'd just seen in Cal Ackerman's eyes.

Chapter 16

The first thing Tish did when she got back to Houston on Sunday evening was make two copies of the engagement party disk. Tomorrow, she promised herself, she would give one to Elysee, keep one for herself, and lock the original up in her safety-deposit box.

After nearly losing her camera to a thief, she wasn't taking any chances. This job was the only thing she had left. She wasn't about to screw it up. She could only give thanks she'd changed the disk before the camera had been stolen.

The second thing she did was quickly review the engagement party video before breaking it down frame by frame. Sitting in her office, staring at the screen, watching Shane and Elysee announce their engagement, seeing Shane give her the ring, just broke Tish's heart.

When Shane touched the small of Elysee's back, Tish felt the warmth of his hand against her own back and recalled the way he'd held her when they'd danced at Louie's. Such a small thing. Why did it feel like such a big deal?

Because his hand—his poor damaged hand that had once been whole, had once belonged to her—was now resting against another woman's back.

Betrayal, hot and salty, rose in her throat strong as brine. Why did she feel betrayed? They'd been divorced for two years. She had no right to feel this way.

Tish sat cross-legged on the floor, heart thumping, eyes filled with tears. She had to get these thoughts out of her head, couldn't stand the pain of them one second longer.

Forlornly, she drew her knees against her chest and fought back the tears that threatened to roll down her cheeks. She'd lost so much, but she refused to cry. She was tough. She was strong. Somehow, she would get through this.

In that moment, she turned where she'd always turned when she no longer had Shane to turn to. Hand trembling, she picked up the phone and dialed Delaney's number.

"I'm back from Washington," Tish said the minute her friend answered the phone. "It's official, Shane's engaged to the President's daughter. It'll be in all the newspapers and on the television news tomorrow."

"I'm coming over right now. What flavor of ice cream should I bring?"

In the background, she heard Delaney's husband, Nick, calling out to her, "Who's phoning this late? Tell them to get some sleep and call back in the morning. Come back to bed, Rosy." Rosy was Nick's pet name for Delaney because when they'd first met, she'd blushed so much.

Guilt took hold of her. She was being too needy and inconsiderate of her friend's new life. No matter how close they were, she couldn't expect Delaney to drop everything and come running whenever she slammed up against a painful memory. Delaney was married now, with a husband of her own to consider. Tish should be respectful of that.

"It's okay," she said, forcing false joviality into her voice, "I don't need any ice cream. But thanks."

"Are you sure?" Delaney sounded bewildered.

"Sure, I'm sure."

"Wow."

"Wow, what?"

"You really must be over Shane."

"Yeah," she murmured. "I guess I've finally come to grips with the fact he's moved on."

"That's terrific," Delaney said, sounding dubious.

"Seriously, I'm okay. You don't need to come over and hold my hand."

"Really?"

"Yeah."

The calmness inside her didn't feel faked. She was comfortable. Safe. Secure. She'd screwed up by leaving the camera bag in the bathroom at the Ritz-Carlton, but in the end, she'd triumphed. She'd saved the engagement party video.

That's all that mattered. She didn't want him thinking his impending marriage to Elysee would destroy her.

"I'm happy for you," Delaney said. "But are you absolutely certain you don't need me to come over?"

"Nope, I'm fine."

"Truly?"

"Delaney . . ."

"It's just that I know you. Even if you don't admit it to yourself, deep in your heart you always hoped that you and Shane would eventually get back together."

"I've come to terms with the fact that's not going to

happen," she said, proud of herself that she was able to say it without falling apart.

"You've made amazing progress," Delaney praised. "I must admit, I was really worried when I heard you were going to be filming Shane and Elysee Benedict's wedding, but I guess this will give you the closure you need to move on."

"Yep." She was feeling fine. Really she was. But maybe it would be a good idea to get off the phone before other emotions bubbled up. "Just wanted to let you know I'm back from DC and everything's fine."

"Thanks for calling. Sleep well."

"You, too." Tish hung up the phone feeling that her last lifeline had just been severed.

Shane lay in his bed at the Benedict ranch staring up at the ceiling, feeling as if he didn't belong. In this place, in the dead of night, he was lonelier than he'd ever been in his life.

As a bodyguard, insomnia came with the territory. It was difficult to sleep when your job required vigilance. But he wasn't a bodyguard anymore. He didn't know what he was. He was Tish's ex-husband, Elysee's fiancé. But who was he deep down inside?

Shane didn't know anymore.

Uncertainty had never been an issue for him until he'd been injured, but now it haunted his every waking hour. He thought of his father. He could hear Ben Tremont's voice in his head saying, *"Self-doubt is a weakness."*

But wasn't supreme self-confidence just as bad as self-doubt? If you didn't have some doubt when you were on the wrong path, weren't you cutting off that inner self who knew what was right? Arrogance was a weakness, too. And in the past, he'd been guilty of it.

Maybe that was what he was supposed to learn from the accident. That it was okay to be unsure. That uncertainty could bring you back into balance if you didn't fight it. He'd been out of balance for so long. Was he too far gone now to find his way back?

Anxiety pushed him to a sitting position. Shane switched on the lamp beside the bed, held up his hand in front of him, searching for answers in the ribbon of red scars crisscrossing his palm. He tried to mime pulling a trigger, but his fingers would barely move. Weeks of physical therapy and he hadn't progressed any further than this?

How long before he could fire a gun again? Would he ever be able to fire a gun again?

That was the million-dollar question. If he couldn't fire a gun, how could he be a bodyguard? And if he wasn't a bodyguard, who was he? His questions brought him full circle without any answers.

A sensation of claustrophobia gripped him the way it had the night he went to Louie's. He felt as if he couldn't breathe, as if the walls were closing in.

And on the heels of that feeling came another feeling. It started in the pit of his gut and dug in deep, spreading throughout his body. It was a feeling he'd honed and cultivated as a Secret Service agent. The instinct that told him something bad was about to happen.

No matter how he tossed and turned and tried to ignore it, he couldn't help thinking that something bad was going to happen to Tish.

In his head, he replayed what had gone down at the DC Ritz-Carlton. What if whoever had snatched Tish's camera hadn't been a tabloid journalist as they'd assumed? What if it had been someone with a far darker purpose?

But what purpose could that be?

Shane didn't know, but the worrisome feeling in his gut wasn't dying down. He had to check this out. He flung back the covers, jumped out of bed. He dressed and then quietly, secretively, as only a good agent could do, he slipped from the ranch house without being detected. Leaving the property wasn't as easy. He had to start his SUV, head down the only access road, get security to open the gate and let him out.

Truth was Shane just had to get off the ranch. He had to check on Tish and make sure she was okay.

Why don't you just call her?

In the middle of the night? And say what? "Sorry to wake you, but I got a feeling?"

Okay, here's the deal—just drive by her place. If everything looks copacetic, then drive on by. She'll never have to know you were there.

He traveled toward Interstate 45. Forty minutes later, he was pulling up to the curb outside Tish's garage apartment in the old-money neighborhood of River Oaks. He'd gotten her address off the business card she'd given Elysee. He suspected she'd moved to this area to be closer to her friend Delaney.

When he saw that the light was on in her apartment, his heart rapped hard against his chest. He blew out his breath. She was awake. Now what?

Good God, Tremont, you're acting like a stalker.

He wasn't stalking her. He was worried about her. His gut was gnawing at him, telling him something was wrong.

What if Elysee finds out you slipped away in the middle of the night to come park outside your ex-wife's apartment simply because you had a feeling?

And what would keep Elysee from thinking, Yeah, right. Then why is her business card in your front shirt pocket?

He clenched his jaw, swallowed back the pain clogging his throat. He did that a lot. Swallowed back his pain; sucked up his sorrow. It was what a man was supposed to do. Shane hailed from a long line of heroes. Heroes didn't whine or complain. They didn't mourn for what they'd lost. They accepted circumstances as they were, buried their emotions, took stock of the facts, and moved on without regrets.

So why couldn't he do that?

Because you're not really a hero. Not like your grandfather, not like Dad. They were real heroes. Real wars. Real men. You're nothing but a glorified babysitter.

He looked down at his damaged hand that could barely hold the steering wheel, and his heart plummeted to his feet. Hell, he wasn't even a glorified babysitter anymore. He was useless. Washed up. Wiped out.

Pity over everything he'd lost grabbed him by the throat, but he refused to let it take hold. To hell with pity. He was going to get the use of his hand back. He would prevail. He was a Tremont and Tremonts were heroes. It was his legacy.

He looked up, realized where he was and cringed. How had he come to this? Sitting outside Tish's apartment, blaming his being here on a gut feeling. It was pathetic. What was he hoping to accomplish? He should either knock on her door or get the hell out of here.

Shane started the engine, but he couldn't seem to make

himself put the Durango in gear. His gaze was locked on Tish's window.

There wasn't another woman like her on the face of the earth.

So why did you let her go?

It wasn't him. He'd tried his best. Ultimately, she was the one who'd turned her back on him. Even if he was the one who finally pulled the plug by walking out the door.

The emptiness he'd been feeling at the Benedict ranch hadn't abated. In fact it was stronger now, as the old memories tumbled in on him. Memories that knotted his throat and misted his eyes.

You're still in love with Tish.

He couldn't still be in love with her. He was marrying Elysee Benedict on Christmas Eve.

Marrying Elysee while his heart still belonged to Tish.

His gut twisted. *Okay, fucking fine.* He would admit it. He was still in love with her. But so what? She didn't love him. If she still loved him she wouldn't have let him walk out that door. She would have told him the things he needed so desperately to hear.

Get the hell out of here. Go back to the ranch. Forget about what you lost. Forget about what your gut is telling you. Tish is building a new life. You're building a new life now with a good woman who truly needs you. You have everything you've ever wanted.

Except for Tish.

Determinedly, Shane fumbled for the gearshift with his bum hand and finally managed to slip it into drive. He stomped down on the accelerator, but as he pulled away, he tossed one last look over his shoulder at Tish's bedroom window.

And that's when he saw a dark figure creeping along her balcony.

After calling Delaney, Tish pushed aside all her sorrow and memories and got down to work. She was running the video disk from the engagement party through her state-of-the-art editing program on her computer.

She would watch a segment, freeze it, and make notes for special effects she wanted to add or cuts she wanted to make. She also jotted down a list of music selections to mix in, but she would need to run her ideas by Elysee before finalizing it.

There was the ballroom where the ceremony had been held. And here came Nathan Benedict and his entourage. She paused the scene and made notes before continuing on to the next segment.

The work held her mesmerized as she slipped into professional mode and stopped seeing Shane and Elysee on a personal level. They were just another high-profile couple getting engaged. She wasn't going to let viewing the video trigger any more emotions inside her. This was a job. That's all it was.

She'd managed to block her emotions so well in fact that she got lost in what she was doing. Time flew, and the first indication of trouble was the smell of gasoline filtering in through her bedroom window.

Where was that smell coming from?

Her nostrils twitched.

Had she left the gas burner on the stove turned on? No, she hadn't cooked since she'd been home.

Concerned, she pushed back her chair and thought she heard a noise from the balcony outside her window. She cocked her head, listening.

The noise repeated.

What was that sound? She furrowed her brow, and strained to identify it.

She heard sloshing. That was it. Like a liquid being tossed from a container.

Slosh, slosh, slosh.

A liquid like gasoline.

Fear lifted the hairs on the nape of her neck. She felt a stab in her gut, like a knife plunging in and twisting as the full impact of the sound registered deep within her psyche.

Someone was outside on her balcony dousing her apartment with gasoline!

Call 9-1-1.

The instinctive impulse hit at the same moment a match sparked outside her window.

Whoosh!

The gasoline burst into flames, lighting up the balcony behind the curtains on the French doors and she saw, barely visible beyond the fire, a hooded figure dressed in black.

Tish stood frozen, unable to believe what she was seeing. Someone was trying to burn her out!

Get out. Get out of the apartment. Get out now.

There was no time to call 9-1-1. She had to depend on her neighbors for that.

Briefly, she thought about trying to save things. Her clothes, her shoes, computer disks, but the room was already growing blistering hot as the heat blew the glass from the French doors.

Smoke billowed into her bedroom.

Hurry, hurry.

She wore only Lycra workout pants and an oversized

T-shirt that served as her pajamas. Adrenaline pumping, heart thumping, she spun on her heels, ran from the room, racing for the only other exit out of the apartment.

The fire crackled behind her like an evil, cackling witch, destroying, eating up her life. Smoke, heavy and black, filled the hallway.

How was it burning so quickly?

Get out.

She paused at the door just long enough to slip her feet into her flip-flops and glanced around for the camera bag backpack she'd hooked over one of the kitchen chairs when she'd gotten home.

Where was the backpack? She had to have it. Her wallet was inside it, her credit cards, her identification, her laptop, the backup disk and the original she'd made of Shane and Elysee's engagement party, and of course her camera.

Smoke curled into her lungs, thick and acrid, and obscured her vision. Frantically, she ran her hands along the back of first one kitchen chair and then the other, desperate to find the backpack.

Had she left it in the living room?

She swung her head around, but the fire was already in the living room, too.

Forget the backpack. Get out or die!

Tish coughed against the billowing plume of smoke, barely able to breathe. Her head spun. Admitting defeat in finding her backpack, she staggered for the door but stumbled over something on her way out.

Her foot hung up on it and tripped her.

She fell to her knees, coughing, choking.

She'd stumbled on the strap of her backpack. It was on the floor underneath the chair.

Lungs aching, she hooked the heavy backpack over one shoulder, reached up to fumble for the lock on the door, determined to get outside to the sweet salvation of fresh, night air.

Her head was foggy, her chest constricting.

Get to your feet. Get out the door. You're almost there.

Her stupid feet wouldn't obey.

The sound of the fire was deafening now, coming closer, swallowing everything in its path with a vicious heat.

Okay, fine. If her legs wouldn't work, then she would crawl out of here.

She grabbed for the doorknob, dragged herself to a sitting position, twisted the knob and tumbled out onto the front stoop. She sucked in a merciful breath of smoke-free air. In the distance, she heard sirens. Some sharp-eyed neighbor had called the fire department. Good thing.

Safe. She was safe.

But then a pair of strong masculine hands slipped around her neck.

Oh my God, it was the arsonist and he was going to finish off what he'd started.

Her eyes burned from the smoke and profuse tears streamed down her cheeks. She couldn't see her assailant's face, but she would fight him with every last breath in her body.

In a blind panic, she cocked her knee and kicked savagely at his crotch. She heard a sharp exhalation of air, knew she had made solid contact. And that she'd probably knocked the air out of his lungs and he couldn't speak.

Yes! her brain crowed in triumph.

Can't stop now. Must get away.

She curled her fingers like claws and went for his face, scratching, searching for his eyes.

He grunted as she dragged her fingernails over his skin, committed to doing as much damage as possible. *Take that, you bastard.*

He grappled with her. He was so heavy. How could she fight him?

The sirens were growing closer. If she could only hang on for a few more minutes, help was on the way.

She blinked hard, desperate to see. She was on her back on the front stoop, perilously near the edge of the eight-foot plunge off the stairway.

If she could just buck him off of her. But how? He was twice her size.

She arched her back, spit and scratched, kicked and clawed. She pulled her knee up, used it as a fulcrum, and levered his legs off of hers. She wriggled and kicked, shoving him closer to the edge.

"Tish!" he gasped, just as she was preparing to kick him over the side. "Stop it, stop fighting. It's me. It's Shane."

Chapter 17

"S o let me get this straight," said police sergeant Dick Tracy. The paunchy man narrowed his eyes at Shane. "You were standing outside your ex-wife's bedroom window in the middle of the night."

Shane and Tish were sitting in front of the Houston PD sergeant's desk, both bloodied and battle-weary. The fire department had shown up to put out the fire but her apartment had been utterly destroyed. Several patrol cars had arrived along with the fire trucks. One of the cruisers had brought them downtown to make their statements and fill out a full report.

Shane's face was raw from where she'd scratched him. Tish had skinned her chin in the scuffle and didn't even remember it. And every time she touched her face, soot came off on her hands.

Clutching a grimy tissue in her hand, Tish longed for a shower. They had Styrofoam cups of rotgut cop coffee in front of them. She'd taken one sip when Dick Tracy had given it to her but hadn't been desperate enough for a second swallow. Where was Starbucks when you needed them?

Tish kept looking from the balding, middle-aged cop to the nameplate on his desk that confirmed he was indeed named Dick Tracy. "Honest to God, your name is really Dick Tracy?"

"Yes," he snapped.

"Dick, not Richard?"

"That's right." Dick Tracy glowered.

Shane kicked her lightly on the ankle, and telegraphed her a silent message with his eyes. *Shut up before you get us into more trouble.*

"Your mother must have had a fondness for comic book heroes," Tish said.

The cop scowled. "I don't know what you mean."

"Naming you after a comic book detective. I suppose you didn't have much choice except to become a cop. A name like that is destined to define your whole career path." Tish was blathering and she knew it, but she didn't want to talk about the fire. Focusing on Dick Tracy's curious name was a nice distraction. "Must be hard to live up to such a moniker, though. I mean here you are in your what . . . late forties and you still haven't made it to detective? That's gotta eat at you. Ouch!"

Shane's kick was more solid this time, his frown darker. *Are you nuts?*

Dick Tracy slid a glance over at Shane. "I can see why you're divorced. What I don't understand is why you were spying on her."

Yeah, Tish thought. *Good question. I can't wait to hear the answer to that one.* She folded her arms over her chest and waited expectantly.

"I wasn't spying," Shane denied.

"Were you stalking her?" Dick Tracy leaned forward, sizing Shane up with a critical eye.

"I am not a stalker." Boldly, Shane also leaned forward until his nose was almost touching the police sergeant's. A shiver skated up Tish's spine. It thrilled her when Shane got all tough and manly.

"Did you start the fire?"

"I did not."

"So." The cop's voice dripped sarcasm. "You just happened to be in the right place at the right time."

"Basically."

"I gotta warn you, I don't believe in coincidences. If you weren't spying on her, stalking her, or looking to burn her house down, why were you there?"

Tish curled her hands into fists. She was anxious to know the answer to this one.

The question had been nagging at her from the start. She knew Shane hadn't started the fire, even though Dick Tracy seemed inclined to believe otherwise. Personally, she didn't have a single doubt on that score. When it came to her physical safety, there wasn't a person on the planet she trusted more than Shane.

Shane made a noise, half-snort, half-sigh. He wasn't looking at Dick Tracy. His gaze was hooked on Tish. "You wouldn't believe it if I told you."

"I might. Why don't you try me?" the cop said, expressing exactly what Tish had been thinking.

"I was there to watch over her," Shane answered, then immediately snapped his jaw shut.

A sudden, inexplicable thrill caused goose bumps to raise up on Tish's arms. Shane had been watching over her? Was this the first time? Or had there been others?

Her gaze searched his face, looking for answers in his

eyes, but he wasn't looking at her. He was focused intently on Dick Tracy, never breaking eye contact, trying to prove he had nothing to hide.

"You were watching over her." A Skeptics-R-Us expression drew Dick Tracy's eyebrows down. He shuffled through the notes on his desk. "Does your fiancée, Elysee Benedict, the first daughter of the United States of America, know that you slipped out of bed in the middle of the night to come into Houston and stand outside your ex-wife's apartment to watch over her?"

Shane didn't answer him.

Dick Tracy swung his gaze to Tish. "You have any idea that your ex-husband likes to swing by in the middle of the night to 'watch over you'?"

She didn't know how to answer that. She looked from Shane to the police sergeant and back again.

"Just tell him the truth, Tish." Shane nodded.

Tish drew in a breath. "I had no idea."

"I don't swing by in the middle of the night. This is the only time I've ever done it."

"The only time?" Dick Tracy pointedly cleared his throat.

Shane shifted in his seat. Tish could tell that talking about this was making him uncomfortable. "Maybe there were a couple of other times, when we were first divorced and she was living in our old house all alone. I just wanted to make sure she was okay."

He'd come back to check on her after the divorce?

Tish's heart and stomach contracted in tandem waves and a pea-sized knot of pain embedded itself in the dead center of her sternum. He'd come back to check on her after the divorce.

"I don't get it," Dick Tracy said. "If you cared enough

about this woman to check on her after your breakup, then why did you divorce her?"

Tish perched on the edge of her seat, muscles tensed, waiting for Shane's reply.

Shane took a sip of coffee, winced, and quickly set it back down on the desk. He was stalling, trying to decide what to say. Tish recognized the tactic. "It's complicated," he muttered at last.

"I'm all ears." Dick Tracy cupped both hands behind his ears.

Breath bated, Tish leaned forward and almost fell off the chair. Would he reveal his true emotions to Dick Tracy? Would she at long last find out what had really propelled him out the door that last morning they were together?

Would he tell the cop about Johnny? Briefly, she closed her eyes and bit down on her bottom lip to stay the tears that threatened to tumble.

"My being there has nothing to do with the fact that someone burned her apartment to the ground tonight."

"No?"

"No."

Shane and Dick Tracy continued their macho stare-down. One minute passed. Then two. The police sergeant finally caved. He dropped his gaze, plucked a pencil from the cup holder on his desk, and started doodling on a Post-it note.

Tish slumped back against her chair. She wasn't going to learn anything about Shane's true motives. Not tonight. Hell, if the police couldn't wring the truth out of him, she'd probably never know for sure.

"Let's take a different approach. Forget the past. Why were you at her place tonight? Why this night, out of all the other nights, did you decide she needed watching over?"

"I woke up with a bad feeling she was in danger."

Dick Tracy snorted and flipped his pencil back in the cup holder. "Psychic, are ya? Wait, wait, don't tell me. You had a vision that someone was going to torch your ex-wife's apartment and try to kill her?"

"I didn't know what was going to happen. I just woke up with this feeling in my gut that she needed me."

Tish couldn't help herself. She gave a half-laugh. "Oh, that's rich. When we were together, when I really needed you, where were you? Off protecting someone else. But now you're engaged to Elysee frickin' Benedict and suddenly your gut's telling you to come look after me?"

"Well, yeah."

Tish rose to her feet, sank her hands on her hips. "Maybe you should discuss these tendencies with a shrink, if you want *this* marriage to last."

"Your wife's got a point," Dick Tracy said.

"We're not married!" Shane and Tish said in unison.

Dick Tracy raised his palms. "Okay, I get it. You're divorced and hate each other."

"We don't hate each other," Shane said.

The cop made a derisive noise. "Look here, I get off duty in an hour. I don't have time for this. Let's just make a statement and you'll be free to go, but I don't want either one of you leaving the area until this investigation is over. Got it?"

They nodded.

"Sit back down"—Dick Tracy pointed to the chair Tish had vacated—"and let's get this over with."

Tish plunked back in her seat and told her side of the story. Then Shane told his.

"Do you have a patrol officer who can take me back to my vehicle?" Shane asked the police sergeant when all the requisite paperwork had been completed.

"Nope. Shift change."

"How are we supposed to get out of here?"

"Oh, don't worry about that. You've got a ride coming." Dick Tracy's eyes gleamed.

"Yeah?"

"I had my assistant call the Benedict ranch. They're sending a car."

"You did that on purpose." Shane splayed his palms on the sergeant's desk.

Dick Tracy shrugged, grinned. "Just doing my job. After all, you can tell the most about a suspect when he's under pressure. If I'm not mistaken"—he nodded toward the entrance—"your ride has arrived."

Simultaneously, Shane and Tish turned, just as the doors of the precinct flew open and a clot of Secret Service agents, led by Cal Ackerman, marched into the station.

And there, in the center of the group, looking as innocent and sweet as Cameron Diaz in *My Best Friend's Wedding,* stood Elysee Benedict.

As the rising sun edged up into the morning sky, Shane found himself stuffed into the backseat of the limo with Elysee on his right side and Tish on his left. Cal Ackerman and another agent sat in the seat across from them. Once upon a time, he would have been sitting next to Cal. Now he was sandwiched between his ex-wife and his wife-to-be.

It was a surreal sensation.

"Here," Tish said, rummaging around in the backpack

that served as her camera bag and coming up with a disk. She passed it to Elysee. "Hang on to this for me. The original burned up in the fire, but luckily I'd made two copies and stowed them in the camera bag."

Elysee slipped the disk into her pocket and looked over at Shane. "Do you think the fire could be related to the disk?"

"I don't know," he said.

Elysee looked back at Tish. "You're coming to stay at the ranch where you'll be safe and that's all there is to it."

"No, no," Tish said. "I can get a hotel room."

"Don't be silly," Elysee said matter-of-factly. "It's the perfect solution. You need a place to stay."

Shane's gaze flashed to Tish's face. He shouldn't be looking at her. Not in front of his fiancée, but he couldn't seem to stop himself. Her hair was disheveled, her mass of corkscrew auburn curls cascading over her slender shoulders. Black soot smeared her cheeks and forehead. Her chin was skinned, marring her peaches-and-cream complexion. He'd always loved the sun-kissed hue of her skin.

Tish averted her eyes, stared down at her lap. Shane realized for the first time that she was wearing her version of pajamas—well-worn workout pants and an over-sized T-shirt.

His old T-shirt.

When they'd been married, he'd bought her sexy lingerie. Teddies and baby doll pajamas and silky nightgowns. She'd worn them to seduce him, but once the garments had been discarded in favor of lovemaking, once they were spent and ready for snuggling, she would get up, dig out pants worn soft from wear and one of his T-shirts, and slide back into bed.

Elysee, on the other hand, was a total girly-girl about her bedclothes. She slept in satin and silk. He knew because he'd been her night shift bodyguard and she'd occasionally get up in the middle of the night, with a gauzy dressing gown over her delicate underthings, and challenge him to a game of chess.

Weird that in waking life Tish was overtly sexual, while Elysee was demure. Yet in their sleeping attire Tish preferred comfort and cotton, while Elysee went for high style and lace.

Women. Who could figure them? Certainly not him. If he could, he'd still be married to Tish.

"We need to swing by Tish's place so I can pick up my Durango," he said as the limo cruised through downtown Houston. To keep from staring at Tish, he studied the carpet, noticed there were little pieces of what looked to be red gravel underneath Cal's shoes.

"I've already dispatched someone to retrieve it, sweetheart," Elysee assured him, still smiling. Her congeniality was almost eerie, but there was something else in her eyes. An emotion he couldn't identify.

Here was another weird thing. Elysee hadn't asked what he'd been doing at Tish's place in the middle of the night. Wouldn't a normal woman be jealous, or at the very least, curious?

Elysee reached over his lap to touch Tish's hand. "I'm so sorry for what happened to your apartment. I'm just glad you managed to get a call off to Shane and he was able to race to your place in time to save you from the arsonist."

Shane tensed, fisted his hands against the tops of his thighs. What was Tish going to say?

"I didn't . . ." Tish flashed a quick glance at Shane's face.

Was she going to tell Elysee the truth? He tensed, bracing himself for what might come next.

Tish shifted her gaze to Elysee, who was looking over at her so wide-eyed and trusting. She cleared her throat. "Yes, yes, I was lucky."

Relief loosened Shane's limbs, but it was quickly replaced by guilt. He shouldn't be getting off this easily. If the roles had been switched he could bet Tish would be grilling him like a steak.

"So it's settled. You'll stay at the ranch until you can get back on your feet," Elysee commented.

Tish sneaked another glance at Shane. He kept his face impassive, although he would have felt more comfortable if someone had detonated a grenade in the limo. He looked across at Cal Ackerman, who was smirking at him. He deserved it. He'd broken the bodyguard's code. Never get personally involved with the person you were hired to protect.

"All right, then."

"Isn't that wonderful, darling?" Elysee linked her arm through his and squeezed tight.

"Wonderful," Shane echoed and forced an optimistic smile. How in the hell had he gotten himself into this? Then he looked down at the hand Elysee was touching. His injury had made him vulnerable in more ways than one.

If not for a sleep-deprived backhoe driver, he would not be in this fix: about to marry one woman while he was still in love with the other. What was he supposed to do about that?

Nothing. You don't do anything.

Indecision held him tight in its grasp, which was bizarre because he'd always made decisions fast and followed through quickly. It was that ability that had driven him out of bed in the middle of the night. His instinct to act was the very same thing that had saved Tish's life, but it had ended him up in this situation.

Indecision took hold. Made itself at home in his chest. Curled up tight against his spine.

Indecision.

The very thing Shane feared most.

"Don't marry him."

"What?"

Four hours after Elysee and her entourage had retrieved Shane and Tish from the police station, Elysee sat at her writing desk. Telephone in hand, she'd just ended a conversation with a department store retailer. Shane was at his morning physical therapy session. Tish had been ensconced in a guest bedroom to try to get some sleep after her ordeal. Elysee blinked at Cal Ackerman, who'd come into the room while she was on the phone.

"Shane." Cal strode across the room toward her. "Don't marry him."

His statement threw her off balance. She settled the cordless phone into its docking station, straightened in her chair and met his edgy gaze. Her pulse quickened. She lifted a hand to her throat. "Why not?"

"Because." Cal took a deep breath. "You deserve someone who loves you."

"Shane loves me," Elysee said, but even as she spoke the words she felt hollow deep inside.

Cal shook his head. "Not the way you should be loved."

He was standing mere inches away, and Elysee could feel the heat emanating off his big body.

She gulped. "What do you mean?"

"You know," he said in a tone that raised the hairs on her forearms.

"I don't." *What a fib.* "If you'll excuse me, Agent Ackerman, I've got a wedding to plan."

He laid a big palm smack-dab on top of the papers in front of her and leaned in close. "You're making a big mistake."

Elysee's knees felt weak. Good thing she was sitting down. She didn't know what to make of this, but suddenly, she flashed to a mental image of a buck-naked Cal climbing out of the shower. She closed her eyes, shook her head, but the image persisted.

"You've overstepped your bounds, Agent Ackerman," she said sharply, unnerved by what she was experiencing. She shouldn't be feeling what she was feeling. Not when she was engaged to another man. "I'll thank you to remember your place."

"Pulling rank?" His tone was amused.

"Yes." She lifted her chin. "I am. I'd appreciate it if you'd step back across the room."

"What's the matter, Elysee?" He dropped his voice. His head was so close that if she turned, his lips would be on hers. "Afraid of what you're feeling?"

She spun away from him, scrambled to her feet, so unnerved she could barely speak. She stood with her back to the wall, struggling to catch her breath. "I'm appalled at your effrontery, sir."

"Who're you trying to kid? Me or you?"

Her hands curled into fists. "Please, you're making me uncomfortable."

"No one's ever made you uncomfortable before?" He arched an eyebrow.

Not like this! She'd never been so upset with someone while at the same time desperately aching to kiss them. *What's the matter with me?*

"Do you value your job, Agent Ackerman?"

"Not as much as I value stopping you from making a major mistake."

The honesty in his words, the serious expression on his face, startled her. "Duly noted. Thank you for expressing your objections. Now, if you'll just mind your own business, we'll forget this entire conversation. Otherwise, I'll have to ask my father to have you replaced."

A knock on the bedroom door pulled Tish from a restless sleep, where she'd dreamed of a shadowy menace chasing her. In the grogginess of half-sleep she remembered the fire and a rush of sadness rolled over her.

Another knock sounded but before she could organize her thoughts for a response, the door opened and Elysee poked her head in. "You awake? "

"Just barely." Tish stifled a yawn.

"Get up, we're going shopping."

"Shopping? Like this?" Tish waved a hand at her rumpled clothes. "It's all I have to wear. I can't go to the mall looking like this." She cocked her head at petite, five-foot-two, size-four Elysee. She was five-nine and wore a size twelve. "It's not like you and I could share the same clothes."

"We're going shopping presidential style."

"How's that?"

Elysee crooked a finger. "Come with me."

Feeling grumpy, dowdy, and decidedly homeless, Tish begrudgingly got out of bed. She ran a hand through her tangle of curls, stuffed her feet into her flip-flops, and followed Elysee out of the room, her curiosity piqued.

Elysee led her through the house to the sitting room where she'd first interviewed Tish. Today, the room was filled with racks and racks of clothes, from Macy's, Nordstrom's, Ann Taylor, and Neiman Marcus. Salesclerks stood in a line, waiting at the ready for Elysee's beck and call.

And then Tish saw them.

Shoes. Boxes upon boxes of shoes. Jimmy Choos, Christian Louboutins, Manolo Blahniks, Dolce & Gabbanas.

Her heart pattered. "What's all this?"

"It's a little difficult for the President's daughter to pop down to the local mall, so the mall comes to me."

This was Tish's biggest fantasy come true. A shopaholic's erotic dream. It was the most amazing thing that had ever happened to a poor girl with a bad credit rating.

"It's awfully nice of you," Tish said, fingering a beautiful silk camisole. "But I can't afford this stuff. My pocketbook is geared more toward Target."

"Sweetie." Elysee patted her shoulder. "This shopping spree is a gift. From Shane and me."

Tish backed up, backed away from all the lovely, lovely clothes. She raised her palms in front of her, and shook her head. "No, no. I can't accept this."

Elysee blinked. "Why not?"

"It's too much. It's too extravagant." *It's from you and Shane. My ex-husband whom I still love.* The whole situation was just too damned weird.

"But you have to have clothes."

"If someone could just give me a ride to the nearest Wal-Mart I'll pick up a pair of jeans, a couple of blouses, a package of underwear, and I'll be good to go." She realized for the first time that she was truly stuck here. The car she'd borrowed from Delaney was parked under the carport near her burned-out apartment.

"Tish Gallagher, you're the first daughter's wedding videographer. You've got to look the part."

She gazed at the clothes again and sighed with longing. "Seriously, Elysee, I can't accept."

"Seriously, Tish, why won't you just let us help you?"

Because I don't deserve it. Because you're so nice and I'm lusting after Shane and you don't even know it.

"If it makes you feel any better, you can deduct the cost of the clothes from the final installment on our wedding video."

"Really?" Now that was an idea she could wrap her head around.

"Really."

"Okay."

"Now, let's shop."

Two hours later, Tish's wardrobe had been replenished. While the retailers were tallying totals and packing up their inventory, Elysee and Tish were served a late lunch of finger sandwiches and pasta salad on the veranda.

"So tell me, what's Shane like in bed?"

"Huh?" Tish choked on a mouthful of raspberry tea.

"Is he forceful?"

"Um, are you sure you really want to discuss this with me, again?" Tish asked.

Elysee lowered her voice. "I don't have anyone else to discuss this sort of thing with."

"What about your girlfriends?"

"Honestly, it's difficult keeping friendships when you're in the public eye." Elysee took a deep breath.

"I'm sure it is."

"So tell me what he's like in bed."

"Elysee, that's personal."

"Was the sex bad between you two? Was that why your marriage fell apart?"

She shouldn't have said what she said next, but she couldn't seem to stop herself from bragging. "If great sex could keep a marriage together, let's just say Shane and I would have been superglued for life."

"Really." Elysee struggled to keep the smile on her face.

Tish felt as if she'd just kicked a puppy. "I'm sorry, I shouldn't have said that."

"No, no, I'm glad you told me. I need to know these things." Elysee took a breath. "So why did you divorce him?"

"I didn't divorce him. Shane divorced me."

"I didn't know."

"Now you do."

A long silence ensued. Elysee toyed with a cucumber sandwich. "Why did he divorce you?"

"Because I didn't need him the way he thought I should and then the one time I really needed him, he wasn't there for me," she said, hearing the bitterness in her own voice.

"That doesn't make any sense." Even when Elysee frowned, she managed to look sweet and innocent. It grated on Tish's nerves.

"Don't let it worry you, Elysee. Your marriage will be fine. You're plenty needy enough for Shane."

It was an awful thing to say. Especially to Elysee, who'd been nothing but kind to her. Immediately, Tish felt like the crud in the bottom of a dirty refrigerator. No, wait, she was lower than that. She was ring-around-the-toilet crud.

Elysee burst into tears, pushed back her chair, and ran sobbing from the room.

Great going, Gallagher. You're turning out to be quite the puppy kicker.

Chapter 18

I don't want to interrupt your workout, but I have a favor to ask."

Shane glanced up to see Tish standing in the doorway of the elaborate gym. Embarrassed by the puny little one-pound weight cradled awkwardly in his right hand, he hid it behind his back.

She looked absolutely breathtaking in a green silk blouse that molded to her lush breasts and designer blue jeans that hugged her sexy ass. His body stirred, responding in a totally inappropriate way.

"Where's your physical therapist?" she asked, sauntering into the room.

"He got a phone call."

"So you're in here all alone?" She craned her neck, looked around the corner at the bank of treadmills. She moved with the grace of a dancer, lithe and totally at ease in her own skin. She ran her hand along the padded cushion on the nearby butterfly machine. She'd always been a very tactile person. Kinesthetic. Physical. Shane clamped his teeth shut, remembering how much she'd liked to touch and be touched.

"You needed to ask a favor?" he said gruffly, to hide what he was feeling.

"Will you give me a ride back to my place?"

"Your place burned down."

"I know, but my car's there. Or rather Delaney's car is there. She let me borrow it after mine got repossessed."

"Your car got repossessed?" The damned weight was getting so heavy, the weakened muscles in his wrist were yelping with pain. He clenched his jaw.

Her cheeks flushed red with embarrassment. She made a face, waved a hand. "I know, I know. I'm irresponsible, unreliable, immature."

"I didn't say that."

She was trying so hard to be tough and brave, enduring a burned-up apartment, a repossessed car. A sudden tenderness swept through him so raw and stark it had him shaking his head. He wanted to pull her into his arms, hold her close and tell her everything was going to be all right. But he had no right to comfort her. He'd given up his right when he'd filed for divorce.

"You were thinking it."

"I was thinking . . ." No he couldn't say what he was thinking. A spasm shot through his right hand. He dropped the weight. It fell to the floor with a loud thunk. He shook his hand trying to free it of the charley horse. "How heavy that weight was getting," he finished, wincing.

"Cramp?"

"Uh-huh."

"Here," she said, stepping across the room toward him, hips swaying in that sassy walk of hers. "Let me."

He started to say no, that it would be all right, but

before he could pry the words from his mouth, she was there, reaching for his hand.

Touching him.

Tilting her head and studying him.

She placed the pad of her thumb in the center of his savaged palm, her fingers wrapping around the back of his hand. Her skin was so warm against his, but he was self-conscious about the scars.

Her thumb kneaded his palm in widening circles. She was so close. Too close.

He could feel the blood pumping through his veins as he stared at her moist, luscious lips. He remembered exactly how they tasted like summer raspberries. A taste he craved.

Swallowing past the lump of aching desire blocking his throat, Shane pulled his hand from hers. "The cramp's gone."

He lied. It wasn't gone. But for the sake of his sanity he had to distance himself from her. Before he ended up doing something that would ruin everything for both of them. He couldn't have her. He was engaged to Elysee and the river of ancient history was too wide to cross.

"Come on," he said gruffly. "I'll give you that ride."

"Yes," she agreed with a quick nod.

Forty minutes later they stood in her driveway, surveying the burned-out ruins of her apartment.

A gasp rose to Tish's lips the minute she grasped the extent of the damage. He watched the impact on her face, saw how her features sank and crumpled. He had an overwhelming urge to reach out and put an arm around her shoulders to steady her, but he did not.

The arson investigator and his team were there, sifting through the rubble.

"Who are you people?" the investigator asked.

"It's my apartment. Or it was," Tish said, eyeing his helpers as they relocated pieces of her charred life and sifted them into different piles.

"You can't be here. The investigation isn't complete."

"We just came for my car." She jerked her thumb over her shoulder in the direction of her landlady's garage.

"All right, but please back away from the perimeter."

"Is everything completely destroyed?"

"Pretty much."

"Do you have any idea who might have started the fire?" Shane asked. He stepped closer to the investigator, his shoes crunching loudly in the red lava landscape gravel that fronted the garage.

The investigator shook his head. "We can't release any information at this time. I'm going to have to ask you folks to get what you came for and be on your way."

"Hey," one of the team members called to another. "I found something intact. It was buried under a stack of burned-up books."

All eyes swung the man's way. He was holding up a bookend, a sculpted little girl with a pail of water in her hand carved from the burl of two banyan trees that had twined and grown together. Somehow it had come through the fire unscathed, probably because it had been buried under the books. Shane recognized it and felt an immediate sorrowful tug in his gut.

He'd bought the Jill half of the Jack and Jill bookends for Tish at a rummage sale while they were on their honeymoon in Galveston. She'd fallen in love with it the moment she'd seen it.

"Remember the day you bought that for me?" Tish whispered.

"I remember," he said gruffly.

"We never did find Jill's mate."

"No Jack."

"Can I have it?" she asked the arson investigator. "Please."

"I'm afraid it's evidence until the investigation is closed."

Evidence of what? Shane wondered. *A memory gone bad? A promise forgotten?*

"All right," she told the investigator, then to Shane she said, "I'm ready to leave now."

Shane walked her to the car and opened the door for her. She slid across the leather. He handed her his cell phone. "Here, take my cell."

"What for?"

"Your cell phone burned up in the fire. You're a woman driving alone in a big city and it's almost forty miles to the ranch. Take my phone."

"But aren't you following me back?"

"No, I've got a couple of things to do first."

They looked at each other. Was that longing in his eyes? Sadness?

She took the cell phone. "Thank you."

He moistened his lips and for one wonderful moment she thought he might kiss her good-bye. "That was weird about the Jill bookend. The only thing that survived the fire intact."

"Weird," she echoed, her eyes hooked on his mouth. The tension, the emotion, the sad yearning for days gone by vibrated the air between them.

"I never found the Jack bookend for you like I promised."

"No."

"I should have found it," he said. "I should have kept my promise."

"It doesn't matter."

"It does matter, Tish. I let you down."

"It's too late for that, Shane."

Was it her imagination or was his hand trembling ever so slightly? She saw the anguish in his eyes. What did he want from her? What did he expect?

"I could go on the Internet tonight, check out e-bay, search for the bookend."

"You don't have time for that. You've got a hand to heal. You're getting married in a month. You've got preparations to make. Besides, what use do I have for bookends? My books are all gone."

"Tish," he murmured her name again.

"I release you, Shane, from any obligations you might still be feeling toward me. You don't owe me a thing."

"But I made a promise."

"Things happen. People aren't always able to keep the promises they made in good conscience. Let yourself off the hook, Shane. I'm not holding it against you that you never bought that other bookend for me."

"You've changed." He looked at her as if really seeing her for the first time.

"I have to go. Elysee is expecting me. We're going to work on the video." She had to get out of here before she did something completely stupid, like telling him she was still in love with him. She started the engine.

"Drive safely." He raised his hand.

She slammed the car into gear, backed out of the

carport, and left him standing there, looking utterly confused.

Seeing the burned-out remains of Tish's apartment brought Shane face-to-face with the realization of how easily she could have died in that blaze. He could have lost her forever.

Until this minute he hadn't fully understood the depths of how much he missed her. Of how he would miss her if she was suddenly gone.

He couldn't let this lie. Last night, someone had tried to kill Tish and he was determined to find out why. Jaw clenched, he climbed into the Durango and drove to the police station.

Dick Tracy was reluctant to speak with him.

"The investigation is ongoing," he said in that non-committal way cops have perfected, when Shane prodded for answers.

"In other words," Shane said, "you've got nothing."

"I didn't say that." Tracy leaned back in his chair, sizing him up with one long, cool, appraising glance.

"And?" The conversation made him feel like a dentist trying to extract impacted wisdom teeth.

"And what?"

Tracy was apparently in no frame of mind to surrender his secrets, but Shane was in no frame of mind to leave this police station without some answers. "Any new leads? Any clues?"

"I don't have to tell you anything."

As Nathan Benedict's future son-in-law and a former Secret Service agent, Shane could have thrown his weight around. He had connections. One well-placed phone call and he could force Dick Tracy to turn over the evidence. But that would take time. He wanted answers now.

"Sergeant Tracy." He leaned across the desk. "You seem like a reasonable man who's just doing his job. Don't make me pull strings."

"You threatening me, Tremont?"

Okay, wrong tactic.

"Not at all," Shane said smoothly when he was feeling anything but smooth. Inside, he felt ragged and edgy. "I'm law enforcement, too. I was hoping you'd share what you've learned."

Tracy considered him a long moment. He opened up his desk drawer and drew out a plastic evidence bag. He tossed it in the middle of his desk. It was a matchbook with Shane's and Elysee's names on it, along with the date of their impending nuptials—Christmas Eve. "Evidence team found this on the ground outside your ex-wife's apartment, along with several cigarette butts. Someone's been watching her. You have any idea who?"

"Those matchbooks were given away at our engagement party. Anyone could have grabbed a handful."

"Not anyone. Only the people with access to you and your fiancée."

"What are you saying, Officer Tracy?"

"I'm saying the culprit is probably someone you know and trust."

Elysee lay on her bed, head buried under her pillow. Tish was one hundred percent correct. She *was* needy. Her neediness was the reason she'd thrown herself headlong into World-Fem and helping Rana. She'd thought that by empowering other women, she could empower herself. Her neediness was what had broken up her first three engagements. Was it also sabotaging her relationship with Shane?

If she were being honest with herself she would admit his need to be needed was the very thing that had attracted her to him. He was the strong shoulder she'd been looking for to cry on and he liked that role.

Was their relationship based on anything more than mutual co-dependency?

It was a troubling thought.

She rolled over, brought the pillow to her chest and stared up at the ceiling with a painful blend of hope and longing. Was there any possibility that she could hold on to Shane? Or was she doomed to make Tish's tragic mistake?

Elysee knew she could never compete with Tish. The woman was so sexy and smart and brave. Elysee had no illusions about herself on that score. She was flat-chested and narrow-hipped and gap-toothed. She had been a solid C student no matter how hard she studied—which was why she hadn't bothered with college. And she was such a coward that she had to call the Secret Service to swat spiders for her. She was a dowdy, dumb wimp.

Don't marry him. The words Cal had spoken to her that morning rang in her head.

But how could she back out now? The last thing on earth she wanted was to hurt Shane. He'd already suffered so much.

Marriage should be forever. If Shane's not The One, it's better to break an engagement than a wedding vow.

Elysee covered her face with her hands as she imagined the tabloid headlines. *Fickle First Daughter Flakes on Fiancé Number Four.* She thought of the engagement party and the money her father had already spent.

Shane was a good man, a kind and honest man. Their

marriage would be filled with mutual respect and admiration. On that score, she had no doubts.

But what about love? quizzed a tiny voice deep inside her. Cal was right. She deserved someone who'd love her fully, completely, wholeheartedly, without any reservations, the way her father had loved her mother. The way Alma Reddy and her husband loved. Could she and Shane ever love each other like that?

She had to find out.

Elysee went to Tish's room, knocked tentatively on the door. When she didn't answer, Elysee tried the handle. It was unlocked. She knocked again, pushing the door open as she went. "Tish?"

The room was empty.

But Tish's camera sat on the dresser, input/output cords hooking it up to the television. Elysee slipped the disk of their engagement party that Tish had given her in the limo out of her pocket and inserted it into the camera. She turned on the television and perched on the foot of Tish's bed to watch.

The sound of her father's voice announcing her engagement to Shane drew her attention to the video. Her stomach wrenched with emotion—regret, sadness, guilt, and an inexplicable feeling of hope. The camera view panned the room, then came back to linger on Shane and circled the room again.

This time, when the camera caught Shane's face, he was looking right into the lens with such an expression of abject longing it took Elysee's breath.

How sad and lost he looked. Why would he look that way on the day of his engagement?

Puzzled, she tilted her head to study his features.

Why was he staring into the camera?

Why was the camera so focused on Shane's face?

Realization hit her like a landslide. It was obvious to anyone with two good eyes and half a brain.

Shane was looking at the person behind the camera and the person behind the camera was fixed on him.

Tish.

In an instant, Elysee's body went as cold as if she'd been doused with ice water.

Shane was still in love with Tish and she with him.

Her stomach churned. Her heart constricted. And here she'd been repeatedly throwing them in each other's path. Oh, Lola had been right. Hiring Tish to videotape the wedding had been a terrible idea.

It's not Tish's fault if he still loves her. You love who you love.

The question was, did she love Shane as much as Tish did?

Elysee realized she didn't know the answer to that question. What she felt for Shane was very calm and quiet and familiar. No Fourth of July fireworks. No angst. No intense yearning. Were her feelings for him predicated on nothing more than admiration, friendship, and gratitude that he'd saved her life?

She realized she did not know. Until now, her life had been dictated first by romantic notions engendered by her mother, and then by her father's expectations. She didn't blame her parents. They'd done what they'd thought best for her. She blamed herself for not questioning her values and beliefs before.

In that moment, Elysee knew what she must do.

Tish was roadkill.

Flattened.

Squashed.

Annihilated.

She drove blindly, not really knowing where she was going. Not caring. Desperate to blunt the devastation suffocating her heart.

Her apartment had burned to the ground. Her ex-husband, whom she still loved, was marrying Elysee and there was nothing she could do about it. Anxious for someone to talk to who wasn't involved with the sainted first daughter, Tish pulled into a shopping mall parking lot, cut the engine, and punched Delaney's number into the cell phone Shane had given her.

"Hello." Her voice came out dry and reedy.

"Tish?"

Relief washed over her. "Yeah."

"Are you all right?"

Tish couldn't speak. Emotion was a wad of tears jammed up tight against her throat. She wasn't going to cry.

"I read about the fire in this morning's paper. I've been calling and calling your cell phone, but kept getting your voice mail. I was so worried."

"I'm fine." Tish finally managed to choke out the words. "My cell phone burned up in the fire."

"I tried calling your mom, but when she hadn't heard from you either, I really started to panic. I had Nick check the local hospitals."

"I'm sorry I worried you."

"I'm just happy you're okay. It scared me when the paper said the fire was a suspected arson and that you were at home at the time of the blaze."

"Yeah."

"Were you hurt?"

"No."

"That's good. I'm so glad you're all right."

"Shane was there."

"Shane?"

"Yeah." She was having trouble putting more than three words together.

"What was he doing there?"

"I don't know." Truly she did not. She wasn't sure that she believed his claim that he'd had a dream she was in trouble. Why hadn't he just picked up the phone and called her? The man was seriously messing with her head.

"Why would someone try to burn down your apartment?" Delaney asked.

"I don't know." She was starting to sound like a scratched CD, endlessly repeating.

"You're really not all right at all."

"No," she agreed. "I'm not."

"Where are you?"

"On my way back to the Benedict ranch. I'm staying there until the wedding." Her voice sounded stronger now. That was good. "But I'll be all right. I'm just shook up."

"Are you sure? You know you're more than welcome to stay with me and Nick."

"I know. Thank you. I might take you up on your offer." Her heart swelled with love for her friend. "But enough about me. How are you doing, Delaney? It seems forever since I've seen you."

"That's because you've been jetting off with the presidential set," Delaney joked. "You're going to get so big you'll forget all about your friends."

"That'll never happen," Tish said fiercely.

"You say that now . . . ," she teased.

"And I mean it."

"I do have a bit of news."

"Oh?"

"I wanted to tell you in person, but Tish, I'm so excited. I don't think I can wait."

"What is it?"

Delaney inhaled a sharp sigh of joy. "Nick and I . . ." She paused.

"Uh-huh?"

"We're pregnant!"

Tish's body went limp and she almost dropped the phone. She sat there gulping in breaths of air.

Delaney was having a baby. Nothing was ever going to be the same between them again. She felt joy for her friend, but at the same time she feared for the tiny life growing inside of Delaney. She knew how precarious that precious life was. How it could all turn on a whisper of a second. Hopes could be dashed. Dreams eradicated.

"Tish? You still there?"

"Uh-huh."

"Did you hear me?"

"I heard you. I'm just stunned. I didn't know you and Nick were trying to have a baby."

"We weren't." Delaney giggled. "We just got a little careless. But Tish, Nick's so happy. You should see him. He already went out and bought a little baseball glove. It's adorable."

"How far along are you?"

"Just eight weeks."

"Are you hoping for a boy or a girl?"

"We don't really care as long as it's healthy. I sort of want a boy, but I think Nick prefers a girl."

"I'm so happy for you two."

And she was. She was! Tish wasn't jealous of Delaney, just deeply sorry for herself. For all the things she'd lost. From her baby to her husband to her home to her clothes. Photographs and keepsakes. Memories of her life up in smoke.

Tish bit down on her bottom lip. She would not give in to self-pity. She was made of sterner stuff. She'd survived losing a baby in the early third trimester of her pregnancy and the dissolution of her marriage. She would survive this, too.

"Why don't you come here? It would be a joy to have you," Delaney said. "It would be like college. Except with Nick hanging around."

She thought of living with Delaney. The eager smiles on her friend's face as she decorated the nursery. The knowing glances she'd exchange with her husband when she thought Tish wasn't looking. She simply couldn't bear it.

"You and Nick need your alone time right now. I'll be fine at the ranch."

"You're sure?"

"Positive."

"If you change your mind, you know where to reach me."

"Thank you."

Silence hung between them. The gulf had already begun.

"I was worried about telling you," Delaney said. "I kept thinking about Johnny. I don't want you to feel . . ."

"Honey, don't you dare worry about that," Tish said, forcing her voice to sound lighthearted and carefree. "I'm fine."

Fine as ground glass.

"I just . . ."

"Listen, I've gotta go. Elysee wants me to go over the engagement party video with her. I'll call you later. In the meantime kiss Nick for me and congratulations to you both."

"Tish . . ."

"Love you. Bye," Tish said and hung up.

For the longest time, she stared down at the cell phone. Briefly, she thought of calling Jillian to see if she could stay with her, but then she remembered Jillian was in San Francisco for six months and she'd sublet her downtown condo. Rachael lived with her roommates, so that was out. And Dixie Ann was in San Diego.

Her house was burned to the ground. She had to be careful with her money. Her best friend was pregnant. She couldn't stay with either of her other two friends. And there was the possibility that whoever burned her apartment wanted her dead. She was stuck on the ranch with her ex-husband and his fiancée.

Things couldn't possibly get worse.

The laughter started deep inside her and built. Shaking her body, rumbling up through her diaphragm, into her lungs, and finally out through her lips until she was laughing hysterically, uncontrollably. Until she couldn't breathe.

Hell, she thought, it was a lot better than crying. At least when you laughed at rock bottom, your eyes didn't get all red and puffy.

Chapter 19

After his return from taking Tish to get her car, Shane went in search of Elysee. He traveled the path from the garage through the gardens, past the place where he'd first kissed Elysee—that sweet, chaste kiss that had caused him to put her up on a pedestal.

He stared down at his mangled hand. He tried to make a fist but could not contract his fingers inward any more than an inch. All this time in physical therapy and this was the best he could do?

Disgusting.

Worthless. He felt absolutely worthless. Last night, he hadn't been able to stop an arsonist from burning down Tish's apartment. Nor had he been able to save her from the fire. She'd saved herself. Not only saved herself but then nearly booted his sorry ass off the stairs.

What kind of man was he now? Broken. Useless. Unable to protect the people he loved. Viciously, Shane kicked at the loose pebbles on the garden path. His heel skidded in the gravel. He lost his balance and fell smack on his ass.

Chagrined, he stared up at the main house and saw Pete Larkin standing on the back porch sneaking a smoke. A fitness trainer who smoked? Just his luck. Shane's humiliation was complete. Someone had seen him.

Scrambling to his feet, he tried to look cool and failed miserably. He limped. His hand hurt. His face was covered in scratches. He was a mess.

Suck it up. Your grandfather stormed the beach at Normandy. Your father made it back from Vietnam in one piece. This is nothing.

He could take the humiliation. He could handle the pain and his physical limitation. What he couldn't handle was having Tish so close, unable to touch her, fighting his desires, all the while remembering he was engaged to the President's daughter.

How had things gotten so damned fucked up?

The temptation to get into his Durango and just drive and drive and drive until he hit water was overwhelming. Too bad he wasn't the kind of guy who ran away when things got tough.

Oh, no? Who the hell bailed out of his marriage? That doesn't sound like the actions of a stick-to-it guy.

The thought clipped him low in the gut. All his life he had believed he was the kind of man who accepted responsibility willingly. He hadn't been a foolish teen. No drunken escapades, no irresponsible sex.

Well, except for that time on the ferry with Tish, when protection and condoms hadn't even entered his lust-soaked mind.

Twice in his life, he hadn't lived up to his image of himself. Once when he'd been so caught up in passion he'd gotten Tish pregnant, and then a year later when he'd walked out on her.

Guilt knifed him. Sliced open his gut, eviscerating him and letting every emotion he'd been trying to hold inside come tumbling out in a rush of messy heat.

There was one big divider between the way he tried to live his life and Shane's actual behavior. One thing and one thing only had led him from the straight and narrow path he'd always walked.

And her name was Tish Gallagher.

But Tish had changed.

Shane had never seen her so calm, so accepting, as he had seen her this afternoon. He didn't know what to make of her transformation. He was gobsmacked.

Face it, Tremont. It's finally over. You should be relieved. Now you can get on with your life.

But he wasn't. He couldn't.

He scratched his head. His hair had grown out. He would need to get it trimmed before the wedding. When he'd first seen Tish again his hair had been nothing but little spikes of stubble all over his head. Now, so many things had changed, yet the most important one was still the same.

He was engaged to marry Elysee Benedict.

And he had Tish's blessings.

Fury grabbed him then. Fisted his gut. Burned his throat. He had no idea why he was so angry, but it felt damn good. Ever since the accident, he'd been walking around in a muddle. He hadn't stopped to ask himself what it was that he really wanted.

What did he want?

Tish. He wanted Tish.

You can't have her.

The strength of his desire knocked him on his ass. For two years he'd fought his desires, hidden his feelings, tamped down his emotions. He'd been a good Secret Service agent. No, he'd been a great Secret Service agent.

But what was he now?

Maimed. Muddled. Lost.

Shane refused to put up with this helpless feeling. He had to do something. Had to prove he was still a man. He had to get his courage back.

By the time he reached the back porch, Larkin had ducked back inside but the air was still redolent with the smell of his cigarette. Shane went in through the rear entrance, past the kitchen where preparations for the evening meal had already started. Elysee was throwing a small dinner party for her charity.

Lola was in the kitchen, confabbing with the executive chef about special dietary restrictions for one of the houseguests they were expecting for the President's visit. She spied Shane and graced him with her usual glare. For some reason, the woman hated him.

"Have you seen Elysee?" he asked Lola.

"I believe she's upstairs in her room."

"Not upstairs, Lola. Here I am."

Shane turned to see Elysee coming into the kitchen.

Their eyes met.

Her automatic smile was the painted-on version she doled out to the media. "Shane," she said. "We need to talk."

His breathing stilled and he felt a supreme sense of calm. "I know."

"Let's go somewhere more private for this conversation."

He realized all the ears in the room were attuned to them. He held a hand out to Elysee. She took it. They turned toward the back door. Shane saw Cal in a corner of the room glaring at him, arms crossed over his chest. When they started out the exit, Cal followed.

"I can handle her security from here." Shane stopped in front of his old partner.

"Can you?" Cal bristled.

Shane narrowed his eyes. "What's that supposed to mean?"

"You can't even hold a gun. How are you going to protect her?" Cal chuffed.

Elysee splayed a hand against Cal's chest. "It's okay. I'll be all right with Shane. We're just going for a stroll around the lake."

The look Cal gave her betrayed the same feelings that stirred inside Shane whenever he looked at Tish. The realization that came to him was sudden but certain. Cal Ackerman was in love with Elysee Benedict. The question was, did Elysee know?

"You've got nothing to fear," he said, reassuring his old partner. "I'll bring her back to you safe and sound."

Cal nodded curtly. "Fifteen minutes. After that, I'm coming after you."

It sounded like a threat. Shane didn't know what to make of this new development. Elysee slipped her arm through Shane's. Cal audibly ground his teeth. He had the feeling Cal would've gladly ripped his throat out.

Neither one of them spoke until they were treading the path leading away from the ranch house and toward the lake—the very place where Shane had proposed.

Elysee took a deep breath and stopped underneath an oak tree overlooking the water. "I don't really know how to say this," she began, but then didn't go on.

He cupped her cheek with his palm. "Whatever you have to say, it's going to be okay."

Her blue eyes, clear and soft, focused on his. "Is it?"

"I promise."

"You're such a good friend; that's why this is so hard for me." She was breaking up with him. He didn't know whether to jump in and help her out, or let her be the one in control.

In the end, he decided she needed to be empowered more than she needed the easy way out. He smiled at her. "No matter what you say next, Elysee, I just want you to know that you'll always be my friend."

"Really?" Her expression was somber.

He leaned down to touch his forehead against hers. "Really."

She exhaled sharply and sank against his chest. "Oh, thank heavens. The last thing I want is to lose your friendship."

"You won't."

She stepped back from the circle of his arms. "You already know what I'm going to say."

He nodded.

"You're still in love with Tish." Elysee's voice caught and her eyes misted with tears.

"Yeah." Darn if he wasn't feeling a little misty himself. "But she doesn't love me anymore."

Elysee laughed.

Confused, Shane tilted his head. "What?"

"You great big fool. She's truly, madly, deeply in love with you."

His heart thumped. "Are you sure?"

"You're not?"

"But I hurt her something terrible."

"She's a forgiving person."

"You really think I have a chance of winning her back?"

"Not as long as I have this on my finger." Elysee twisted off her diamond engagement band. She took his hand, placed the ring in his palm, and closed his fist around it. "Although Daddy's going to be disappointed. He really likes you."

"This isn't about your father."

"I know."

His gaze searched her face. "Elysee," he said and slipped the ring into his pocket. "I'm sorry if I hurt you in any way."

"You didn't hurt me." She smiled warmly. "You gave me a precious gift."

"What's that?" he asked gruffly.

"Unconditional friendship. Unfortunately, we both mistook what we were feeling for love. True love is something deeper," she said softly. "It's what you have with Tish. It's the thing I've been searching for my entire life, but I just haven't been able to find."

"It might be right under your nose," he said.

"What do you mean?" She canted her head.

"Cal Ackerman's in love with you."

Audibly, she sucked in her breath and her eyes brightened. The wind gusted, blew tendrils of blond hair about her face. "Did he say something to you?"

"No."

"Then how do you know there's something there?"

"The look in his eyes, the possessive way he glares at me whenever I touch you. Dead giveaway."

"I'm not sure that's enough to go on."

"It's up to you to find out."

Elysee tapped her foot in frustration. "Why can't men just say what they're feeling?"

"Something in the masculine gene prevents it, I guess," he said, thinking about Tish, about all the things they'd been through, about all the things he'd never been able to say to her but should have.

She snorted. "More like pure hardheaded stubbornness if you ask me."

"How do you feel about Cal?"

"I don't know how I feel about anything right now."

"That's understandable."

"Three days after our official engagement and it's all over." She ruefully shook her head. "My shortest engagement yet."

"Maybe next time, you should just elope." He grinned.

"Maybe I will." She grinned back.

"You're going to find him, Elysee," he reassured her. "The man you're supposed to be with. And when you do, you're going to know with absolute certainty."

"The way you knew about Tish?"

"Yeah." His voice cracked oddly.

"What happened between you two? What was it that broke apart a love that seemed so strong?"

Shane couldn't answer that. He couldn't tell her about Johnny. It was too painful. Instead, he shook his head. "I lost my faith in love."

She touched his shoulder. "We all have crises of faith."

"Not you. Not about love. That's one of the things that I admire most about you. Your resilience, your unwavering belief in happily ever after."

"Some people call it romantic foolishness."

"They're wrong. You gave me hope. You gave me back

my faith. And that's a gift I'll never forget." He leaned down and kissed her cheek. "Thank you."

He straightened and she beamed up at him, her warm smile filling his heart with their special friendship.

"We better get back," she said. "You've got something very important you have to do."

"What's that?" he asked.

"Go find Tish and tell her everything she needs to hear."

While Shane and Elysee were walking around the lake, Tish had returned to the ranch to retrieve her camera equipment and her clothes and get the hell out of there before she ran across her ex-husband and his bride-to-be. She hurried past the Secret Service agent positioned in the hallway near her bedroom. She found the montage of photos of Shane and Elysee spread out on the desk the way she'd left them that morning.

Seeing their happy faces was a knife to her gut. How was she ever going to put this video together? Looking at the pictures over and over, feeling that constant weight on her heartstrings would be torture.

The sudden urge to go shopping was overwhelming.

No, no. That was a cop-out. She knew it now. Shopping was the way she'd smothered her feelings. No more smothering. No more denial. She would embrace the pain. It was the only way through it.

You can do this. You're not a coward. See this thing through.

Once and for all, she would prove she was a consummate professional. Nothing was going to stop her.

Haphazardly, she tucked the pictures back into the

photo albums. She grabbed the stack and stood up. A clipping floated out, drifted to the floor.

Tish leaned over to pick up the piece of paper.

It was an article from *People* magazine about the backhoe accident on the UT campus. The headline read SECRET SERVICE AGENT SAVES FIRST DAUGHTER'S LIFE.

There was a photograph of Shane lying in a hospital bed looking frail and pale. His head was shaved, his scars fresh. The picture hit her with a visceral punch. Bile rose in her throat and her body went cold all over. For the first time she recognized how close Shane had truly come to dying.

Tish couldn't bear looking at the photograph, seeing him so helpless. That wasn't her husband. That wasn't her Shane. Breathing heavily, she flipped the clipping over, pressed the article facedown on the desk.

Resolutely, she again hoisted the photo albums in her arms. As she did, her gaze slid over the flip side of the *People* article.

It was a piece about an Indian woman working with the WorldFem organization to put a stop to the horrific practice of honor killings. Because of her work, she'd been placed on a death list, targeted by an assassin. Tish's eyes drifted to the photograph. She'd seen this woman before.

At Shane and Elysee's engagement party.

A thought stirred at the back of her mind, not yet fully formed. Yes, this was definitely the woman she'd seen. Could this woman be the key to why someone had tried to steal her disk?

Pondering that question, Tish took the third copy of the disk from her purse and slipped it into the camera, which was hooked to the DVD player. Seconds later, she was reliving the engagement party.

Fast-forward through the pomp and circumstance. Fast-forward through Shane giving Elysee the ring and kissing her. Fast-forward through Nathan Benedict announcing their engagement. Fast-forward past the congratulatory toasts.

To the part Tish was searching for.

Elysee was surrounded by well-wishers, blushing prettily, innocently. Then the camera caught a furtive woman wearing a scarf over her head hovering in the shadows. Tish watched as Elysee made her excuses, slipped through the crowd, headed toward the woman. They shook hands and Elysee led her through the French doors and out onto the patio.

Her pulse quickened. She didn't even remember filming this. Her mind must have been too befuddled by the engagement.

The camera angle swung away from Elysee to put Shane in the foreground. He was talking to Cal Ackerman. The camera lingered longingly on his face, spelling out for anyone who wasn't too blind to see that the person behind the camera was hung up on her subject.

Tish yanked her eyes off Shane and searched the background. Dammit. There wasn't any more footage of Elysee.

Wait, wait. There it was. Out on the patio when she'd accidentally left the camera on without knowing it.

It was the mystery woman and Elysee was handing her something. Was the footage of this woman the real reason someone had wanted her disk in the first place?

Tish had no answers. None of it seemed to have anything to do with someone burning down her apartment.

Were the two incidents even connected? She rewound the tape.

The camera moved again, back to focus on Shane. Was she besotted with the man or what? There were other people in the frame behind Shane. The Ambassador from India was speaking in a language she vaguely recognized as Hindi, to a man who had his back to the camera. They were both eyeing Rana Singh.

She still didn't get it. Something was going on, but it was over her head. Whatever was on this disk held no meaning for her, but it definitely meant something to the person who was on it.

"Turn off the video and eject the disk," a voice from the doorway commanded. Too late, she realized she'd left the door to her bedroom ajar.

Startled, Tish turned and immediately let out a gasp of shocked surprise.

For there, pointed at her face, was the business end of a very large handgun with a silencer attached to it.

Chapter 20

Pete Larkin motioned toward Tish. "Hand me the disk."

"What?"

"Don't make me shoot you."

"Who are you? What do you want?" she asked.

"Just the disk."

"Why would you want the disk of the engagement party unless—"

"I'm on it and it's not a flattering camera angle," he growled. "Give me the disk."

"You speak Hindi," she said, as a terrible thought took root in the back of her mind. Larkin was the man talking to the Indian Ambassador on the tape.

"Fluently."

"You've been to India."

"Many times.

"Oh my God," Tish gasped as her suspicions crystallized. "You're the death squad assassin I read about in

People magazine hired to kill Rana Singh. That's why you want the disk. It can incriminate you."

"Ding, ding, she's smarter than she looks, folks." Larkin ripped the disk from her hand and stuffed it in his front pocket then lowered his gun, pressing it firmly against her rib cage.

"Pick up your car keys," he commanded, nodding to where they rested on the desk.

Once she had the keys in her hand, he took the gym towel that was slung around his neck and used it to cover the gun in his hand. He wrapped his arm around Tish's shoulder.

"Here's what's going to happen," he said. "We're going out the side exit. If we meet someone on the way out and you give any indication of what's going on, I'll kill them. Got it?"

Tish nodded. She had no reason to doubt his sincerity. The cold, calculating look in his eyes told her he was very capable of carrying out his threat.

"Walk at a steady pace, neither too fast nor too slow," he instructed. "When we get outside, walk to your car, get in on the passenger side, and scoot over behind the wheel. Now let's go."

He muscled her out of the room and forced her to walk down the corridor beside him. Larkin had slung his arm around her waist, his gun pressed icily into her side.

Tish had fleeting thoughts of escape, but before she could even form a plan, Larkin whispered, "Forget about trying to make a run for it. I have no compunction about shooting you here if I must."

The flagstone walkway was wet from water sprinkler overspray. Now Larkin's other hand was at the back of her neck and he was pushing on her spine with his thumb, keeping her in line by putting pressure on her nerve endings. He guided her around to the back of the house where visitors parked in a covered lot.

"You're doing fine. Just keep it up."

When they reached the Acura she did as he'd instructed, getting in on the passenger side, sliding over to the driver's seat. He slid in after her, never taking the gun from her side.

"When we get to the security checkpoint, give a friendly little wave and keep driving. The guards don't pay as much attention to who's leaving as to who's coming in. If you so much as raise an eyebrow I'll kill you both. Do I make myself clear?"

"Yes."

"Good. Now drive."

"You're not going to get away with this, you know. There are cameras hidden all over the place. When I don't come back, the Secret Service will review the security tapes and hunt you down."

"Wrong. I'm CIA. I know exactly where the security cameras are and how to disable them," he bragged.

"If you're CIA, how come you're working as a physical therapist at the President's ranch house? Not much foreign intelligence going on in Katy, Texas. Doesn't seem like a job they'd give to their best agent."

His scowl deepened. "I got sent here when Elysee was engaged to her previous fiancé, Yuri Borshevsky. He had KGB ties. Someone had to keep an eye on him—since I speak twelve languages including Russian and Hindi, guess who got picked?"

"Still, it seems like a menial assignment. Babysitting, almost."

"It is." Larkin gritted his teeth. Clearly this was a touchy subject. "Now shut your mouth and drive."

Her life was in her own hands. She had to do something to get away from him or he was going to kill her. Of that she had absolutely no doubt.

Drive off the road.

"If you try to drive off the road," he said, reading her mind, "you'll be dead before your head hits the steering wheel."

"Lovely imagery. Thanks for that."

"Just wanted to let you know I'm not screwing around."

"There's one problem with your threat."

"And what's that?"

"If you kill me now you'll never know who all I gave copies of the disks to."

"You made copies?" His voice hardened.

"Lots of them."

"You're lying."

"Are you willing to take that gamble?" She snuck a glance at him. His eyes narrowed, glaring, and his jaw tightened. She could see his mental cogs turning.

He swore violently and pressed the gun against her temple. "Who else has copies?"

The feel of the end of the gun against her head was more chilling than finding a rattlesnake in her bed. Her body went cold with fear; her fingers blanched white on the steering wheel. Her mind raced desperately around the possible avenues of escape.

Stay calm. You've got to stay calm or you're lost.

"We're in traffic. Someone could see you with that gun pressed to my head and call 9-1-1," she said quietly. "Why don't you put it out of sight?"

She could tell it irritated him to have to do what she said, but she also knew she'd made an excellent point. He slid the gun down the side of her head, past her neck, and repositioned it against her rib cage. It was only slightly less terrifying there than having it pointed at her skull.

"Hang a left at this next traffic light and remember my finger is on the trigger. You make a wrong move and the gun goes off."

"And you've got one hell of a mess to deal with."

"I've dealt with worse."

"Still," she said, struggling to keep hysteria at bay by sounding flippant and carefree. "You'll never know how many copies of the disk I made."

"It's a risk I'm willing to take. In fact, I think you're lying. I don't think you made any copies at all."

"But you'll never know for sure."

"Oh, I'm sure I know a way to persuade you to talk." His voice sounded so sinister, she dared a quick glimpse at him. His features were maniacal, and she knew this was no mission sanctioned by the CIA. He had to be a rogue agent who'd lost all sense of boundaries. One look at his ominous face and she knew he was talking about torture. Horror sickened her stomach. She had no doubt he was completely capable of carrying out such an awful deed.

Please don't let me throw up, she prayed.

She had mistakenly thought that by telling him she'd made copies of the disk he would spare her life, because there was no way of knowing whether she was telling the truth or not. She'd never counted on torture. If this deranged lunatic tortured her, she knew she would end up telling him anything he wanted to hear. Including the fact that she'd given a disk to Elysee.

Dear Lord, she'd placed the President's daughter squarely in the line of fire.

You have to get away from him. It's the only chance you have. It's the only chance Elysee has.

"Take the overpass," he instructed. "Drive at the speed limit. Not one mile above or below."

"Where are we going?" she asked, really not wanting to hear the answer but frantic for some kind of information that would help her form a plan.

"To the shipping channel. To the docks."

"Why are we going there?"

"Not that it's any of your business, but I've already made arrangements for the disposal of two bodies. A third corpse shouldn't pose much in the way of an added inconvenience." His grin was pure evil. "There's a lot of places to torture someone down along the waterfront where screams go unheard."

After his talk with Elysee, Shane hurried to Tish's bedroom to tell her that they'd broken the engagement, but she wasn't there. He went in search of anyone who might know where Tish had gone. The place was in a bustle because the President was coming in. He couldn't find any staff members who'd seen her.

Until he spoke to one of the valets, who told Shane he'd seen Tish get into her car with a man just a few minutes earlier. Shane pressed for a description but the valet said he hadn't been close enough to get a good look at the guy.

Shane thought about phoning Cal, but hesitated. He no longer had any idea who he could trust. For all he knew, Cal could be behind the arson fire. He hated to believe it of his former partner, but at this point, everyone who'd been staying at the ranch that had been at the engagement party was suspect. Especially Cal, since he smoked and had access to those matches. Especially since Shane had seen bits of red lava rocks—the very same red lava gravel that was in the garden outside Tish's apartment—underneath Cal's shoes in the limo the night of the fire.

Call Tish.

But, of course. He was so frantic with worry, he hadn't thought of the simplest solution first. He went into Tish's bedroom, picked up the cordless phone, and called his cell.

It rang six times, then switched to voice mail. He left a message asking her to call him immediately and hung up. That's when he realized Tish's camera was hooked up to the computer monitor and photos were scattered across the desk.

Tish might be a little flighty at times, but when it came to her work, she was a dedicated professional. She would never have gone off and left her camera on or her editing equipment strewn around. He examined the camera and saw the disk was missing.

Alarm jolted through him.

He stabbed his fingers through his hair, blew out his breath and let out a short but emphatic curse. Something had happened to interrupt Tish from her work. Where had she gone?

And with whom?

He pivoted. On his way back out the door he saw a decorative glass bowl filled with the same matchbooks Dick Tracy had found at the scene of the fire. He scooped up a handful as he went past and stuffed them into his pocket, convinced they held the key to the person with whom Tish had gone.

His training told him not to jump to conclusions, but his gut told him his fears were valid. Someone had taken Tish and her camera disk from the engagement party, he guessed. And he feared it was someone who meant her serious harm.

Shane's father had taught him that in times of crisis he should always listen to his gut and not to his head. Listening to his head had sent him walking out on his marriage when he should have paid attention to what his gut had told him.

Instinctively convinced Tish was no longer on the ranch, he raced back to his Durango, got in and zoomed to the security checkpoint at the front gate. The guards had changed shifts, so the officer in the guard shack hadn't seen Tish leave, but it had been logged in that Tish and a passenger had left the grounds seventy minutes earlier.

"Passenger?" Shane asked of the guard. "Who was the passenger?"

"It doesn't say here, sir."

"Male? Female?"

The guard lifted his shoulders in a helpless gesture. "No notation was made regarding the sex of the passenger in the car with Ms. Gallagher. Would you like me to call the other guards at home?"

"No." Shane didn't have time for that. Besides, he had another plan. He would track her via the GPS device in his cell phone. Wherever she was, he could target her location.

Once he had a plan of action, Shane calmed. He would find her and when he got hold of the sonofabitch who'd taken her, his retribution would be both swift and relentless.

He felt a surge of protectiveness for Tish unlike anything he'd ever felt before. It was far stronger than his sense of duty, far deeper than his patriotism and his honor code. It wasn't about revenge. This wasn't about his ego. This was about Tish's safety. She needed him—this time, he was determined to be there for her.

The sun was slipping down to the horizon as Larkin shoved Tish ahead of him through the maze of shipping pods lining the docks. Huge freighters lay tied up at their berths. There was a lot of activity around the new arrivals, but Larkin stayed clear of those areas, guiding her farther and farther away from any dockworkers and her possible salvation.

Larkin shunted her down dark and musty rows of heavy metal containers, and the smell of fish and brackish water was thick in her nose. With all the noise and hustle, it was doubtful anyone would have heard her cry for help. The gun poking hard into her back deterred Tish from even trying to call out.

Finally, he told her to stop beside one of the pods positioned right at the edge of the water. "Open it up," he said.

Oh God, was this where he was going to torture her and kill her? Was this pod to be her coffin?

She hesitated, unable to make herself open the door.

He jabbed her in the spine with his gun. "Do it."

She obeyed his demand, struggling to unlatch the heavy metal door. As she worked on it, his pager went off. Cursing, he tugged it off his waistband and squinted at the display. For a brief second his concentration left her and went to the pager. Her eyes went to the water: If she jumped off the pier could she swim away from him?

Or would she simply be a sitting duck in the water, a perfect target for his bullets?

"Sonofabitch."

"What is it?"

"The President is arriving at the ranch in an hour and he wants a training session and a massage when he gets there," Larkin fumed. "He treats me like I'm his frickin' servant."

"Well, he is the President of the United States."

"Like I have time for this crap."

"You better show up. If you don't, someone might get suspicious of your whereabouts," Tish said.

He cursed again. "Okay, in you go."

"What?"

"The pod." He waved his gun. "Get in there."

"But it's dark inside." She peered nervously into the black depths. "It smells like mice."

"You'd rather I just shoot you now?"

"I'm in." Tish hopped into the pod.

Larkin slammed the door on her and turned the lock. She pressed her ear against the door, straining for the sound of his footfalls walking away.

He was gone.

Relief weakened her limbs and she sank to the floor of the pod, wrapping her arms around herself to stem the uncontrollable shaking that suddenly gripped her body.

Inside the shipping container was airless and empty. Tish had never known darkness could be so deep and black, except for in her own mind, in her soul, after she'd lost the baby.

And then she'd lost Shane.

Mentally, she had whirled out of control, spinning

wildly, madly—a dizzying dance of consumer excess. Buying, shopping, throwing away money. Until she'd lost momentum and like a wobbly dreidel, fallen over, top-heavy, spent and out of balance.

Time passed.

She didn't have any idea how long it was. It could have been mere seconds. It could have been a dozen hours. She might have dozed. She might have only hallucinated that she dozed. She might have dreamed that she hallucinated about dozing. The isolation and visual deprivation were disorienting.

I'm going to die. I'm going to die in here alone without ever telling Shane that I still love him.

Shane arrived at the docks just after dusk. The location scared the hell out of him. He knew someone could easily go missing down here. He found the Acura parked behind an abandoned warehouse on the far side of the shipping channel.

That's where his search ended, when he peered in the window and spied the cell phone he'd given Tish lying on the console. Shane's gut spoke to him, and it was yelling some pretty ugly things.

You weren't there for her when she needed you most, Tremont. Face it, you failed her. If she dies, it's all your fault.

He gulped. Guilt and fear hitched a ride from his throat to his stomach and settled in like bad indigestion. He stepped away from the car, eyes scanning the night, senses attuned for danger. His Sig Sauer was nestled in its shoulder holster, but it gave him little comfort. Fear badgered him, too. *What are you going to do? Shoot with your left hand?*

Yes.

Your target better be as wide as a Wal-Mart.

He heard a sound in the darkness behind him. He whirled, simultaneously reaching for his gun, but his reaction time was too slow.

"Got the draw on you, Tremont," said a voice from the darkness. "Throw down your weapon."

"What the hell is going on here? Who are you? Where's my wife?" Shane demanded, searching the shadows for a face.

Surprise tripped down his spine when he saw Pete Larkin emerge with his own Sig Sauer pointed at Shane's head.

"Throw it down," Larkin repeated. "You're worthless with the thing anyway. I know what kind of shape your hand is in."

"What are you doing, Larkin?"

"Stop yapping and do it." Shane tossed his weapon on the ground. Larkin retrieved it and tucked it in his waistband.

Rage engulfed Shane, red-hot and blind. It wasn't long ago that he could have as easily killed Larkin as look at him. "What the hell is wrong with you? Where's Tish? Is she alive? If you've done anything to her, I swear I'll kill you."

"Don't sweat it. I'll take you to her. Reunite the lovebirds. Put your palms on the back of your head, turn around, and start walking toward the water."

Calm down. You're no good to Tish in an irrational state. Remember your training. Detach from your emotions.

"What's this about?" he asked, struggling to keep his

voice calm when he wanted nothing more than to launch himself at Larkin and rip his throat out.

"Something you shouldn't have gotten involved in. It was none of your damn business. Nothing to do with you. Either one of you."

"Clearly." Shane's mind was racing as he tried to formulate a plan. He didn't want to act too prematurely, didn't want to disable Larkin before the man led him to Tish. "Who are you working for?"

"CIA."

"Fucking spook."

"You think that's an insult?" Larkin laughed. "Take a left at the next shipping container and don't try anything or I'll blow your kneecaps off."

"You don't scare me."

"Then you're very stupid. I have no problem with killing anyone who gets in my way."

"I'm guessing your superior officers have no idea what you're up to. Since when is a wedding videographer a threat to national security?"

"Those spineless pencil pushers. Please. They don't have a clue what it's really like out here in the field."

"What did Tish do to deserve this?"

"She took my fucking picture."

"And?"

"She got my voice on tape."

"Sounds like your fault for doing business in a public place."

"It was Sumat Kumar's idea," he grumbled.

"The Indian Ambassador?"

"He wanted the meeting at the engagement party so I could see Rana Singh."

"He hired you to assassinate Elysee's former nanny?"

"And some rebellious Indian chick whose father is some kind of cabinet minister in India. He wanted her dead for marrying a guy he didn't approve of." He smirked. "Imagine if we had honor killings in the States. All the teenage girls would be dead."

"So what were you getting out of the deal?" Shane asked, as his mind frantically tried to come up with a plan. The only reason Larkin would be telling him all this was if he intended to kill him.

"Besides a shitload of money, you mean?"

"Besides that."

Larkin smirked again. "Kumar's promised to give me detailed info on their nuke capacity. The CIA won't give me another shit babysitting assignment like Yuri Borshevsky after I drop that little Turkish delight in their lap."

"All this for two honor killings?"

"These dudes are rabid about keeping the practice alive. They don't want their women getting uppity."

"So you're just going to kill these women in cold blood for your personal gain?"

"Shut up, Eagle Scout, and take a right."

Shane did as Larkin said, his mind in high gear as he mentally tried out several possible ways to overpower the other agent. But every idea he formulated would have to wait until he found out what Larkin had done with Tish.

They stopped next to a padlocked shipping pod sitting near the edge of the dock. Larkin pulled a set of keys from his pocket, tossed them to Shane. He reached for them with his bad hand and missed. They fell to the dock.

"Pick them up."

He did.

"Third key on the ring."

He found the key.

"Open the pod."

He did.

"Get inside." Larkin snatched back the keys.

Shane walked in, fully expecting to be shot in the back of the head. But to his surprised relief, Larkin slammed the door and locked him up inside.

Chapter 21

Tish woke with a start when the door opened. She was curled into a ball on the floor and by the time she jerked her head around, the door had closed again.

But someone was in here with her. She could hear them breathing.

"Hello," she whispered. "Is someone there?"

"Tish?"

The sound of her ex-husband's voice sent joyous rapture reeling through her heart. "Shane!"

They found each other in the dark, mouths melding, arms embracing.

"Tish, Tish, you're alive. You're okay." He rained kisses on her face.

"How did you find me?"

"Through the GPS tracking in my cell phone."

"Larkin got you, too?"

"Yeah, I didn't see it coming. I had feared it was Cal Ackerman who'd torched your house—he had red lava rocks in the tread of his shoes and he smokes. I never suspected Larkin."

"I don't understand what's going on."

He told her then about his talk with Dick Tracy; the matches, the lava gravel; how Larkin revealed he had agreed to assassinate Rana Singh and Alma Reddy for Sumat Kumar in exchange for cash and detailed information about India's nuclear weapon capacities.

"Larkin got a beeper message that the President wanted a workout session and a massage at the ranch. That's probably where he was headed when he left here. If he didn't go, he'd blow his cover. I suppose you ran into him on his way out."

"Yeah."

"I told him I made copies of the disk."

Shane made a disturbing noise. "Did you?"

"Yeah."

"How many?"

"Two. One burned in the fire and Larkin took my copy."

"Who has the other one?"

"Elysee."

He made that noise again, clearly frustrated.

"I know."

"Larkin will be back as soon as he completes his obligation to the President. It's an hour to the ranch and an hour back. A workout session and massage will last a couple of hours. We have about four hours to come up with a plan to defeat him or we're dead," Shane said.

They fell silent.

"We're stuck here," she said after a long while.

"We'll probably die here."

"At least I'm with you," she whispered.

He held her close and she listened to the steady strum of his heartbeat. In spite of her fear she was overjoyed to be held in his arms once again, if only for a little while.

"We might as well sit down," he said. "I have a feeling we're going to be here for a while."

They settled in on the hard, cold metal floor and he tucked her into the crook of his arm.

Emotion knotted up tight inside her. There was so much she wanted to say to him, but she had no idea where to start. She lay with her head pressed against his chest, feeling his warmth, listening to the beat of his heart.

"Shane," she whispered.

"Yes."

"I need to talk."

"What about?"

"You, me, the divorce . . . Johnny."

He didn't say anything.

"You still can't talk about your feelings? Even with two years' distance?" She heard his ragged intake of breath. She waited. Finally, finally, when she'd just about given up, he spoke.

"It hurt me deep, Tish, that you wouldn't talk to me about the credit card trouble you were in. Why did you hide it? I was your husband. It was my job to help."

"I didn't talk to you because you shut me out!"

"How did I do that?"

"With impossibly high standards. Perfect credit scores and checkbook balanced to the penny. It was overwhelming. You were overwhelming."

"You honestly believed I would put money above your feelings?" He sounded stunned.

"I was afraid you would judge me harshly and I didn't want to disappoint you, Shane. What can I say? I hid the debt from you because I was ashamed." She paused, struggling hard not to cry.

"Tish." The whisper of her name twisted from his

throat. She heard the anguish in it and a corresponding pain settled over her heart. "I really let you down."

"No more than I did you."

"Explain it to me now. Why did you buy all those things? Why did you rack up credit card charges we couldn't afford? Help me to understand."

"If I knew the answer to that then I wouldn't have done it, or I could have stopped."

"Was it to fill some kind of emotional void? Did it have something to do with your childhood? Was it about your mother emphasizing the importance of latching on to a man with money?"

"Partially, I'm sure."

"What else?"

"What do you mean?"

"Was I the cause in some way?"

"I don't know."

She wished she could see his face. His voice hitched. "I felt so betrayed when the creditors started calling and I found out exactly how much in debt you'd sunk us. Those cards were in my name, Tish. It was my account. I was responsible. You went behind my back and sullied my name."

"Well, you like being responsible," she snapped. "Why was it such a problem?"

"Was that the way you wanted me to feel? Like you'd cheated on me? Were you trying to get back at me for not being there when you went into labor with Johnny?"

"I don't know," she repeated.

"I think you do know. Maybe not on a conscious level, but maybe subconsciously you were trying to get back at me for not being there when you needed me most."

"No, subconsciously you're feeling guilty for not

being there when I needed you most. Don't project your guilt onto me."

"If that's not it, then what were you getting back at me for?"

"I wasn't getting back at you. I was just trying to relieve my own pain." Her voice cracked loud and echoed off the metal walls of the pitch-black shipping container. "You didn't even seem to notice how I was suffering. You forgot about Johnny so easily."

"You're wrong. I didn't forget." His tone was brittle.

"You made me take apart the nursery before I was ready to let go. You never talked about him. You cut me off whenever I tried to talk about him."

"Tish, I couldn't talk about him. I'm the strong one. I'm the protector. Don't you get it? If I talked about him, I couldn't have stayed strong for you."

"Dammit, Shane, that's the problem. You want to take care of everyone. Like you're ten feet tall and bulletproof. But if you're always the strong one, your loved ones never get the chance to prove their strength, or to help you. It's lopsided and unfair."

Silence stretched in the void of darkness.

"I never thought of it that way."

"Well, think about it. You grew up with all that flag waving, gotta-live-up-to-the-family-legends-and-be-a-hero stuff. Not that you shouldn't be proud of your family history, but come on, nobody can live up to all that hype. By always striving to be this great heroic figure, you never let yourself be a real human being with less than honorable impulses."

"I struggle plenty with my less than honorable impulses," he said. "I just try not to show it."

"But that's what you've got to do! Let me see that my

big hero is reluctant once in a while. That he's conflicted over his decisions. That he's not some frickin' perfect Dudley Do-Right who makes everyone else feel like dirty rotten scoundrels because they can't live up to his standards."

"You mean like this?" Even in the complete blackness, his mouth found hers with unerring accuracy.

The minute their lips touched, Tish was electrified. She felt like a desert flower joyfully blooming after a rare soaking rain. God, how she'd missed him!

Their tongues met, starving, two years without this delicious meal. They kissed and kissed and kissed. The joining of their mouths was more intense than that night on the ferry. This was a kiss of reunion.

Of forgiveness.

Of coming home.

They melted into each other, eyesight cloaked by the blanket of blackness. But they didn't need to see. They knew each other so well: by touch and taste, smell and sound.

She uttered a low sound and slipped her arms around his neck. His fingers knotted in her hair, his energy blazed as hot as her own. They were tuned to the same frequency, both vibrating with heightened awareness of each other.

The ridges and swirls in her fingertips traced the landscape of his face as they kissed; absorbing the subtle yet distinct changes in terrain from the apples of his cheeks to the hollows below. She moved, feeling the shape of his head like a sculptor. Her fingers traveled over him with complex precision, felt with delicate, indefinable intuition. She ran her hand through his hair and traced the ridge of the scar at his temple.

Wounds.

They both had so many wounds.

How different things might have been if they could have had this conversation two years ago. If they'd both been able to find balance in their lives.

Transcended. She was transcended and emotionally reborn.

Balance.

It was what she'd been after all along. With balance came closure.

Closure. It was where Elysee had been trying to lead her. She'd found it now, in this dark container, with her ex-husband, whom she still loved with all her heart but was finally able to let go on to his new beginning.

He kissed her harder, as if sensing her changing mood, pulling her back with him to the passion, to the flame. His tongue swept her up in a divine pleasure that she'd thought lost to her forever.

It was as thrilling now as it had been before. Maybe even sweeter now, because of what they'd been through, of all that they'd suffered.

His hand snaked up underneath her shirt and he ran his hot palm up her belly. She moaned softly, encouraging him, shooting the rapids of desire, riding the river of reward. She didn't care if this was right or wrong. She wanted him.

Tingles of anticipation started at the base of her neck, crept across her face, over her scalp, darted along her shoulders, trickled down her arms and finally shuddered softly down her spine.

She sat in his lap, between his spread thighs: such big, muscular thighs, full of power and promise.

He tried to pull her shirt over her head with his injured hand, but he kept dropping the hem. "Dammit," he swore.

"Shh," she said. "Let me."

Stripping off her shirt and then unhooking her bra, she flung her garments away.

"Ah," he said. In the darkness, his mouth found the hardening tip of her nipple. Tish sucked in her breath at the delicious shock of his warm moistness suckling her tender breast.

He curved one arm around her waist, pulling her closer against him. She sighed as a strange blend of electricity and chemistry fused with her emotions and sent a surge of bittersweet pleasure flashing through her.

The blackness surrounded them, encompassed them, defined them. She could feel his erection through the material of his pants, prodding against her pelvis. He rubbed his beard-stubbled jaw along her sternum, his mouth seeking her other nipple. The sensation sent a fresh set of chills tripping over her spine.

He pulled lightly on her nipple and she sank closer to him, pressing her pelvis into the seam of his jeans. She pressed her head alongside his, nuzzling him like a colt. He laughed and the sound was of delight.

He went for her lips again, but in this sightless chamber ended up kissing the tip of her nose.

She had been so foolish. So blind. To her faults and motivations, to his needs and expectations.

All this time, she'd fled from him. She'd hidden from him in shopping malls and behind cash registers. She'd run away down the long corridor of the past two years, through the labyrinth of her own distrustful mind.

Run away, not just from him, but from her betrayal of him. Of what she had done to their marriage. Run from the searing pain of loss. All this time wasted. All this extra heartache because she hadn't had the courage to face her emotional pain, accept it and move through it.

By diverting her mind from the truth with shopping sprees and spending binges, she'd never given herself permission to heal. She'd frittered away money to lift her spirits, to stuff up the holes in her heart. But there was no stuffing up the holes with pretty clothes and designer shoes. No easing of her sorrow, just a numbing of her soul.

"Tish," he whispered and she felt his body tense. "What is it? What's wrong?"

"Johnny," she whispered. "All these mistakes were from losing Johnny."

She cried then, fully, completely grieving for the lost child who'd vanished before he'd ever really been theirs.

Shane held Tish tight and just let her cry, being strong for her now in a way he hadn't been before. Not trying to soothe her, just letting her go with it. Letting her feel the grief.

The next thing he knew, he was crying, too. His body shook with great, silent sobs.

They held on to each other in exquisite agony. In their pain, they came together.

United.

"I'm sorry, I'm so, so sorry, sweetheart. I'm so sorry I failed you."

She clung to him and he to her. He rocked her in his lap, her bare breasts against his chest.

Through the glaze of his sorrow-soaked heart, Shane began to feel something more. Something beyond the anguish stirred. Something primal and rich, life at its most organic.

Their chances of getting out of this alive were slim. Death lay so very close by. But if he had to die, at least he was with Tish.

Paradoxically, in these last moments of impending annihilation, Shane had never felt more alive. He realized that before now the very thing that had most appealed to him about Tish was also the thing he had feared most. Her passion.

If he succumbed to passionate love, along with its acceptance he must give up the notion of free will and self-control.

He'd tried to avoid losing control when they were married. Encouraging her to clamp down on her feelings, to sweep under the rug any emotions he found too disturbing. He'd been wrong about that.

Shane found her lips by sliding his mouth from the top of her head downward, kissing everything he found along the way. Her forehead, an eyebrow, the bridge of her nose.

Intensity rose off her like heat from a radiator. Her skin quivered beneath his fingertips. He fumbled out of his clothes and she shimmied from hers—both panting, both aware of every nuance, every sound, every scent in the darkness.

Once they were totally, gloriously naked and lying side by side on a bed of their piled clothing, he draped his wounded hand across the dip of her waist and tugged her against him.

"We shouldn't be doing this, Shane. It would kill Elysee if she knew."

"Didn't I mention Elysee and I broke up?"

"You did not."

"I meant to the minute I found you. I guess I got distracted."

"Who broke it off? You or Elysee?"

"We both did. We realized what we had was nothing more than a strong friendship. And I realized something else."

"What was that?"

"I never stopped loving you."

"I never stopped loving you."

Joy saturated his bones, pumped through his heart, hummed in his veins. He had her back!

She kissed his chin. He relished the sweet caress of her tongue. Her touch went straight to his brain, spun magic.

"I haven't made love to another woman since the last time I made love to you," he whispered, breathing in the scent of her silky hair.

"Not with Elysee?"

"We haven't shared anything more than kisses. It's like being in some damned Regency romance novel," he said.

"Good, because I haven't been with anyone else either," she confessed. "No one else could measure up to you."

"Oh, Tish." He squeezed her tight, buried his face in her hair.

He kissed her again because he couldn't help himself. He didn't want to help himself. She was all around him. His nose filled with her spicy scent. The sound of her quickened breathing was in his ears. The feel of her smooth, high breasts pressed against his. He had to have her or die.

Desire ignited, surged through his blood, snatching him up on a swell of love.

This felt too right. Too good. Too damn vital to be the wrong thing.

She kept kissing him, doing incredible things with her devilish tongue. God, how he'd missed kissing her. He groaned loudly and plunged his fingers through her hair.

His penis ached, hard and taut, surging in anticipation. Hungry for the caress of her fingertips. If they were going to die, he wanted to die with Tish embedded in his brain while he was embedded inside of her.

She licked a heated trail down his throat to his chest and playfully nibbled at a nipple. Shane sucked in a deep breath and forgot all about dying. Every cell, every nerve fiber in his body was attuned to what was happening between them.

His balls pulled up hard against his shaft, crying out for her attention. His breathing shortened, quickened. As if reading his mind, she reached down to gently stroke the head of him, her whisper-soft fingertips gliding over his skin.

Helplessly, he thrust his pelvis forward, pushing his penis against her palm.

Tish murmured a sound of feminine power. It was hard for him to let her take the lead, but he knew they both needed it this way. Her, so she could feel strong again. Him, so he could let his needs be met rather than having to be the one to always meet her needs. She needed to be needed. It was finally dawning on him how much power he'd denied her by insisting on taking care of her. He was just now learning that it was okay to be helpless once in a while. To let someone else take the wheel.

Her lips engulfed his erection, her tongue performing

magic against his aroused flesh. He groaned aloud. All this time without her. God, he'd been such a damnable, proud fool.

His heart pounded, his excitement intensified. He suddenly felt shy and unsure. What was the protocol here? There were no rules for this. No code of behavior to follow.

"Shh," she murmured, briefly breaking contact. "Let go, relax. For once just let me take care of you."

Reeling from the rush of it all, Shane surrendered his need for control and let Tish have her way.

Soon, he felt his climax rising, pushing up through him. Tish must have sensed it, too, because she broke contact, dragging her moist warm lips from his engorged penis.

She straddled him, her soft inner thighs rubbing against his hips. He gasped, but she dropped her mouth on his, silencing him in a rush of red-hot kisses.

His Tish, just as daring and passionate as always. Damn, he wished he could see her.

Chuckling deep in her throat, she rocked back on her knees, took him in the palm of her hand, guiding his throbbing head into her slippery crease. His hands went to her waist. His right hand couldn't grip her tightly, but he was holding her nonetheless. That little miracle was all he'd really needed.

He raised his trembling hand and curved it around her breast. The weight of it felt glorious against his savaged palm. "Such breasts," he murmured. "Such beautiful, beautiful breasts."

Tish cupped her hand around his hand cradling her breast and slowly, she began to move. "My wounded warrior," she whispered. "My big, strong, wounded man."

She moved up and down in a languid rhythm, halting her upward momentum only when it seemed he would fall from her velvet clutches. Down and up. Down and up again.

Her tempo increased. Shane stiffened. He was close. On the edge of explosion. He felt the current of it start deep inside him, rising up on a torrent of release.

He felt her tense as her internal muscles began their rhythmic squeeze. She hugged him inside her, held him close as the clutching spasms of her orgasm gripped him, too.

And in one hot, spectacular gush they came together. The simultaneous release rippled through them like ocean waves against rocky shores.

Tish collapsed against his chest, their bodies slick with the aftersheen of great lovemaking. He wrapped his arms around her as their hearts slammed against their chests and their breathing came in hungry gasps.

He buried his face in her hair, inhaled the sweet, honest scent of her. He'd never felt as vulnerable as he did in this moment of reunion, and yet he'd never felt more invincible.

This wasn't mere lust he felt. It wasn't just love. They were bonded for life. Even if stupidity and blind grief over losing their son had separated them for two long years, they'd never really been apart. He knew it now. They were connected on an eternal level that mistakes and heartaches could not destroy. They were two parts of a single beating heart.

Now and forever.

Then he realized something profound. Their separation had been necessary for them both to grow to this point. They'd had to be apart in order to learn the lessons they were supposed to learn. They'd rushed their relationship before, letting chemistry and passion sweep them past the getting to know you stage.

If Tish hadn't become pregnant, they wouldn't have married as quickly as they had. Shane had never regretted marrying her, not even in those bleak days after the baby's death. What he did regret was letting his pride and guilt get in the way of what had been truly important. He'd been so ashamed that he hadn't been there for her when she'd needed him most, that he'd let her down in the most fundamental way; he'd turned away from her emotionally. In doing so, he'd pushed her to desperate measures.

It was difficult for him to admit his weakness, but he needed Tish. Without her, he was out of balance, as she was without him. He felt the message sear into his soul.

In that moment, he realized something else. He'd become involved with Elysee because of that deep longing to be connected again. But he'd never been connected with her. He'd picked Elysee because she was safe. With her he would never have to feel the kind of pain he'd felt with Tish. But the absence of pain also meant the absence of pure joy. Caring passionately about someone meant you might get singed a little. Nor could you get hurt without caring passionately.

But they were together again. Newly minted and starting over. The joy of it was almost more than he could believe.

And then he remembered Larkin.

Chapter 22

Elysee sat in her bedroom, replaying the engagement party video, knowing she'd done the right thing by ending her engagement to Shane, but feeling embarrassed that she'd now gone through four fiancés. What was the matter with her? Why did she keep picking the wrong men? She stared at the video as if it held the answer to her questions. Why couldn't she find the kind of love that had bonded Shane and Tish together so tightly in spite of all their troubles?

What did she want out of life?

What was her heart's deepest desire?

Elysee realized she did not know. Until now, her life had been dictated, first by romantic notions engendered by her mother, then by her father's expectations. She didn't blame her parents. They'd done what they thought best. She blamed herself, for not questioning her values and beliefs before now.

She'd just let everyone tell her what she was supposed to believe, whether it was her parents or her friends, or the men she took up with or even America's perception of her.

The engagement party played on—the participants laughing, talking, and celebrating. She was so caught up in her own identity crisis she barely noticed that she was caught on screen passing Rana the money meant to ensure Alma Reddy's safe passage into the United States.

This was pointless. Reviewing the evidence of yet another failed engagement was not going to solve anything. Elysee sighed and got to her feet.

Hindi. Beneath the noise of the party, Tish's tape had caught someone speaking in the language taught to Elysee as a child by her nanny. Someone was speaking words she could not believe she was hearing.

Ambassador Kumar was ordering someone to take out a hit on Alma Reddy. Her murder was to take place the minute she set foot on American soil.

With dawning horror, Elysee realized Alma was arriving tonight.

Shane and Tish dozed in each other's arms and woke sometime later to the sound of a freighter ship docking nearby. In the darkness, they scrambled to their feet, fumbled for their clothes, and got dressed.

Several minutes later, the door to the pod opened with a metallic groan. The beam from an ultra-bright flashlight blinded them.

"Change of plans," Larkin called out. "Alma Reddy isn't on this ship the way she was supposed to be. So I'm killing you two first, but before we get to that, I need to know how many copies you made of the disk and exactly where they are. And in case you need a little incentive, sister," he said to Tish, "I'm going to smash every bone in your hubby's fucked-up hand with this nifty little silver hammer I brought along with me until you tell me everything you know."

It had taken some doing, but in the hubbub of her father arriving at the ranch and with Lola's help, she'd managed to give her Secret Service detail the slip. Elysee had never been to the docks before. She'd tried frantically to reach Rana on her cell phone, but had had no luck.

She'd lied to Lola and told the secretary she was sneaking off for a rendezvous with Shane. Lola let Elysee use her car and provided a distraction for the checkpoint security. Elysee had no idea who she could trust besides Shane, and she hadn't been able to find him. She didn't want to take the chance of leading a killer to Alma Reddy.

Alma was due to arrive on a freighter at midnight and Elysee had to be there to warn her. Once she knew both Alma and Rana were secreted away someplace safe, she'd call Cal Ackerman to come pick her up.

She arrived at the docks just in time to see the freighter come pulling into the shipping channel. It was awfully dark down there and pretty scary with all those big containers stacked everywhere. Plenty of places for a hired assassin to hide.

Up ahead, along the waterfront, she saw a flashlight beam bobbing, a beacon in the darkness.

"Rana," she whispered. She had to get to Rana and warn her. She rushed ahead into a little clearing amid the containers, but stopped short in the shadows when she saw Shane and Tish, their hands bound in front of them with duct tape, being held at gunpoint by Pete Larkin only a few feet away from where she stood.

Her heart slammed into her chest. What to do? What to do?

Call 9-1-1.

She reached into her pocket for her cell phone, flipped it open, and pressed the 9.

In the quiet darkness that single soft beep was deafening.

Larkin's head came up.

Their eyes met.

Elysee whirled.

Larkin dove.

She dropped the phone.

He grabbed her ankle, pulled her down on the dock.

She shrieked.

He yanked her by the front of her shirt with one hand and pulled her to her feet, while simultaneously spinning toward Shane, his gun outstretched. He caught Elysee's neck in the crook of his arm, then pressed the gun against her temple.

"Don't move, hero," Larkin threatened.

Elysee held her breath.

Shane's eyes met hers.

Larkin began backing up, dragging Elysee with him.

Shane launched himself at Larkin.

Instinctively, instantaneously, Larkin swung the gun around and fired without aiming in Shane's direction.

Elysee heard a gasp of pain. "Shane?"

Her eyes widened. Shane hadn't been hit. Tish had been standing right behind him.

With a soft "Oh," Tish crumpled to the dock.

Shane whirled around just in time to see her collapse. He made a guttural sound of despair and dropped to his knees beside his ex-wife.

"You bastard!" Elysee cried.

Using a self-defense technique Shane had taught her, she reached up and pressed in just the right spot on Larkin's carotid artery. Two seconds later he lay incapacitated on the ground.

"Secret Service," Cal Ackerman's voice rang out from behind them all. "Don't anybody move."

The pain in her shoulder burned like liquid fire. Tish opened her eyes to find herself in a hospital bed.

Where was she? How had she gotten here?

She blinked and glanced around. Shane was perched in a chair at her bedside looking weary and sad, gazing down at his wounded hand. Elysee stood at the window, arms crossed over her chest, staring at something on the street below. Lola was kicked back in a recliner across the room, tapping something into her laptop. And Cal Ackerman was leaning his shoulder against the doorjamb.

She reached over and touched the thick bandage at her collarbone. Ouch!

Her head felt muzzy, her memory vague. The last thing she remembered was making love with Shane in the shipping pod. She smiled. They were a couple again.

"Hey, you guys?" she croaked, pushing the words past her dry lips.

"Tish!" everyone said in unison.

Lola closed her laptop. Elysee moved away from the window. Cal stood up straight. And Shane, an exhilarated smile on his face, took her hand.

"How are you feeling?" Shane asked. "You okay?"

"Fine, fine, just confused. How'd I get here? How long have I been here? I'm starving."

"You've been unconscious for two days," Lola said.

"Two days!" Her gaze flew to Shane's. He nodded, confirming what Lola had said. "What happened to my shoulder?"

"Larkin shot you," Shane said through gritted teeth, "but the bullet was a clean through-and-through. When you fell you hit your head, and that's why you've been out. If it hadn't been for Elysee's quick thinking, Larkin would have killed all three of us."

"Only because none of you trusted me enough to let me know what was going on." Cal glowered. "If Elysee hadn't been wearing her tracking device . . ."

"Elysee saved us?" Tish laughed, feeling giddy and happy to be alive.

"What's so funny?" Elysee asked. "You don't think I'm capable of saving someone?"

"No, no, not at all."

"I'm tougher than I look." She blew on her fingernails and rubbed them against her shirt in a comical gesture that said, "Yeah, I bested a badass rogue CIA agent and it was easy."

Everyone laughed then.

"So what became of Larkin?"

"He's in big-time trouble. Thanks to your videotape, he'll be going to prison. Ambassador Kumar is in some pretty hot water himself."

Tish shifted her gaze to Elysee. "What about Rana and Alma? Are they okay? Did Larkin get to them?"

"They're both fine," Elysee said. "Rana had never really intended to ship Alma via freighter. It was just a story she concocted because she knew how ruthless the men coming after Alma could be. She had to stay two steps ahead of them. Rana didn't clue me in, thinking it would be safer for me if I didn't know Alma's real travel route. She never dreamed I would end up going to the docks."

"It would have been smarter," Cal chided, "if you hadn't ditched your bodyguard."

"Good thing you showed up," Shane said. "I hate to think what would have happened if you hadn't been there."

"But how did you know Larkin would be there?"

"I didn't know for sure it was Larkin, but your video-tape led me to the docks."

"My videotape?"

"You caught Ambassador Kumar on tape hiring Lar-kin to murder Alma. They were speaking in Hindi and I understood it. So ultimately, Tish, you were the one who broke the case," Elysee explained.

"There was so much left to chance." Tish shook her head. "If Shane hadn't given me his phone with the GPS tracking, if you hadn't watched the video, I'd be dead. Thank you, Elysee, for saving my life."

Elysee smiled. "I think everything happened the way it did for a reason. We're connected. All of us."

Tish smiled back, recognizing the truth of it. They were all connected in some way.

"Your mother's been here," Shane said, "and your friends Delaney and Rachael. Jillian called from San Francisco. Everyone's been pretty worried about you."

"My head's so fuzzy. I really don't remember much of what happened."

Lola said. "Cal confessed that the reason he had red lava gravel on his shoes from the garden outside your apartment was because he'd gone there to tell you that Shane was still in love with you."

"You knew?"

"Please," Cal said gruffly. "I knew you two were meant to be together the night you took him home from Louie's."

Tish glanced over at Shane. Their eyes met and his smile tipped up at the corners. She was barely aware that Elysee, Cal, and Lola had tiptoed out of the room.

"I think we're alone now," he whispered.

"I thought they'd never leave." Her gaze took him in. He was dressed in faded blue jeans and a white button-down shirt with the sleeves rolled up. He managed to look both crisp and relaxed.

His face was full of tenderness. "I got something for you."

"Oh?"

He reached behind him for something on the floor and pulled up a package wrapped in a turquoise bow.

"You got me a present?" Her grin widened.

"Open it."

Eagerly, she pulled off the ribbon and lifted the lid. The minute she saw it her heart stilled and her bottom lip started to quiver. "Shane, it's magnificent."

From the box she lifted the Jack bookend, a perfect match to her Jill. "Where did you find him?"

"E-bay, and I paid a pretty penny for express-mail shipping. Jill's in the box, too. Dick Tracy brought her by yesterday. The investigation's closed since Larkin confessed to starting the fire."

Tish took Jill from the box, sat her next to Jack in her lap. They were together again, balancing each other.

"Thank you," she whispered. "Thank you."

"No," he said. "Thank you for loving me and never stopping."

She slipped out of bed and settled into his lap. Kissing

him lightly on the lips, she slid her arms around his neck. He held her close. She could hear the steady lub-dub of his heart.

They sat there in the hospital room, gazing into each other's eyes, drinking each other in. All this time, never knowing, they'd been on a journey back to each other.

She stared into the depths of his breathtaking brown eyes and her heart filled with contentment. They were better now than they'd been. Stronger, wiser, braver.

"My love, my life, my wife," he whispered. "For now, forever, for always. Marry me again, Tish. This time we'll do it right."

There was only one thing to say. With a sweet sigh of pleasure, Tish said, "Yes."

Epilogue

Adjusting his boutonniere in his parents' backyard, the ex–Secret Service agent, turned business manager to his high-profile videographer wife, scanned the crowd.

All the usual suspects were there. Tish's friends—Delaney with her rounded belly and her husband, Nick; Jillian, who'd just made Assistant DA in Harris County; Rachael, who was still single and searching; Shane's parents and his sister, Amy; Tish's mom, Dixie Ann.

The special guest of honor, one class act, Elysee Benedict, was present. Cal was there, too, keeping an eye on Elysee.

They had so many friends, such a loving family. They were so blessed it was hard to believe that they had once gotten so off track. But that detour had taught them a very valuable lesson neither one of them would ever forget.

Balance. That was key. Shane had learned to stop identifying with an impossible image of heroism that he could never achieve and accept himself, flaws and all.

Tish had learned to ask for what she needed rather than burying her emotions under excess spending.

Some big changes had been made, and they were all for the better.

Once the vows had been taken and the ceremony completed, his beautiful wife tugged off her wedding veil and handed it to her friend Rachael with a bold wink. Then she pulled him off to the side for a big kiss.

"I love you, Shane Tremont. I have from the moment you punched that bald guy on my behalf at Louie's."

"And I love you, Tish Gallagher Tremont. From the first night you took me to bed and wouldn't let me touch you."

He wrapped his right arm around her waist with the hand that was now almost healed. "I never stopped loving you, not one time during all the sadness and confusion over losing Johnny."

"Shh," she said. "It's okay. Everything is as it should be."

"I have a very smart wife."

And that's how Shane Tremont, middle-class boy from small-town America, found himself remarried to the love of his life.

About the Author

Lori Wilde is the bestselling author of more than forty-five books. A former RITA finalist, Lori's books have been recognized by the Romantic Times Reviewers' Choice Award, the Holt Medallion, the Booksellers Best, the National Readers' Choice, and numerous other honors. She lives in Weatherford, Texas, with her husband and a wide assortment of pets. You may write to Lori at P.O. Box 31, Weatherford, TX 76086, or e-mail her via her home page at www.loriwilde.com. Lori Wilde teaches Romance Writing Secrets via the Internet through colleges and universities worldwide @ www.ed2go.com.

Can two people with broken hearts find love with the last person they'd suspect... each other?

Please keep reading for an excerpt from *Rocky Mountain Heat* (previously published as *All of Me*)

AVAILABLE WINTER 2019

Chapter One

Houston deputy district attorney Jillian Samuels did not believe in magic.

She didn't throw pennies into wishing wells, didn't pluck four-leaf clovers from springtime meadows, didn't blow out birthday-cake candles, and didn't wish on falling stars.

For Jillian, the Tooth Fairy and the Easter Bunny had always been myths. And as for Santa Claus, even thinking about the jolly fat guy in the red suit knotted her stomach. She'd tried believing in him once, and all she'd gotten in the pink stocking she'd hung on the mantel were two chunks of Kingsford's charcoal—the kind without lighter fluid.

Later, she'd realized her stepmother put the coal in her stocking, but on that Christmas morning, while the other kids rode bicycles, tossed footballs, and combed Barbie's hair, Jillian received her message loud and clear.

You're a very bad girl.

No, Jillian didn't believe in magic or fairy tales or happily-ever-afters, even though her three best friends, Delaney, Tish, and Rachael, had supposedly found their true loves after wishing on what they claimed was a magic wedding veil. Her friends had even dared to pass the damnable veil along to her, telling Jillian it would grant her heart's greatest desire. But she wasn't falling for such nonsense. She snorted whenever she thought of the three-hundred-year-old lace wedding veil shoved away in a cedar chest along with her winter cashmere sweaters.

When it came to romance, Jillian was of the same mind as Hemingway: *When two people love each other, there can be no happy ending.* Clearly, Hemingway knew what he was talking about.

Not that Jillian could claim she'd ever been in love. She'd decided a long time ago love was best avoided. She liked her life tidy, and from what she'd seen of it, love was sprawling and messy and complicated. Besides, love required trust, and trust wasn't her strong suit.

Jillian did not believe in magic, but she did believe in hard work, success, productivity, and justice. The closest she ever came to magic were those glorious courtroom moments when a judge in a black robe read the jury's guilty verdict.

This morning in late September, dressed in a no-nonsense navy-blue pin-striped Ralph Lauren suit, a cream-colored silk blouse, and Jimmy Choo stilettos to show off the shapely curve of her calves and add three inches to her already imposing five-foot-ten-inch height, Jillian stood at attention waiting for the verdict to be read.

On the outside, she looked like a dream prosecutor— statuesque, gorgeous, young, and smart. But underneath the clothes and the makeup and her cool, unshakeable countenance, Jillian Samuels was still that same little girl who hadn't rated a Christmas present from Santa.

"Ladies and gentlemen of the jury, have you reached a verdict in this case?" Judge Atwood asked.

"We have, Your Honor," answered the foreman, a big slab of a guy with carrot-colored hair and freckled skin.

"Please hand your decision to the bailiff," the judge directed.

Jillian drew a breath, curling her fingernails into her palms. Before the reading of every verdict, she felt slightly sick to her stomach.

The bailiff, a gangly, bulldog-faced middle-aged man with a Magnum P.I. mustache, walked the piece of paper across the courtroom to the judge's bench. Judge Atwood opened it, read it, and then glared at the defendant over the top of his reading glasses.

Twenty-three-year-old Randal Petry had shot Gladys Webelow, an eighty-two-year-old great-grandmother, in the upper thigh while robbing a Dash and Go last Christmas Eve. Gladys had been buying a bottle of Correctol and a quart of 2 percent milk. He'd made off with forty-seven dollars from the cash register, a fistful of Slim Jims, and a twenty-four pack of Old Milwaukee.

"Will the defendant please rise?" Atwood handed the verdict back to the bailiff, who gave it to the jury foreman to read aloud.

Head held high, Petry got to his feet. The man was a scumbag, but Jillian had to admire his defiance.

"Randal LeRoy Petry, on the count of armed robbery, you are found guilty as charged," the foreman announced. As the foreman kept reading the verdicts on the other charges leveled against Petry, Jillian waited for the victorious wash of relief she always experienced when the word *guilty* was spoken. Waited for the happy sag to her shoulders, the warm satisfaction in her belly, the skip of victory in her pulse.

But the triumph did not come.

Instead, she felt numb, lifeless, and very detached as if she were standing at the far end of some distant tunnel.

Waiting . . . waiting . . .

For what, she didn't know.

People in the gallery were getting up, heading for the door. The court-appointed defense attorney collected his papers and stuffed them into his scuffed briefcase. The guards were hauling Petry off to jail. Judge Atwood left the bench.

And Jillian just kept standing.

Waiting.

It scared her. This nonfeeling. This emptiness. Her fingernails bit into the flesh of her palms, but she couldn't feel that either.

"You gonna stand there all day, Samuels, or what? You won. Go knock back a shot of Jose Cuervo."

Jillian jerked her head around. Saw Keith Whippet, the prosecutor on the next case, waiting to take his place at her table. Whippet was as lean as his name, with mean eyes and a cheap suit.

"Chop, chop." He slammed his briefcase down on the desk. "I got people to fry."

"Yes," Jillian said, but she could barely hear herself. She was a bright kite who'd broken loose from its tether, flying high into a cloudless blue sky. Up, up, and away, higher and higher, smaller and smaller. Soon she would disappear, a speck in the air.

What was happening to her?

She looked at Whippet, a weasly guy who'd asked her

out on numerous occasions, and she'd shattered his hopes every single time until he'd finally given up. Now he was just rude. Whippet made shooing motions.

Jillian blinked, grabbed her briefcase, and darted from the courtroom.

Blake.

She had to talk to her mentor, District Attorney Blake Townsend. He would know what to do. He'd tell her this feeling was completely normal. That it was okay if the joy was gone. She would survive.

Except it wasn't okay, because her job was the only thing that gave her joy. If she'd lost the ability to derive pleasure from putting the bad guys behind bars, what did that leave her?

The thing was, she couldn't feel happy about jailing Petry, because she knew there were thousands more like him. She knew the prisons were overcrowded, and they would let Petry out of jail on good behavior after he'd served only a fraction of his sentence to make room for a new batch of Petrys.

The realization wasn't new. What was startlingly fresh was the idea that her work didn't matter. She was insignificant. The justice system was a turnstile, and her arms were growing weary of holding open the revolving door.

She was so unsettled by the thought that she found it difficult to catch her breath.

Blake. She needed to speak to Blake.

Anxiety rushed her from the courthouse to the district attorney's office across the street, her heels clicking a rapid rhythm against the sidewalk that matched the elevated tempo of her pulse.

By the time she stepped into the DA's office, she was

breathing hard and sweating. She caught a glimpse of her reflection in a window and saw that her sleek dark hair, usually pulled back in a loose chignon, had slumped from the clasp and was tumbling about her shoulders.

What was happening to her?

The whole room went suddenly silent, and everyone stared in her direction.

"Is Blake in his office?" she asked the DA's executive assistant, Francine Weathers.

Francine blinked, and it was only then that Jillian noticed her reddened eyes. The woman had been crying. She stepped closer, the anxiety she'd been feeling morphed into real fear.

She stood there for a moment, panting, terrified, heart rapidly pounding, staring at Francine's round, middle-aged face. She knew something bad had happened before she ever asked the question.

"What's wrong?"

The secretary dabbed at her eyes with a Kleenex. "You haven't heard?"

A hot rush of apprehension raised the hairs on the nape of her neck. "Heard what? I've been in court. The Petry case."

"I . . ." Francine sniffed. "He . . ."

Jillian stepped closer and awkwardly put a hand on the older woman's shoulder. "Are you okay?"

Francine shook her head and burst into a fresh round of tears. Jillian dropped her hand. She'd never been very good at comforting people. She was the pit bull who went after the accused. Gentleness was foreign.

"This morning, Blake . . . he . . ."

Jillian's blood pumped faster. "Yes?"

"It's terrible, unthinkable."

"What?"

"Such a shame. He was only fifty-six."

Jillian grit her teeth to keep from taking the woman by the shoulders and shaking her. "Just tell me. What's happened?"

Francine hiccoughed, sniffled into a tissue, and then finally whispered,

"Blake dropped dead this morning in the middle of Starbucks while ordering a grande soy latte."

THE NEXT FEW DAYS passed in a fog. Jillian went about her work and attended her cases, but it felt as if someone else was in her body performing the tasks while her mind shut down, disconnected from her emotions. She'd never experienced such hollow emptiness. But she could not cry. The tears stuffed up her head, made her temples throb, but no matter how much she wanted to sob, she simply could not.

Francine had learned from Blake's doctor that he'd had an inoperable brain tumor he'd told no one about. That new knowledge cut Jillian to the quick. He hadn't trusted her enough to tell her he was dying.

The morning of Blake's memorial service dawned unseasonably cold for the end of September in Texas. Thick gray clouds matted the sky, threatening rain. The wind gusted out of the north at twenty-five miles an hour, blowing shivers up Jillian's black wool skirt.

She still couldn't believe Blake was gone. Speculation about who would be appointed to take his place swirled through the office, but, grief-stricken, Jillian didn't give the issue much consideration. Blake was gone, and no one could ever replace him in her heart.

Learning of her mentor's death compounded the feelings of edge-of-the-world desolation that had overcome her during Petry's trial. She'd met Blake when he'd been a guest lecturer in her summer-school class on criminal law at the University of Houston. He'd found her questions insightful, and she'd thought he was one of the smartest men she'd ever met.

Their attraction was strictly mental. They admired each other's brains. Plus, Jillian had lost a father, and Blake had let a daughter slip away. When Blake had been elected district attorney about the same time Jillian graduated from law school, his offer of a job in the DA's office was automatic.

Jillian didn't question if it was the right step for her. Blake was there. She went. Other than Delaney, Tish, and Rachael, Blake was the closest thing to family she could claim.

The memorial service was held in an empty courtroom at the Harris County Courthouse. Law was Blake's religion. Saying farewell in a church didn't seem fitting. Francine had made all the arrangements. The room was jam-packed with colleagues, opponents, allies, and adversaries. But there was no family present. Blake had been as alone in the world as Jillian.

A poster-sized photograph of Blake sat perched on the judge's bench. Beside it was the urn that held his ashes. The smell of stargazer lilies and chrysanthemums permeated the courtroom. Jillian took a seat in the back row of the gallery. Her head hurt from all the tears she'd been unable to shed. Her throat was tight. Her heart scraped the ground.

Suddenly a memory flashed into her head. One night, four months earlier, she'd gone over to Blake's house for dinner to celebrate putting a cop killer on death row. She'd expected Blake to be in a good mood. He was supposed to be cooking her favorite meal, spaghetti and meatballs. She'd brought a bottle of Chianti for the occasion. Instead, after he'd invited her in, he told her he'd ordered takeout Chinese and then he'd gone to sit in the bay window alcove overlooking the lake behind his property, a wistful expression on his face.

She sat beside him, waiting for him to tell her what had happened, but he did not. Finally, after several minutes of watching him watch the birds landing on the lake for the evening, she'd asked, "Blake? Is something wrong?"

He tilted his gray head at her. He looked so tired, and he gave her a slight smile. "You should get married," he'd murmured.

"Huh?" She'd blinked.

"You shouldn't be here hanging out with an old man. You should be dating, forming relationships, finding a good guy, getting married."

She hadn't expected the hit to her gut that his words inflicted. "You know I'm not a big believer in marriage."

Blake had looked away from her then, his eyes back on the birds and the lake. "You deserve love, Jillian."

She had no answer for that. "Marriage didn't work out so well for you."

"Because I screwed it up. God, if only I could go back in time . . ." He let his words trail off.

"Did something happen?"

He glanced at her again, and for just a second she saw the starkest regret in his eyes. Regret tinged with fear. The look vanished as quickly as it had appeared, and she convinced herself she must have imagined it.

"Nah." He waved a hand. "Just an old man getting maudlin."

The doorbell had rang then. The delivery driver with their kung pao chicken and steamed pork dumplings. The rest of the evening Blake had been his usual self, but now, looking back on the moment, Jillian couldn't help wondering if that was the day he'd been diagnosed with the brain tumor.

She blinked back the memory. Her nose burned. *Oh, Blake, why didn't you tell me you were dying?* He'd worked up until the last minute of his life and then died so tritely in Starbucks.

Jillian's heart lurched. She felt inadequate, useless. And guilty that she hadn't seen the signs. She remembered how his vision seemed to be getting worse. How lately he'd been making beginner mistakes when they played chess. She thought they were close friends, and yet he hadn't told her about his illness. Hell, she might as well admit it. She felt a little excluded. He hadn't trusted her with his darkest secret.

Just before the service began, the doors opened one last time and Mayor Newsom swept inside with Judge Alex Fredericks, followed by Alex's beautiful young wife with a towheaded toddler on her hip. The minute Jillian spied Alex and his family, she felt the color drain from her face.

Nausea gripped her.

The last time she'd seen Mrs. Fredericks had been on

Christmas Eve of the previous year. At the same time Randal Petry had been shooting Gladys Webelow at the Dash and Go, Jillian had been ringing Alex Frederick's doorbell in the Woodlands, dressed only in a denim duster and knee-high cowboy boots. Learning for the first time that her new lover was married with a family.

Jillian sank down in her seat and prayed neither Alex nor his wife spied her. Newsom ushered them to the front of the room, where they sat side by side in three empty folding chairs. The service lasted over an hour as one person after another took the microphone to remember and honor Blake. Jillian had prepared a speech, but when the officiating minister asked for any final farewell words, she stayed seated. She couldn't bear standing up there in front of Alex.

He had been the biggest mistake of her life.

Her friends urged Jillian to open herself up to a relationship. They'd made her start to hope that she could find love, that there *was* a man out there for her.

And hope was such a dangerous thing.

Alex was handsome and charming and at just thirty-six already a criminal court judge. They looked good together, both tall and athletic. Her friends were all falling giggly in love, and Jillian dared to think, *Why not take a chance*? For the first time in her twenty-nine years on the planet, she'd put her fears aside, opened herself up, and let a man into her heart.

And then she'd found out about Mrs. Fredericks.

Idiot.

She should have known better. No matter what anyone said, there was no such thing as magic. No happily-ever-after. Not for her anyway.

"If there's anyone else who'd like to say something about Blake, please come forward now," the minister said. "If not, Mayor Newsom has an announcement he would like to make, and then we'll conclude the service with a closing prayer."

The minister stepped away from the microphone and the mayor took his place. Newsom shuffled his notes, cleared his throat, and then launched in.

"We've lost a great man in Blake Townsend. He's irreplaceable. But life goes on, and Blake wouldn't want us standing in the way of justice," Newsom said as if he had a clue what Blake wanted. "Since all his friends and colleagues are gathered here in one place, it seems the best time to announce the appointment of our new DA before my formal press conference this afternoon."

A murmur rippled through the crowd.

It was crass and inconsiderate, announcing Blake's successor at his memorial service, but classic Mayor Newsom. The guy had the class of a garden trowel. Jillian caught her breath and bit her bottom lip. She sensed what was coming and dreaded hearing it.

"Judge Alex Fredericks will be the new Harris County district attorney." Newsom turned to Fredericks. "Alex, would you like to say a few words?"

Anger grabbed her throat and shook hard. No, no! It could not be true.

Jillian would not sit still and listen to this. Bile rising in her throat, she charged for the door. Reality settled on her shoulders, even as she tried to outrun the inevitable. She hurried across the polished black marble floor of the courthouse, rushing out into the blowing drizzle, gulping in cold, damp air.

She didn't see the Tom Thumb delivery truck. She just stepped off the curb and into its path.

A horn blared. Tires squealed.

Jillian froze.

The truck's bumper stopped just inches short of her kneecaps.

She stared through the windshield at the driver, and he promptly flipped her the bird. She smiled at him. Smiled and laughed and then couldn't stop.

The driver rolled down the window. "Get out of the road you crazy bitch."

Great, terrific, you almost get run over and you're laughing about it. The guy's right. You are crazy.

She wandered the streets, not paying any attention to where she was going and ending up walking the path through the city park she and Blake had walked many times together, engaged in friendly legal debates. She wondered what he'd think of Alex as his replacement. Blake hadn't known about her relationship with Alex. She'd been too ashamed to tell him.

Her mind kept going back to the memory of the night Blake had told her she should get married, and the more she thought about it, the more convinced she became that had to have been the day he'd gotten his diagnosis. The death sentence he'd shared with no one.

The rain pelted her, and Jillian realized she'd been walking in a big circle for the last thirty minutes. Ducking her head against the quickening rain, she hurried to her office. The place was empty. Everyone else had probably gone to lunch after the services were over. She shrugged out of her coat, dropped down at her desk, and closed her eyes.

"Blake," Jillian whispered out loud. "What am I going to do without you?"

All her girlfriends were married now, getting pregnant, having babies, living lives so very different from her own. She'd used Blake to fill the void. Every Thursday night, they'd played chess together. He'd make dinner, because Jillian didn't cook, or they'd go out to eat, her treat. He was the one she called when she had trouble with a case, and she was the escort he took to political functions. Many assumed they were having an affair. But she'd never felt any of those kinds of feelings for Blake, nor he for her. He'd always been like the dad she'd never really had.

Except now he was gone.

"Ms. Samuels?"

She opened her eyes to see Alex Fredericks standing in the doorway.

His gaze was enigmatic, his stance intimidating.

Jillian thrust out her chin, refusing to let her distress show. "Yes?"

"I want to see you in my office."

She stared. Was the bastard about to fire her? Ever since she'd ended their affair, whenever she appeared in Alex's courtroom, their relationship had been adversarial. She'd lost more than one case she might have won if there'd been another judge on the bench.

"Don't you mean Blake's office?"

"I'm the new DA," he said. "It's my office now, and I want to see you in there immediately."

Jillian wanted to tell him to go to hell, but she held her tongue and got up.

Other employees were filtering into the building. She followed Alex into Blake's office. A fresh surge of anger